HANNAH JO ABBOTT

Walk with Me

To my parents, Tim and Donna McDow,
who always believed I would be a writer.

Acknowledgement

Thank you to The Lord for giving me this idea and allowing me to write this story.

Thank you to my wonderful husband who has pushed, prodded, and encouraged me along the way. I could never have done it without you!

And THANK YOU, THANK YOU to my beta readers who fell in love with these characters the same way I did and who gave me the confidence and encouragement to finish the book and send it out into the world.

Chapter 1

*P*aige Kelly climbed into the driver's seat of her ten-year-old minivan, shut the door and sighed a tired, heavy sigh. "Why do I even wear these shoes?" she asked herself out loud, pulling off the thin, black flats. "No support, and I'm on my feet all day. Ridiculous." She pulled her long, chocolate brown hair out of the tight ponytail and let it fall around her shoulders. With her head leaned back on the cracked leather of the headrest, she closed her eyes and took a few deep breaths. It had been a long day at work waiting tables and she was thinking that a nap sounded pretty good. "No time for that," she said with a mix of sadness and determination. She turned the key in the ignition, raised the volume on the radio, and started her drive home.

Paige had lived all of her twenty-two years in Pine Haven, Alabama. As a child she had made a game out of counting the number of cars that passed on a drive through town. Today she only saw seven on her way home. From work she wound around a country road before reaching Main Street.

The drive took her through the business part of town where several shops stood on either side of the two-lane road. Wide sidewalks allowed people to easily come and go to browse through the shops. Spring had always been her favorite season, a break from the cold of winter, but also a time of cool refreshment before the coming of the blazing southern summer heat. But Paige didn't take time to notice the bits of green and yellow sprouting up from the ground while she hurried home. Just outside of town she turned down a narrow, paved road. The road was lined on either side by white, wooden rail fencing and a half a dozen houses dotted the neighborhood spread out over a few acres each. A few minutes later she pulled through the driveway and into the garage of a spacious, two-story, brick house.

Once the car was parked in the garage she stuck her shoes in her bag and walked through the door in her bare feet. Even though she was home from work, her day was barely half over. She hung her bag on the hook by the door. Paige didn't bother changing out of her work uniform of black pants and a plain white button-up shirt, but walked through the laundry room straight to the kitchen. It was a large room with granite counters wrapped around the back corner and deep brown cabinets filling the space above. A large granite top island stood in the middle, and that's where Paige got to work. She pulled an apron over her head and hummed to herself as she began to gather ingredients and place them on the counter. She stood on a step stool so her five foot, five inch frame could reach the top shelf of the pantry. She had just started opening a can of green beans when she heard the front door open and close and the sound of two pairs of feet running down the hallway.

"Hey, Paige!" came the loud greeting from eight-year-old Lucy. "Can we have a snack?"

"Yeah, can we have a snack?" asked Lucy's twin brother, Joe. The two looked strikingly similar with their dark hair and blue eyes. Both kids wore jeans, simple T-shirts, and tennis shoes and carried backpacks over their shoulders.

"Yes, you can," Paige answered matter-of-factly. "But first go wash your hands and let's check your folders. Do you have homework tonight?"

"Yes," said the girl.

"No," said the boy at the same time.

Paige cocked her head and gave him a look that said he better tell her the truth.

"OK, yes." He resigned as he shifted his weight back and forth from one foot to the other, "but I did most of it in class, I only have two problems left."

Paige tried to hide the smile, but couldn't help it. Joe was just too smart, "Alright then, snack and then homework before playtime, OK?"

"OK." The twins agreed and hurried off.

Paige set her dinner preparation aside and began to cut an apple into slices. As she arranged it on two plates with some peanut butter, Joe and Lucy returned to the other side of the island from Paige where they sat on hightop barstools. She asked them about their day at school while they ate and pulled out their books. Once they were settled she turned her attention back to dinner while she helped Lucy with her math homework.

"Oh yeah, I almost forgot." Lucy looked up from her paper and pushed her shoulder-length hair behind her ear. "I need you to sign my field trip form for Monday, we're going to the strawberry patch, remember?"

"Of course, I remember." Paige smiled. "Get me the form now before we forget."

Lucy dug in her backpack as she spoke. "Paige?"

"Yeah, Lu?"

"You're going on the field trip with me this time, right?"

Paige looked at the younger girl. She remembered how disappointed she had been on the last field trip when Paige didn't go. "Yes, I am. I promised I would," she assured her.

"Yay!" Lucy said. "Amy said her mom goes on all the field trips and she asked me why my mom can't come."

Paige's heart thudded, she cleared her throat to speak. "What did you tell her?"

"That my Mom and Daddy are gone to heaven."

Paige swallowed hard so the tears wouldn't have a chance to surface. Even though it had been three years, every mention of her parents still brought Paige to a complete halt and left a sickening feeling in her stomach. "That's right, Lucy. But I promise, you can tell her your big sister will on your next field trip."

"Thanks, Paige."

Joe had been sitting quietly, but he was listening to Paige and Lucy. "I'm done with my homework now. Can I go play?" he asked.

Paige saw the hint of sadness in his eyes and nodded to him.

"Me too." Lucy said and hopped down from her stool. The two put away their papers and hung their backpacks on the assigned hooks in the entryway before going to their rooms to play.

Paige turned to put a dinner casserole in the oven then went to start a load of laundry. She made her way around the house

4

straightening up as she went, picking up an out-of-place book or toy and putting it away. She stopped at the small desk to the side of the kitchen and looked over the family schedule and list for the next few days. She liked a place for everything, and everything in its place. At least that she could control. Before she knew it, thirty minutes had gone by and she heard the timer on the oven. She set the casserole on the table and looked out the window when she heard a car in the driveway.

Moments later her brother and sister walked through the door. At sixteen, Shepherd Kelly liked to think of himself as the man of the family. With his dark hair and strong features, he was unmistakably related to his sisters, but truly masculine in his looks. He had just come from baseball practice and still wore his practice uniform. He had picked up thirteen-year-old Zoey from her tumbling class on his way home.

"Hey guys," Paige said. "I'm about to put dinner on the table."

"Okay, I'll just be a minute to clean up," Shep replied. Zoey was already up the stairs.

"That's fine," she told him. "Zoey," Paige called out. "Wash up and come help me set the table." She turned to her brother before he could get out of sight too. "Shep, thank you for picking Zoey up, I'll be honest, I was a little afraid you would forget," Paige admitted.

"Is that why you put an alarm on my phone for when I left practice?" Shep gave her an accusing look.

Paige was obviously caught. "Well," she stalled, "Okay, yes, it is."

Shep laughed. "I knew it. But, ummm, maybe it's a good thing you did."

"Seriously? Did you really forget?" Paige stared at her brother. "Sort of. But it's just that I wasn't thinking about it when I got in the car, so I can't say whether I would have actually made it home without her, but..." he trailed off.

"It's alright." Paige waved a hand in the air as if sweeping the offense away. "Just don't delete that reminder, I set it for every Thursday."

"Gee, thanks for the confidence." Shep said sarcastically. He sounded a little hurt.

Paige stopped to look at him, but she had no response. She wanted to trust Shep, and his recently acquired driver's license really helped out with the family schedule. Still, he was just a teenage boy and she just never knew how much he could handle. "I'm sorry, Shep."

"It's alright, you were right anyway," he said as he headed for the stairs.

Paige shook her head and sighed. She wished she knew how to help him grow up without embarrassing him.

As he went, Zoey came back down the stairs to help Paige. Zoey was one sibling Paige had a hard time connecting with and she tried to make special time for her when she could. Paige asked questions about her day at school and her tumbling class while they set the table. Zoey mostly responded with one-word answers. She spoke politely, but didn't offer any unnecessary information. They finished the task in near silence and Paige turned to call the other kids.

"Joe, Lucy, wash up. Dinner's ready." Paige called to the twins.

Within a few minutes dinner was on the table and the family began to gather in their seats. Paige looked at the clock and tried not to worry that her eighteen-year-old sister, Peyton, was fifteen minutes late getting home from cheerleading practice. *Practice probably just ran a little late*, she thought as she bit her bottom lip.

"I'm starving," Shep declared as he entered the kitchen fresh from a shower.

"We will wait for Peyton," Paige said with a look.

"Can you at least call her and see where she is?" He whined as he took his seat.

"I don't want to distract her if she's driving." Paige replied, but there was no need to call anyway. Peyton walked in the door at that moment.

"Hey, sorry guys. Coach kept us overtime to work on a new stunt. I'm sorry, Paige," Peyton said. She dropped her gym bag and hurried to the kitchen sink to wash her hands and take her seat. She wore a t-shirt and a cheerleading practice skirt with her tennis shoes. Her dark hair was in a high ponytail that made her blue eyes look big and bright.

"It's alright, you're here now." Paige breathed a little more easily. She mentally did a head count of all her siblings around the table, *one, two, three, four, five,* then aloud she said "Shep, will you please ask a blessing?" Everyone bowed their heads.

Everybody's home, Paige thought to herself. *Everybody made it home safely.*

Chapter 2

"Hey Shannon, can you toss me the sanitizing spray?" Paige and her coworker were wiping down tables in the dining room after the lunch rush. It had been a busy day in the country club restaurant where she worked as a waitress, but the tips were good and Paige was happy. She could use the extra money.

"Here you go," said Shannon as she passed the cleaner bottle. "Want me to sweep up?"

"Sure, if you'll do that I'll just finish up these tables here and then I'll put on fresh coffee for the afternoon."

"Okay, deal." Shannon and Paige were a good team when it came to sharing tasks and getting things done and Paige always appreciated the days she worked with her friend. The dining room had seating for seventy. Dark cherry tables and chairs were spread throughout the room. Large windows on one side opened up to a view of the golf course and the back wall featured a large stone fireplace. At the front entryway there was a long counter with hightop leather stools and beyond the counter was the door to the kitchen. Paige and Shannon finished straightening up and had a bit of a break during the early afternoon lull. They knew there might be folks in for coffee, and the occasional late lunch order, but the dining room was most likely going to be quiet for a while. Paige pulled a stool up to the back side of the counter and helped herself to some coffee. Shannon joined her and the two made easy conversation.

"So how's the scratch on the car?" Shannon asked.

"Ugh," she groaned and covered her face with her hand. "It's alright, it's not really that big of a deal. I just can't believe Shep didn't look before he backed up. The car door beside him was obviously open. Just in his blind spot I guess." Paige sighed.

"Yeah, it could happen to anybody. He's trying so hard." Shannon defended him.

"I know, and he's doing well. He can just be in such a hurry and not pay attention. It worries me when I think about him out on the road. And, of course, he resents that I worry about him, or that I threaten to take away the keys. I just don't know what to do."

"It's a tough spot for you to be in. And for him, really. I know he loves you and Peyton, but two older sister's trying to keep him in line? Come on. That has to be a blow to his ego."

Paige nodded in agreement. "I just wish that I could give him an older male perspective. He looks up to his coaches and older guys on his team, but is that really enough?"

"Have you thought about trying to connect him with one of the men from church? It would be nice to give him sort of a father figure," Shannon saw Paige wince at this phrase. "....Or you know, like a sort of uncle or something."

"That would be nice. I just don't know any men at our

church well enough to ask that sort of favor. And I'm sure they're all busy with their own families."

"It's still a thought. Maybe you could ask the pastor for a suggestion or if he knows someone who would be willing to do that kind of thing."

"I'll think about it," Paige said, but she didn't seem committed to it. "So tell me about your date the other night." Paige turned the attention to her friend with a wink.

"Oh my gosh, you know it wasn't a date. My mom just wanted me to go out with 'her friend's son' that she thinks is 'a handsome young man.'" Shannon spoke while doing air quotes with her hands.

"Yeah, so, was he handsome?"

"Actually, yeah he was pretty good looking."

"So tell me about it," Paige insisted.

"Oh I don't know. I mean, he was nice I guess, just not really somebody I would see myself with. You know, he seems all corporate, ready to take on the world, and I'm a waitress. He probably has a membership at some country club, and I work for one."

"I know what you mean. But this is just temporary for you. You're not far off from graduating with your degree." Shannon was a senior at the college thirty minutes from town, and worked her hours at the club around her class schedule.

"I know, but still, it just seems like we're in different life phases."

"But you wouldn't always be," Paige said.

"You don't even know this guy. Why are you pushing?" Shannon asked.

"I don't know, I'm just thinking out loud I guess. You know your mom wants you to be happy."

"I have plenty of time to find a guy, on my own timetable, not necessarily my mom's." She laughed. "But what about you, Paige, don't you want to be happy?"

"Good grief," Paige rolled her eyes at her friend, but then paused and thought for a second. "I don't even think about that. Between working and getting kids ready for school and planning meals and buying groceries, and cleaning house…" She counted on her fingers as she spoke, then took a deep breath to continue. "And making sure that everybody makes it through the day alive. I'm not sure that I have time to think about being happy. I'm just trying to survive."

"I'm sorry, Paige, I didn't mean to upset you." Shannon frowned.

"It's alright, it's just reality." She shrugged.

"I think you should ease up on yourself a little. You're doing a great job with the hand you've been dealt. I just wish you could have a little fun once in a while."

"I have fun with you, don't I?" asked Paige as she nudged Shannon with her elbow.

"Yeah, in between waiting tables. But when was the last time we hung out and did something outside of work?"

"I guess it has been a while."

"Then let's do it! When can we have a girls' night?" Shannon begged.

"We'll plan something soon. I'll think about it." Paige gave her usual brush off comment. The pair went back to work and the conversation was dropped.

. . .

Russell Pierce sat in his office and stared at the sign on his desk, "Operations Manager". Then he stared at all the boxes on the floor and tried to decide where to start unpacking and setting up his office. He still couldn't believe he was the new Operations Manager at Shady Pines Country Club. It was a dream job for him, really. He thought back to his first summer working as a caddy on the golf course and all the different jobs and paths that had taken him away and brought him right back to the place of his first real job. And at such a young age, too. He knew that at twenty-seven there would be plenty of people who didn't think he could handle this position. But he knew this place - the club, the golf course, the tennis courts, the restaurant, even the locker rooms - as much as he knew his childhood home, and he was confident that he could take on the responsibility.

He ran his fingers through his dark brown hair and tugged on the collar of his shirt where it was brushing against his neck. A knock at his door startled him, and the General Manager poked his head in. "Getting all set up, Russ?"

"Yes Sir, Mr. Thompson." Russell stood up to greet the older man, his six-foot frame towering over his desk.

"Now Russell, you're in a management position now, not a junior caddy carrying around my clubs anymore. Call me Bob."

"Sorry, Mr…err, Bob, old habits."

"That's alright, glad to know you've got manners, but we're colleagues now."

"Thank you, sir." Russell ran his fingers through his hair again. He knew this would be a hard habit to break. Mr. Thompson, Bob, was the picture of professionalism in his work at the club. In his late sixties, he still had a full-head of gray hair and a strong game on the golf course. He had been the manager since Russell was a teenager and it seemed strange to think of him as an almost equal.

"Have you had any trouble finding things?"

Russell smiled and gestured around his office. "Only what's still in boxes."

"Be sure and let your assistant, Lauren, know if you need any help. And the tech guy will be in later to get you all set up on the network and get your email. I think he's got you down as droopy drawers pierce at Shady Pines dot com."

Russell blushed. "I was hoping people would have forgotten that one by now," he said of the old nickname from an unfortunate caddying incident.

"Not a chance." Bob laughed. "Good to have you back."

"Thanks."

"See you around," Bob said as he closed the door.

Russell got up to move some items from one of the boxes and thought to himself, *An Assistant? I can't believe I'm in a position to have my own personal assistant. I must be getting somewhere in life.* Just then the bottom of the box he was lifting fell out and all the items inside crashed to the floor. He had to laugh. *Maybe not. I guess God is just trying to keep me humble.*

His cell phone rang and he could hear the sound coming from one of the boxes, but he wasn't sure which one. He began to open boxes and shuffle through items as quickly as possible and by following the sound he found the phone. "Hello?" he answered.

"Hi honey, how's your first day going?" came the familiar voice of his mother, Gladys Pierce.

Russell smiled and looked at his watch. "Pretty good so far, especially since I just won a bet."

"What bet?" she asked.

"The bet on how long it would take you to check up on me today. I said one o'clock, but Jack and Sam didn't think you would make it past lunch."

"Oh, they give me no credit." She brushed off the joke from her three sons. "Besides I just wanted to see how you're doing."

"I know, Mom. I'm doing fine. Everybody is being nice to me and the bullies didn't steal my lunch."

"I'm glad to hear that," Gladys said.

Russell thought for a second. "Actually now that I'm thinking about it, I never stopped to eat lunch. I just dove right in this morning with a department head meeting first thing and since then I've just been trying to get situated and unpack."

"Do you need me to bring you something to eat?" She asked eagerly.

"That's alright, Mom. I'll grab something." He definitely didn't want his mommy bringing him lunch on the first day.

"Alright. So tell me, how's the apartment?"

"About the same as my office right now, still boxes everywhere and lots of unpacking to do."

"I still wish you would come back and live in your room at home. Then I wouldn't have to worry if you eat or not."

"Mom, I'm a grown man. I think I'm past the point where it's acceptable to live with my parents. But if it will make you feel better, I'll let you cook me dinner tonight, and maybe even bring you my laundry."

"I'll be happy to do whatever you'll let me. I'm just happy to have you back in town."

"Thanks Mom. But I've got to run now, need to get some work done."

"Of course, I'll let you go. But get something to eat."

"Yes, ma'am."

Russell hung up the phone, grabbed his keys and stood to leave his office. He knew he was a grown man who could take care of himself, but he had to laugh that he needed someone to remind him to eat a meal. *Maybe that's why I need an assistant,* he thought.

Russell quickly headed down the hall toward the front door of the building. He looked down to check his pocket for his cell phone just as he rounded a corner. Then it happened.

A girl carrying a large box walked around the corner from the other direction, and Russell looked up just before he ran right into her. As they collided the box went flying and the blow knocked the girl backwards and she fell to the floor. Russell barely managed to stay on his feet as he tripped over her. Silverware and napkins from the box landed all over the hallway. He tried to right himself and take in the situation all at once. He looked at the girl, obviously in shock from being trampled, but after a moment she jumped up and began to quickly pick up the items.

"I'm so sorry." Russell went to her. "Here, let me help you."

"It's alright," said Paige.

"No really, it's my fault, I guess I just wasn't paying attention, it's my first day, and I forgot to eat lunch, and I was just in a hurry."

"It's alright," Paige said again. She scooped up the last of the items into the box and began to lift it to carry again.

"Here, can I carry that for you, please?" Russell begged apologetically.

"No, that's alright, I've got it." Paige answered.

"No, really, I feel terrible, at least let me help."

"No thanks, I can handle it myself," she said and went on around the corner without another word.

Russell stood not really knowing what to do and feeling so bad for…he didn't even get her name. This girl he had just trampled. Obviously she was an employee, but that was all he knew. If she had left as much as a fork, he would have felt like she was Cinderella running away from the ball. As it was, he had nothing to know who she was or where he could find her to fully apologize. *I guess I was right,* he thought, *God is still trying to keep me humble.*

Chapter 3

"Mom, I'm here," Russell called out as he walked into his parents' house. He had stopped by his apartment after work and changed into khaki shorts and a light blue golf shirt. He made himself at home as walked through the formal entryway. The house smelled of freshly baked bread and coffee. The short hallway opened up into the main part of the house. The focal point was the sunken living room where the Pierce family had gathered many times over the years. There were hardwood floors throughout and white built-in cabinets set off the light blue color of the walls. A large, tan, sectional couch made the space look cozy and welcoming, and next to it were two comfortable wingback chairs reserved for "Mom" and "Dad", also known as Jim and Gladys Pierce. The living room was only separated from the kitchen by two steps up and a long counter. Gladys had designed the kitchen herself many years ago so she could prepare meals for her family and the many friends that came into their home. It was her favorite room in the house, and that's where Russell found her.

"Hey there." Gladys stopped her meal preparation to give her youngest son a hug and a kiss on the cheek. "I want to hear all about your day." She went back to the counter where she was cutting vegetables. She was a lovely woman with a strong personality. As she described it she was "aging gracefully", her short blonde hair still dyed to cover the gray roots. She was dressed in white capri pants and a flowing top in a floral print. Her sandals revealed a perfect pedicure that matched the color of her fingernails.

Russell thought about his day and of the girl he had run over. He laughed to himself, but didn't mention that episode to his mother. "It was interesting, but good. Mr. Thompson told me to call him Bob, I don't know when I'll be comfortable with that." He leaned on the counter as he spoke.

"Of course you should, you're working with him now. But you're right, it does seem strange," she said. She finished the salad she was preparing and starting buttering bread from the warm loaf on the counter.

"I know, it does. Can you *believe* I have this job?" Russell asked, "I mean, *really?*"

"Yes, I can," Gladys said proudly, "I have always known you could do whatever you wanted to, and from the time you were fourteen and started working there you would say 'I'm going to run this club someday.' And now your hard work has paid off."

"I'm not exactly 'running the place', but it's definitely a lot of responsibility. And I guess it is mostly because of all the time I've already put in there. That's what Mr. Thompson said when they called to ask me to interview for the position."

"I'm just happy to have you back in the area. You have no

idea how much it means to me for you to be here so we can see you all the time."

"Yep, that's right, as long as you keep feeding me," Russell said and patted his stomach with both hands.

"You bet we will. And you know we would love for you to come to church with us on Sunday. We have a great community there…and there are a lot of singles there too." Gladys feigned casualty with the last part.

Russell knew that look though, he was used to his mother always being eager to marry him off. "Mmhmm, I bet there are. We'll see, I want to check out a few churches to find where I fit best. But it's so weird, I still picture you guys at the church where we grew up."

"I know, honey, but after Pastor Miller retired it just wasn't the same. We loved being there while all of you were kids, but things change. And we felt like it was an exciting time to be part of something new and growing. That's what we love about our church now. I think you would like it too, there are lots of good opportunities for you to jump in and get involved."

Russell shrugged his shoulders. "Like I said, we'll see," he said, "What's for dinner?"

At that moment, Jim Pierce came in from the back patio with a plate in his hand, "Steaks," he called out. He entered from the side door that connected directly from outside into the living room, he looked like an older version of his son, with dark gray hair and dressed casually in a golf shirt and khaki shorts.

"Hey Dad, what's going on?"

"Just the same old, same old, son. How's everything with you?"

"Pretty good. Just trying to get settled in at work and at the apartment."

Jim walked over to his wife to set down the plate of meat and gave her a quick kiss on the cheek. "Has your mother tried to set you up with anyone yet?"

Gladys playfully elbowed her husband in the ribs. "No, I have not," she declared.

"Oh, but I think she's trying," said Russell leaning on the counter. "She's talking up your new church and telling me how many singles there are, I can only assume she means females."

"Yep, she's trying, but sounds like she hasn't nailed down anybody specific yet, so you may be alright for now." Jim's eyes twinkled as he spoke.

Gladys rolled her eyes at them both and finished up the salad she was making. "You both better stop teasing me or no dessert for either of you."

"Okay, okay, we'll stop." Russell held both of his hands up in surrender. He looked over at the plate of steaks and noticed how many there were. "Are we expecting someone else?"

"Well I didn't know how hungry you would be since you can't remember to eat on your own," his mother joked. "No, I'm kidding, your brothers are coming over too, I hope that's alright."

"Yeah, sure. I'll be glad to see them, especially since I haven't been picked on enough since I moved back."

"You know they love you," Gladys said.

"Mmhmm," was Russell's only response.

Russell finished helping his mother with the food and was washing up when the front door opened to a whirlwind of activity.

"Uncle Russ!" came the loud cry from his four-year-old nephew.

"Hey Luke, what's up man?" Russell scooped him up and held Luke at eye-level to talk.

"I got a new truck, wanna see?" Luke asked.

"Of course, I do."

"Daddy, can I please show Uncle Russ my new truck?" the boy yelled across the room.

"Yes, you can, but let's have dinner first." Jack Pierce, dressed in a suit and tie, walked across the living room to the kitchen counter and gave his younger brother a hug, "Although it might be past Russy's bedtime." He pinched the younger man's cheek.

"Ha ha, very funny." Russell rolled his eyes and walked across the room to his sister-in-law. "Hey Carrie," he kept his voice to a whisper, since she was holding their eight-month-old daughter, Caroline, who was sound asleep.

"Hey Russell, so glad to have you back," Carrie whispered back.

"Thanks, it's nice to be here. You had better put her down in the other room before you-know-who gets here and wakes her up."

"We're heeeeeeeeeeeeeeeere!" a voice boomed from the front door.

"Ooops, too late." Carrie smiled and hurried her sleeping daughter from the room.

Samuel Pierce never entered a room quietly, the middle child of the three brothers, he was the definition of extravert, never met a stranger, never had a shy moment in his life, and lived to entertain everyone. "Hey Russy," he greeted his brother, "the kids are so glad you're here, they've been saving a spot for you at the kiddy table."

"Aww, that's just too kind, they really shouldn't have." Russell replied with a rye smile.

"Hey Russell." Sam's wife, Izzy, was not far behind Sam. She was a match for his personality and as the mom of three boys, she fit right in with her rambunctious brood.

As all the family entered the house and hugs were passed all around, Gladys tried to calm the noise and gather them together. "Alright, alright, everybody, dinner is ready so everybody to the table."

Parents rushed the kids to wash their hands before coming to the table and shouts of "Sit next to me" and "What's for dinner?" rang out through the dining room as everyone gathered.

The dining room was just off the kitchen and it featured a long, farmhouse style table with benches on each side. Once everyone was seated, Jim cleared his throat and took his wife's hand. They all joined hands together and as Jim said "Let's thank the Lord", from the oldest to the youngest they all bowed their heads. "Dear Lord, thank you for this time together, thank you for our family and for the food you have provided. We are blessed beyond measure, and we praise you for that. Be with us in all we do. Amen." Jim looked up and glanced at all the faces around the table. "Let's eat" he said with a smile. With that everyone dove in and started reaching for plates and passing dishes around. The table was filled with the steaks and salads, as well as baked potatoes wrapped in foil and a plate of chicken fingers for the kids.

"So how was your first day, baby brother?" Jack started the conversation back up.

Again Russell's mind went to the major incident of the day,

but he pushed the thought away. "Pretty good, you know, just played a round of golf, had a leisurely lunch, went for a steam. Typical day." Russell took a bite and waited for Jack's response.

"I knew it, they must be afraid to give you any real responsibilities around there," Jack baited him.

Russell felt his agitation beginning to grow. "Actually, I have a great deal of responsibility." There was an edge in his tone. "I will be overseeing all the day to day operations, directly under the general manager. They seem pretty confident in my abilities."

Jack held up his hands in surrender. "Okay, Okay, chill, I'm just joking."

"Maybe I've had enough of the joking." Russell stared at his brother.

"Boys, that's enough." Jim spoke firmly, "Let's have a friendly dinner, alright? Don't give each other a hard time anymore."

"Yes, besides we're celebrating." Gladys spoke up, "We are thrilled for Russell to have this new job, and he's back in town and the whole family is together. That's something to be thankful for."

Everyone around the table nodded in agreement. Carrie and Izzy launched into a discussion about what they had done over spring break and the tenseness fell away.

Russell sat quietly eating his steak, he knew how happy his mom was for him to be back, and he wanted to be happy too. *When will I stop being the baby?* he wondered. *What do I have to do to prove it to them?* He didn't have an answer, but he knew that he would do whatever he could to make them see. He would take this job as a new opportunity to show them that he was grown up and should be treated like the adult that he was. Then they would see. *They have to*, he thought, *they just have to.*

Chapter 4

*P*aige stopped at the counter to straighten her apron and check that her hair was securely pinned out of her face. She hurried to finish up the cup of coffee that she would need to make it through the day. She skimmed the board with the daily specials to familiarize herself with the menu and as she walked out through the kitchen door Shannon nearly ran into her.

"Oh man...I'm sorry, Paige," Shannon apologized as she moved past her.

"Good grief, that seems to be happening to me a lot lately." Paige tugged on her apron, "I must be difficult to see these days. Maybe I'm becoming invisible," she spoke mostly to herself.

"Huh?" Shannon said as she rushed to grab her apron.

Paige shook her head. "Nothing. Never mind. What's the matter with you anyway? You're late."

"I *know!* I can't believe it, I was up most of the night studying for my exam and then my alarm didn't go off this morning. I was going to get up and study some more before work, but not only did I miss studying, I barely got a shower and got here. You know how I hate being late."

"Yeah, I know, I'm sorry."

"And, of course it's the day that new manager is coming in."

"Who?" Paige asked.

"Oh you know, the new 'Operations Manager.'" Shannon said with air quotes. "Another suit, another boss, you know."

"Oh right, I forgot about that. Well, I don't think he'll be in charge of the restaurant staff."

"Who knows? I mean, the restaurant does fall under 'Operations', so it's possible."

"True. But I wouldn't worry too much, you're not going to get fired for being late one time." Paige seemed calm and unconcerned.

"I sure hope not." Shannon poured a cup of hot coffee and drank it as fast as she dared. "Let's just get ready to work and try to have a normal day."

The two went around setting up the dining room, making sure all the chairs and tables were straight and putting out silverware wrapped in napkins.

Paige set out menus of the day while Shannon changed out the flower arrangements on the tables. They worked in silence for a while. They only had twenty minutes before they opened for breakfast.

While they were still preparing, Mr. Thompson came in followed closely by another man.

"Good morning, ladies," Mr. Thompson said cheerily.

Both of the girls put on their smiles and greeted him. "Morning, Mr. Thompson."

"I would like you to meet our new Operations Manager,

Russell Pierce. Russ this is Shannon and Paige, some of our wait staff."

Paige looked at the man standing beside Mr. Thompson and her stomach wrenched. She felt herself freeze in shock as her mouth fell open and her eyes opened wide. Just as quickly she tried to gather herself, she smiled and hoped her emotion didn't show on her face. Maybe he wouldn't recognize her.

Russell shook hands with Shannon. "Nice to meet you," he said. He turned to shake hands with Paige and when their eyes met a look of recognition flashed on his face. Paige pretended not to notice and confidently reached out her hand. "Hi," was all Russell managed.

"Hi, nice to meet you." Paige's voice shook ever so slightly and she averted her eyes searching for something to busy herself with.

Mr. Thompson didn't seem to notice Russell's reaction and quickly began discussing the workings of the dining room. "They're just getting ready for breakfast. Guests shouldn't arrive for a few more minutes. Breakfast is open until eleven."

"Of course." Russell refocused on Mr. Thompson and began taking in the room. "And what about the afternoon?" he asked.

"Lunch is available from eleven until three to accommodate everyone, and then the bar is open all day for coffee, drinks and a selection of desserts for the remainder of the afternoon until dinner starts at five p.m."

"And how many people are there on the wait staff?"

"Paige?" Mr. Thompson waited for her answer.

"Shannon and I handle the morning, and then two to three other girls come in for lunch, depending on the day, then there's a dinner crew of eight people, plus several additional weekend staff and a few people who fill-in as needed. Our total on staff right now is twenty-two, but we will add additional servers during the summer months."

"And Paige, you're the manager?"

"Ummm, no." Paige looked to Mr. Thompson.

"Oh no, not a manager, just one of our faithful employees. Paige has been here the longest of our wait staff though, she stays on top of things." Mr. Thompson smiled.

"Oh, well, very nice. I'm sure I'll be seeing both of you ladies frequently, I have a caffeine addiction that I just can't break."

"We'll be happy to help with anything we can." Shannon chimed in.

"Thank you. Now, do I get to meet the chef?" Russell asked.

"Of course," Mr. Thompson said, "Let's head back to the kitchen." The two men walked through the kitchen door and out of the dining room.

Paige breathed a sigh of relief. She put her head in one hand and leaned on the closest table with the other.

"Whoa, can you believe he thought you were a manager?" Shannon whispered loudly, "I mean, not that you couldn't be a manager, you totally could, but wow."

Paige lifted her head and went back to her work a little too quickly. Shannon seemed to pick up on her odd behavior.

"What's the matter, Paige? That's a compliment to you," she walked over to look her friend in the face.

"I know. I'm sorry." She stopped her work and put her hand to her face, she felt hot.

"What is it?" Shannon seemed concerned.

"Well you know how I said I've been getting run into a lot lately?"

"Oh yeah, I thought that's what you said."

"So, the other day, I ran into the new manager. Like literally, ran into him."

"Really?" Shannon's eyes were wide.

"Yeah, I was carrying that big box down the hall and as I came around the corner he ran smack into me. The silverware went everywhere. I was so embarrassed, he probably thought I was rude, I don't think I even told him my name."

"Oh. Well it sounds like it was his fault, not yours. You shouldn't be embarrassed. Besides, he's kind of cute."

"Oh, you know I didn't mean that," Paige came back quickly, "It was just embarrassing to look clumsy at my job."

"I wouldn't worry too much about it. Besides, like you said, he probably won't make decisions about the restaurant."

"Right." Paige agreed. "Who knows?"

. . .

Back in his office, Russell leaned back in his desk chair and stared at the ceiling. Mr. Thompson had shown him all around the club. He had seen the restaurant, the locker rooms, the pool, the tennis courts, the golf course and every back closet, office and restroom on the grounds. And now all he could do was sit mentally kicking himself for his reaction to Paige.

I should have apologized, he thought to himself. *I should have admitted that I knew she was the one I ran into the other day. But she brushed me off like she didn't want me to say anything. Maybe she was embarrassed. But she shouldn't be, I should be...I am!*

Russell sat and tried to think why this incident was bothering him as much as it was. Clearly it was just an accident and she wasn't injured. Still he felt badly that he had caused it. Here he was trying to be professional and be the big, bad boss who could handle this job, and on his first day what does he do, but run over the waitress? Not exactly how he pictured things starting off.

He didn't have any more time to think about it though, since Mr. Thompson, Bob, knocked on his door at that moment. "Come on in," Russell said.

"So what did you think of the place? Has it changed much?" Bob had left for a meeting after their tour saying he would drop by later to talk.

"You know I love this place. And no, it hasn't changed much at all. Some of the people are different, but the feel is the same. It's like coming home," Russell replied.

"I'm glad." Bob smiled and gave a slight shake of his head. "Mostly anyway. I'm glad you feel comfortable. But that's something I would like to talk to you about, a project I would like you to take on."

Russell leaned in, curious as to what was forthcoming.

"The club feels the same because it is the same. Not many changes have been made over the years, and mostly for good reasons. We have steady membership and generations of families who come to the club year after year, and they like to feel like you do, like it's a second home. They don't want drastic change. But…" Bob leaned back in his chair and linked his fingers behind his head. "…that doesn't mean there can't be improvements now does it?"

"No sir, of course there's always room for improvement."

Bob leaned back up to the desk. "Yes, exactly!" he said as he pounded the desk with his fist, then he pointed at Russell. "And I want you to find it."

Chapter 4

"Find it?" Russell raised his eyebrows. "Find what?"

"Find the room for improvement." Bob sounded so excited. He stood from his chair and paced the office.

"Me?" Russell said before he could stop himself. Suddenly he felt very much like the fourteen-year-old junior caddy that had stood before Mr. Thompson, and he was asking for his opinion.

"Yes! You know the club, but here you are, with a new and fresh set of eyes and ears. You can look at each area of the club with a critical eye and find those ways we can improve. Find the little details and changes that can make the club the best ever. It will be a time of refreshment, with new ideas that are young and inspiring."

Russell wasn't sure what to say. Of course it wasn't like he could turn him down or say no, this was his job, this was his boss giving him a new responsibility. But could he do this? Could he start walking around departments and making changes to procedures that had been in place since he was a teenager? He stared at his desk for a minute thinking through what to say and how he would tackle this assignment. *This is it.* He thought, *This is my chance to really do something here. I'll do it. I'll take it on and make the club the best it's ever been. Then they'll see.* He looked up with confidence, "That sounds like an amazing opportunity and the perfect way to start my career here. I won't let you down, Bob."

"I know you won't, Russ. I can't wait to see what you find once you start digging. Get ready to start taking notes and see what you can find. You can get started first thing Monday morning in the restaurant." With that Bob gave him a thumbs up sign and headed out of his office.

Russell watched him go and thought of how he intended to

do everything in his power to keep his promise to Bob. But as Mr. Thompson walked out Russell's confidence melted away, because Monday morning he would walk in and start looking for problems and improvements to be made in the restaurant. And big, bad, boss Russell suddenly felt panicked at the thought of once again coming face-to-face with a certain dark-haired waitress.

Chapter 5

❧

"Paige, that casserole was delicious, I've got to get your recipe." Susan Johnson, the wife of one of the church deacons, commented as she handed Paige a completely empty and wiped clean casserole dish.

"Oh thank you, it's really pretty simple. I'll email it to you," Paige told the older woman. It was Friday night after a church family service and potluck dinner and Paige was in the kitchen helping clean up. She made a mental note to send the link from the webpage where she had found the recipe just earlier that morning. She had been planning to make something for the dinner all week, but she didn't get around to deciding what to make until the last minute.

"Paige, look what Abby made me." Lucy came running up to her sister with a crafted bracelet in her hand and pointed to her friend. Just as Paige was going to comment on how cute it was, Joe ran past and snatched it out of her hand.

"Keep away!" he shouted. "Can't catch me."

"Hey! Give that back!" Lucy squealed.

"Joe, give that bracelet back to your sister now." Paige raised her voice slightly as the twins ran down the hallway near the kitchen. "I'm sorry," she apologized to Susan. "They're driving each other crazy a lot lately."

Susan seemed unruffled by the exchange, "I understand, my two are the same way. 'He pulled my hair,' 'She ate my cookie,' 'He made that mess, not me.' I can't imagine that it's easier when they're twins. I don't know how you do it, Paige."

Paige gave her a small smile as she gathered her things and headed down the hall after the kids. She never knew how to respond when people said things like that. She had been looking for Shep earlier and had no luck finding him. The twins had headed towards the church gymnasium, so she followed them. Fortunately when she walked in she quickly spotted the kids, and she finally saw Shep on the basketball court playing with a few other guys. She saw to it that Joe gave Lucy back her bracelet and told them to get ready to leave, then she approached the sideline.

"Shep, it's time to go," she called out. He either didn't hear her or was choosing to ignore her. Paige assumed it was the latter. "Shep!" she called out, louder this time. She began to consider walking out and standing in the middle of the court until he acknowledged her.

. . .

Russell leaned against the wall of the fellowship hall where many church members were still visiting after the potluck dinner. He thought back to when his mom had asked him to come to the meal that night. He had turned her down, reminding her that he really wanted to find his own church, on his own time. But somehow she convinced him that even if he didn't want to eat, he could come afterwards to help her load the tablecloths and centerpieces that she was taking to the event. Now he stood waiting around for her as she made her rounds of talking to people and seeing to different needs.

Gladys and Jim had only started attending Pine Haven Community Church after Russell graduated college and was off on his own. It wasn't the church where he grew up and he didn't really know many of the people. He grew tired of waiting for her, so he began to wander around the campus. He knew she would find him when she was ready. He walked down the hall and into the gym where a bunch of kids were chasing each other and a group of high school boys were playing basketball. He neared the edge of the court to watch, then he turned to his left and stopped, frozen in place.

Paige Kelly. There she was. Standing in the gym. The sight of her stopped him in his tracks. He watched for a moment as she spoke to two younger children. He noticed that she was carrying an empty dish and some sort of craft that looked like it had been made by a child. At that moment Russell nearly stopped breathing. *She's a mom.* He thought to himself. He couldn't remember seeing her with a wedding band on, and immediately thought *She's a single mom.*

What happened next puzzled him even more as she began calling for one of the high school boys on the court. She seemed frustrated that he was ignoring her. *She's much too young to be his mother,* Russell thought. He was still too shocked to fully consider other possibilities, but before he knew what he was doing he found himself walking towards her.

Paige called out to Shep one more time as the teens dribbled the ball closer to her side of the court. "Shep, it's time to go right now."

"Want me to get him for you?"

Paige jumped as Russell appeared at her side and spoke. She glanced over her shoulder and obviously recognized him. She shook her head and seemed to avoid eye contact, "No thanks. I can handle it myself."

With that she walked onto the court and interrupted the ball game, she just stood and stared at the teenage boy. Obviously embarrassed, he walked off the court with a quick "Later guys."

Paige walked alongside him and gathered the two younger kids, then they all walked out the door together.

Russell stood watching them leave, unable to look away and unable to stop thinking about them even after they were all out of sight. *What just happened here?* He thought to himself. He tried to make sense of the family, but couldn't quite figure it out. Just then Gladys walked in the gym and called to Russell, he turned and walked towards her.

"There you are," Gladys said, "I didn't know where you wandered off to."

"I figured you would find me when you were ready," he replied quietly.

Russell didn't notice the concerned look his mother gave him, "Are you alright? You have a strange look on your face."

"Yeah, I'm fine."

Together they walked back to the fellowship hall and began gathering tablecloths. Gladys was chitchatting about some of the people who had been at the dinner and what the tastiest dishes had been. Russell was halfheartedly listening and making occasional "mmhmm"s and "yeah"s. Gladys finally stopped, set down the tablecloth she was folding and put her hands on her hips, "Alright Son, what's going on. Your mind is a million miles away right now."

Russell looked up at his mother a little surprised. "Oh, I'm sorry," he said, "I was just thinking." He looked at her and knew she was not going to let this go. He sighed, placed his hands on the table in front of him and leaned over as he spoke. "Do you know a girl named Paige?"

"Paige Kelly?" Gladys immediately seemed interested.

"Yeah, that's her."

"I've never actually met her, but I know who she is, yes. Did you meet her tonight?"

"Well no, she works at the club, in the restaurant."

"I didn't know that." Gladys said. "So you met her at work?"

"Yes," Russell thought back to his shining moment of trampling her in the hallway, "something like that."

Gladys waited for him to say more, but he didn't. "And you saw her here tonight?" she asked.

"Yes." Still he didn't say anything else.

"So…" Gladys tried.

"What do you know about her, Mom? I saw her with some kids, but then also a teenager? I'm confused. Are they hers?"

"Hers? Oh, you mean are they her kids? No, those are her siblings, Paige is the oldest of four or five I think," Gladys explained.

Understanding dawned on Russell and strangely he felt relieved. "Oh, that makes much more sense. So she was just taking them home? Her parents don't come to the church?"

Gladys' eyes turned sad, "No, Russell, her parents are gone."

"Gone?"

"Yes. I don't know the whole story, it happened before we

came to the church, but her parents both died, I believe in a car accident, a few years ago. Paige has been taking care of her brothers and sisters ever since."

A weight washed over Russell so strongly that he felt the need to sit in the nearest chair. As the baby of the family he had been brought up without any of the responsibility of an older sibling, he couldn't even imagine taking care of a family all on his own, especially when she was barely more than a kid herself.

Gladys walked over to put her hand on Russell's shoulder. Obviously he was upset by this news. "I'm sure it's hard. I don't know her personally, but that would be hard on anybody. She seems to handle it so well, but I'm sure she could use a friend."

Russell went back to folding tablecloths as he thought about Paige and her family. He didn't think he could ever do anything like that, but she seemed to be doing well and in her own words, she could handle it. His mother's statement struck a cord in his heart, but surely she had friends. She didn't need him. He decided to put her out of his mind. He had plenty of his own business to worry about.

Chapter 6

*T*he weekend came and went quickly for Russell. He filled the time running errands, making a few purchases for his apartment and trying to get settled into his new place. Monday morning he rose at five a.m. for his usual morning routine. He quickly dressed in a T-shirt and athletic shorts, and didn't bother to look in the mirror before he laced up his tennis shoes and went for a quick jog around the block. He didn't like to listen to music or talk while he ran, but tried to let the quiet sink in while he woke up and gathered his thoughts for the day. The spring morning was still cool enough to enjoy the weather. The trees were beginning to come alive with green and there were a few flowers just starting to bud. The morning air smelled crisp and fresh after a light rain the night before. Once back at his apartment he showered and dressed in dark grey dress slacks, a blue button down shirt and a blue and gray striped tie. He headed into his small kitchen and reached for the coffee maker. Just then he remembered that even with all the stores he had been to over the weekend he never picked up any coffee, and now he was completely out. All the good vibes from the morning vanished. *Just great. Great way to start a day and an entire week,* he thought. *I guess I'll just have to get some at the club.* Inwardly he groaned that he would have to wait that long for his caffeine buzz to kick in, but there wasn't much else to do. He grabbed his wallet and keys and headed out the door.

His drive to the club was short and he zoned out and drove on autopilot to the place he had been so many times. But once he reached the drive to the club he couldn't help but notice and enjoy the scenery. No matter how many times he drove it, he always thought it was the most beautiful spot he had ever seen. The large wrought-iron gate decorated the entry way with the letters "SPCC", Shady Pines Country Club. The drive lined with pine trees, wound up the hill past the outdoor swimming pool and the tennis courts. At the top of the hill sat the clubhouse. It was a beautiful, two-story brick building complete with restaurant, event center, pro shop, men's and women's locker rooms and steam rooms, a large indoor pool and the staff offices. The front of the building had a circular drive with a covered awning and four large brick columns framed the wide glass doors. To the side of the clubhouse was a small parking lot reserved for the executive staff, where Russell pulled around and parked.

He entered the building through the side door, but before heading to his office, he walked to the restaurant in hopes of getting some coffee. He slowed a bit as he came to the restaurant door, but once inside he refused to admit to himself that he was relieved to see Shannon at the counter instead of Paige. He was also very happy to smell freshly brewed coffee.

"Hello, Mr. Pierce," Shannon greeted him. "Can I get you

something?"

Russell felt a little strange at being called "Mr. Pierce," but it reminded him how his position had changed here and he felt proud of the title. "I was hoping for some coffee," he said.

"Sure thing." Shannon reached for a cup and poured him some.

Russell took the cup and immediately took a sip. He always drank his coffee black. He stood for a moment and let the taste linger. Even though he knew it wasn't that quick, he imagined the immediate rush of caffeine to his brain and believed that he felt more awake and ready for the day. After a moment he realized Shannon had spoken to him again.

"Can I get you anything else?" she asked.

"How about topping this off? I have a feeling it's going to be a long day. If you don't mind I'll take it with me."

"No problem, Mr. Pierce," Shannon said as she filled the mug again.

He thanked her and turned to go, coffee in hand. When he reached his office, Russell laid down his things and sat down at his desk. For the next thirty minutes he read and responded to emails and clicked through his favorite online news sites to catch up on the goings on in the world.

Precisely at 8:40, Bob knocked on his office door. "You ready, Russ?"

"Sure am, Mist...uh, Bob." Russell grabbed a notebook and pen and started down the hall with his boss.

Bob spoke as they walked down the hall toward the restaurant. "I didn't tell any of the staff the plan for having you take a look at each department. Of course word will get around that that's what you're doing, but I didn't want them to know which day you were going where. I don't want them getting set up and ready for you, I just want you to see what a normal day is really like."

Russell nodded in understanding as they walked through the door and up to the counter. Shannon was there again and greeted him.

"Oh hi, Mr. Pierce, Mr. Thompson. Can I help you with something?" Shannon asked.

"Hello, Shannon," Bob started. "Actually, I would like you to just continue on with whatever you're doing. Mr. Pierce here is going to be visiting the restaurant today just to see how everything works. He'll be taking some notes and asking some questions. Please help him with whatever he needs, but try to just keep doing what you normally do."

"Yes sir. Happy to help any way I can." Shannon said.

Bob stopped suddenly and looked around the restaurant as if something was missing. "Is Paige here?" he asked.

"No sir, she's off today."

"Off?" he asked.

"Umm, yes sir. She went on a field trip with her younger sister."

"Oh. Hmm. Well, alright." He paused for a moment as if considering something and then dismissed it.

"Thank you, Shannon. Can I also get a cup of coffee to take?"

"Yes, sir." Shannon poured a cup and handed it to him.

"Thank you." Bob said, "Alright, have a good morning, Russ," and he turned to go.

Once he was gone Shannon looked at Russell. "Don't mind me," he said. "I'm just gonna walk around a bit and take a look at things. I'll let you know if I have questions."

Shannon went back to work and Russell sat down at a table near the corner. For a while he simply observed. Another waitress, there to fill in for Paige, was working in the dining room for breakfast. A few members came in for breakfast, but most just wanted coffee or something small like a bagel or muffin. Russell made a note. A couple of people came in and sat with their laptops and connected to the available wireless to do some work.

Russell thought about his last job, where he too had carried his laptop with him everywhere and frequently worked in coffee shops or places where he could connect to the internet. As a salesman he had had a lot of personal responsibility to acquire new clients and maintain accounts, but he also had a lot of flexibility with his time. He thought about how he had spent a week working from the beach and calling his clients on the phone. They had no idea he was practically working on vacation, but it didn't matter. His time was his own and he had the time and the resources to do what he wanted to do. Eat out, travel, play golf, even work itself was like a hobby since he always enjoyed talking to people and selling became second nature to him. But the culture of the office and company was mostly young, single guys out to do the best for themselves. There was a lot of competition and not much camaraderie. He had given up some of the freedoms when he took on the job at Shady Pines. Here he had a more structured eight-to-five schedule and a responsibility to be in the office every day. But he knew he was ready for a more mature work environment and a place where people were working towards a common goal, rather than their own individual success. A place that felt more like a family.

A place where I could have a family. The thought surprised him a bit. Of course he had always thought he would come back to Pine Haven before he was ready to settle down and have a family, but he still had a lot he wanted to do before that. He was in no rush to get married, like his mom wanted, but somewhere down the road he could see himself in his hometown with a wife and a couple of kids. *Way down the road,* he told himself. That thought brought him back to the present and the task at hand. He wrote down a few more notes on the comings and goings in the dining room. He knew he needed to look over the kitchen soon, but he just sat in the quiet for a few minutes. Before he knew it, he found himself praying silently.

Thank you, Lord, for this opportunity. I still can't believe I'm back here, in the place where I grew up, in my dream job. I love this place and these people, and besides all that, they couldn't have made me a better offer. Thank you for this blessing. I want to honor you in it. Show me how I can do that.

Bless others.

The words he heard in his heart were as clear as a bell.

Bless others? He asked The Lord.

Bless others.

Lord, I've been an independent guy, looking out for myself and my own interests for quite a while. I've always known I should put others first, but I don't even know if I know how to do that. I confess that to You, please forgive me. Please open my heart to love people and show me how I can help others.

Paige.

Russell stopped at the name that was so clear he could almost here it out loud. He waited to hear something else, but that one word seemed to hang in the silence.

Paige, Lord?

Paige.

I can't help her. I wouldn't even know how and she doesn't seem to need any help, she does pretty well on her own. And she definitely doesn't want my help.

Walk with Me.

Russell looked down at his notes and tried to put Paige from his mind. Of course, God wanted him to care about people and help those that he could, but Paige wasn't someone he could help anyway. He tried not to think about the strong impression about her as he picked up his notebook and headed to the kitchen.

The room was a little loud with the sounds of pots and pans and the voices of the kitchen staff. The air smelled of fresh herbs and garlic. James, the chef, greeted Russell as he came in and offered him a taste of the upcoming lunch special.

"Garlic pesto chicken with penne in tomato cream sauce," James said. "Best thing on the menu, better get'cha some." The chef was professionally trained, without a doubt, but his southern accent was thick.

"Thanks, James," Russell said. "Not now, but maybe I'll take a break and have some for lunch after while."

"Alright, Mr. Pierce. Let me know if I can help with anything." Shannon had filled him in on Russell's task for the day.

"Will do, James. Just taking a look around for now."

He walked around the kitchen trying not to get in the way of James' team. The kitchen staff consisted of James, his sous-chef, and three other kitchen assistants responsible for various tasks. Russell started by taking a look at the pots and pans hanging above a prep table and dozens of knives neatly organized on a magnetic wall for quick use. "That's a pretty neat knife display," he commented.

"Oh yeah, it works pretty well. Makes it easy to find what I need and get to work. That was actually Paige's idea." James said.

Russell's heart thudded loudly at the name. "Really?"

"Oh yeah, she's great at ideas for organization and set up in the kitchen. She's always coming up with new ideas for making the kitchen and dining room run more smoothly."

"Hmm, that's good," Russell replied absentmindedly. He ran his fingers through his hair and continued his observations. He noticed the shelves filled with frequently used ingredients and spices. Each space was clearly labeled with what went where. On the end of the shelf was a large clipboard with a list of all the staple foods on the shelf and a check box next to each item.

"What's this?" he asked.

"That's our reorder list. Anytime we notice we are running low on an item on the shelf we go ahead and put a check mark so we know it's time to reorder. It saves a lot of time on Fridays when we are doing our orders. Paige made that list."

"Okay, good." Russell made a note. He went on to the back room with the large walk-in freezer and more of the larger containers of staple foods as well as specific items needed for the week's specials. There was another clipboard like the one on the kitchen shelves with a list of these items. On the wall next to the freezer there was a large bulletin board. Neatly pinned on the board were three different groups of papers, Russell lifted the pages to read them. The first was the current week's menus with the usual items and the daily specials, it also included an order list of staple items that had been needed and the items needed for the specials. Behind the list was a set of recipes for the week. The next two stacks were similar, but were for the following week and the week after that.

James came to the back room to get something from the freezer. "Oh you found the menu board I see. That is my lifesaver. It was…"

"Let me guess." Russell held up his hand and interrupted. "Paige's idea?"

James smiled. "Yes, it was." He paused and took a breath, "Mr. Pierce, let me be a little honest with you. I *love* to cook." He closed his eyes and held his hand over his heart as he spoke. "I have been in the kitchen since I was a little kid and never dreamed of doing anything else. I am creative and I spend all my brain energy thinking about food and new ideas for dishes and dining. But when I came here, I was a mess. I would have beautiful ideas for specials and amazing desserts, but I would find out that we were out of coffee because I hadn't ordered it on time. Or we would run out of the special an hour into lunch. I was pretty sure I could get fired any day. But Paige came in and started looking around the kitchen. She asked me questions like, 'What's on the menu for next week,' or 'What do we need to order?'. Easy, basic things that I should have known, but I didn't. I couldn't think to the next day, much less the next week." He stopped and rubbed his chin as he thought. "Every day Paige checks the order list and looks over the shelves to see if we're running low. Every other week she sits down with me on Wednesday during the afternoon lull and helps me plan two weeks worth of menus so we're far enough ahead to have everything we need. I don't know what I would do without her. I can cook, but without her the restaurant would fall apart."

Russell looked back at the man and then stared again at the lists on the board. He let a thought roll around in his head, then said "Thank you, James, you've been more help than you know."

James went back to his kitchen. Russell finished looking around the back room, freezers, refrigerators and cabinets. He found everything neatly organized and in tiptop shape. He returned to the dining room and enjoyed some of the chicken dish for lunch while watching the activity of the lunch hours. He took a few notes on the number of people and the wait staff and headed back to his office once the rush died down.

Back in his office he absentmindedly stared at the pages of his notebook. He tried to focus on the words on the paper, but all he could think about was what James had said. He was supposed to meet with Bob to discuss what he saw and give suggestions for improvement in just a little while. So far he could only think of one thing to suggest and he had a feeling Bob would not like it. He wasn't sure he really liked it, because of how the idea might come across.

Paige, he thought, *she runs that restaurant. She takes care of her family, and manages a household, and works her job, and even though it's not her job, she runs that restaurant.* He wanted to skip over the idea, he wanted to walk away and say the restaurant was in great hands and leave things alone. But he also couldn't shake his strong impression that The Lord had placed on his heart. He ran his fingers through his hair and began making a different list, a list of reasons why Bob should agree to this idea.

At five minutes to three o'clock Russell took his notebook and headed to Bob's office. He walked down the hall away from the direction of the restaurant and rode the elevator to the second floor. He opened the door to a smaller office where Bob's assistant, Sarah, worked and waited for her to tell Bob he was here and give him permission to go in.

Chapter 6

"Mr. Thompson will see you now. Can I get you anything to drink?" Sarah asked.

Russell held up the water bottle in his hand. "No, thanks." He opened the door to Bob's office and stepped in. The office was much larger than Russell's, or any other office in the building, for that matter. At the entry way was a seating area with two leather couches facing each other and a deep blue wingback chair all surrounding a dark brown coffee table. A large flat-screen television hung on the wall nearby, a national news channel played on the screen with the volume muted. As Russell walked across the room he passed the door to the private bathroom and then a long row of four wooden bookcases filled with hardback books and a few first editions. He came to Bob's desk, a large, decorative wooden desk with a matching hutch and credenza, and looked behind it to the full glass wall that opened up to a view of the golf course. He could see that today was a perfect day for golf, beautiful sunshine, and spring temperatures made it a great day for walking along the lush green hills and paths.

"Good afternoon, Mis...Bob." Russell shook his head, still trying to shake the habit.

Bob turned from where he stood looking out the window. "Hey there Russ, I almost forgot about our appointment. I was thinking about canceling the rest of my day and heading out for a round." He smiled. "But I decided I probably better stick around." Bob was known as a professional business man, on time and on task. But everyone knew the only thing he would blow off work for was time out on the course. "I hope that this meeting is going to be worth it," he laughed.

Russell hoped so too. He tried to put on a smile to cover his nerves. "Yes, sir."

Bob took a seat and motioned for Russell to do the same. "Well tell me what you think of the restaurant."

"The restaurant is great." Russell took a seat and opened his notebook. "It's clean and efficient and the food is delicious. I would love to sit in on dinner to see how things go at that time of day, but lunch was very busy and the staff handled it exceptionally well. All the members seemed pleased. I'm sure many of them eat lunch frequently and know what they like, but today's special was also a big hit. My first impression is that breakfast is pretty slow, we might look at some options for either encouraging more members to eat breakfast here, or cutting back on the number of options available to serve fewer people. However, the staff ratio still seems good for the number of people that came in, so that's good."

"Mmhmm, yes, alright, what else?"

Russell looked back at his notes. "The kitchen is amazing, James is truly gifted. But what's really impressive is the organization and efficiency in there. They've got lists and notes for everything that is happening and it seems that they have all the food ordered in a timely manner and make sure that little goes to waste."

"That's wonderful, that helps the members being served as well as the bottom line," Bob said frankly.

"Yes, I thought so too. And that brings me to my main suggestion."

Russell paused and Bob leaned forward in anticipation. Russell took a deep breath and silently prayed *Lord, help me know how to present this.* "I told James how impressed I was with the system and the way things work, and the thing is, he told me all of that was done by Paige."

Bob looked surprised. "Paige? The waitress?"

"Yes, sir. James was pretty candid about his lack of organizational skills and said that Paige is the one who set up all the systems and makes sure that things run smoothly."

For just a moment Bob looked like he didn't quite know what to say, then he half-coughed, half-laughed and said, "I always like to see some employee initiative, glad to know we have people who like to step up and put forth some creativity and ideas without instruction."

"Yes, I agree." Russell hesitated ever so slightly and then boldly pushed forward with his idea, "and that's why I think we should give her a promotion."

"What?" This was clearly not what Bob expected to hear. Just as Russell expected he immediately seemed to dislike the idea.

"Paige has been running the restaurant, doing far more than her responsibilities as a waitress call for, and she hasn't received the recognition or the compensation for it. James serves as both the manager and the cook, but as a creative person, managing doesn't really fit well with his skill set. I believe it would be in our best interest to make Paige the restaurant manager." Russell sat back in his chair and waited.

Bob started to say something, but then paused and leaned back in his own chair. He turned to look out the window and thought for a moment. Finally he spoke. "What if we talk to James and require him to take back over the responsibilities himself? Especially if the systems are already set up, surely he can keep using them."

Russell had prepared to fight for this. "Yes, sir, we could do that. However, I believe that either Paige will simply continue to work in the same capacity and not be compensated for it, or she will realize her abilities in this area and she'll begin to look for a position elsewhere."

Bob seemed to take that in.

Russell continued, "I took the liberty of pulling Paige's work record from our H.R. office." He laid a paper on the desk and pointed to some numbers. "She has rarely ever missed work when she was scheduled, and even though she's out today, it looks like she has only requested a few days off in her time here over the last three years. Also, I feel that I should point out that several of the restaurant employees already look to Paige as a leader and you yourself asked her questions when I toured the restaurant that made me think that she was a manager. Like I said, she's already doing this job. We don't need to know if she's qualified or if she can handle it. We just need to decide if we value her enough to give her the title and the financial compensation and benefits she deserves." Russell felt bold and sure of himself now.

With that last line said, Bob could hardly argue the point. He sighed and folded his hands on his desk. "Alright Russell. We can do it. We'll give her the job, but I want to reevaluate in two months and see how it's going and what the restaurant looks like at that time."

"Yes, sir, that seems fair," Russell agreed. "I think that you will be pleased with what you see, and honestly it's the best recommendation I can make for improvements to the restaurant. If Paige has had that much success without it officially being her job, I believe we will see vast improvements when she is putting her all into it."

Bob nodded. "Yes, we'll see."

Russell stayed a few minutes more to discuss what they would offer Paige as a salary and benefits, and Russell agreed to send an email to human resources to set everything up.

Chapter 6

As Russell left Bob's office he waved to Sarah and started for the elevator. He wanted to go straight to the restaurant and tell Paige about the job, but halfway there he remembered that she wasn't there today. Disappointed that such good news would have to wait he contemplated the best way to tell her.

Lord, I may have only jumped the first hurdle. I don't know her very well, but I have a feeling the bigger one may be convincing her that she deserves the job.

Chapter 7

⟨⟨⟨ ❦ ⟩⟩⟩

"*L*ucy watch your step. Be careful." Paige held her hand behind her youngest sister while climbing onto the trailer pulled behind a tractor. They took their seats on the floor and huddled close to allow the other children and parents room to sit. They were on Lucy's field trip to the strawberry patch. They would ride the trailer out to the field where they would pick their own berries and load their buckets to take home. Paige was already thinking through the things she would make with the fresh strawberries. Lucy chatted excitedly with her classmates. Paige sat quietly and watched the younger girl interact. She was so full of life and happiness, laughing at a silly joke and squealing with delight as they rode over the bumps in the dirt road. Paige thought about how carefree Lucy was and tried to remember a time when she didn't have a care in the world. An image flashed in her mind, *she sat at the kitchen counter eating a snack, swinging her feet from the stool and making silly faces with....*Paige shook her head and put away the thought. No use daydreaming about days passed, only this moment mattered right now. She looked out at the view beyond the trailer, trees lined the path of the dirt road that they were riding along. The area was shaded and a little cool, but then they came around the bend and the area opened up to the strawberry patch. As they came out of the trees the blue sky brightened and the sun shown on the beautiful spring day. Paige pushed back the sleeves of her light jacket, she wore a t-shirt underneath and jeans that were probably a little too big. Her tennis shoes were comfortable and worn in from a few years of use. During spring in Alabama it was hard to know whether to wear shorts or a coat, the weather could change in a moment, she wanted to be prepared with layers.

"Come on, Paige!" Lucy shouted, getting her attention and the two climbed down together. Paige handed Lucy her bucket as she ran to catch up with her friends.

"Don't go too far," Paige called after her, but knew that it was futile, since her sister was already far away. She sighed.

One of the moms walked up behind Paige and spoke. "It's no use trying to keep up with them at this age. I've given up." Paige looked at the woman who was dressed in designer jeans and knee high brown boots, a crisp white shirt and a fitted blue blazer.

"Oh yeah? I try, but she definitely has a lot of energy." Paige smiled and pulled her jacket closer around her university t-shirt.

"Yes, energy all the time." The woman seemed somewhat annoyed. "That's why I try not to come on these things, but my daughter wouldn't stop begging me, so I finally gave in this time."

"Oh." Paige let her word hang in the air since she couldn't think of a response to the woman.

"I'm Rachel, by the way. Everly's mother." She reached out to shake hands.

Paige recognized the name. Lucy wasn't close with Everly, but she had mentioned her before, she seemed to be the class drama queen. Paige reached out her hand. "Hi, I'm Paige…"

"Do you know how long we will be here?" Rachel interrupted. "I've got a meeting at two o'clock that I can't miss."

"Oh." Paige looked at her watch. "I think we're officially done once the kids are done picking the strawberries, then we're supposed to eat lunch at the picnic area before they go back to school. I would think we will be done before then."

"I drove my car separately just in case. If I need to leave would you be willing to watch Everly for the rest of the time?"

Paige tried not to show the shock on her face. "Oh, umm, sure, I guess I could do that."

"Thanks. You know how it is, just have to take care of everything, all the balls are up in the air." Rachel threw in a light laugh at the end.

"Yes, I do understand that," Paige said, more to herself than the other woman. She picked up her pace trying to keep Lucy in her line of sight.

"Frankly, I would rather be at work anyway. Everly is just so demanding all the time." She rolled her eyes and threw up her hands for emphasis. "I don't have a moment to call my own when she's around. I don't know how people do it with more than one, I cannot even *begin* to imagine."

"Mmhmm," Paige muttered quietly.

"Do you have more?"

"More what?" Paige asked.

"More kids, besides your daughter…what's her name?"

"Oh, ummm, well…" Paige paused trying to decide what to

say. This happened often. People usually assumed she was the mom, but she could still never decide how to handle it. Once she started explaining she usually ended up telling more than she meant to, and that usually led to sympathy or pity and Paige wanted neither of those. "Her name is Lucy, but I'm not her mom."

"Oh, well that explains that, I thought you looked a little young." Rachel looked embarrassed and did the laugh again. "I thought she must have been a little surprise! But you must be the nanny."

Paige gritted her teeth. This woman was far from pleasant and she had no desire to tell her life story to her. "No, I'm her sister."

"Oh, her sister," Rachel paused trying to find the words she wanted to ask. "So you, umm, you take care of her? Like all the time?"

"Yes, I'm her legal guardian." Paige left it at that.

"Oh," Rachel finally seemed to have run out of things to say. She awkwardly fiddled with her cell phone.

Something about the woman made Paige want to tell her how important Lucy was to her and how she wouldn't miss a minute with her, but she didn't. She simply walked faster and glanced over her shoulder to say, "I had better catch up with Lucy, she's really been looking forward to this and I would hate to miss out on that time with her. Nice to meet you."

"Oh yeah, nice to meet you too," Rachel said and went back to her phone.

Paige walked along the lines of strawberry plants observing the other kids and parents. Some of the mothers stood together in a huddle discussing the class, some of the latest gossip and upcoming school events. A few of the parents picked strawberries alongside their kids, some of the kids picked strawberries and others were simply running in and out of the field. Paige walked closer to Lucy and saw her chatting with one of her friends, her bucket was only about a fourth of the way full and she looked like she had tasted more than a few berries. Paige smiled. She walked to the lane closest to her sister and waved a little when she caught her eye, but she didn't bother her. She could play with her friends, Paige just wanted to be close enough to her. She started picking a few of her own strawberries. The plants were full of beautiful, ripe berries and she carefully picked through and chose the best ones to add to her bucket. She was dreaming about strawberry short cake and strawberry ice cream when Lucy ran up to her nearly jumping up and down "Paige, Paige! Look at all my strawberries!" Her bucket was close to full now.

Paige smiled. "I see. That's great Lu! I have been thinking about all the yummy things we can make with them. What do you think about strawberry ice cream?"

"Can we make some today?" Lucy squealed.

"Yes, yes, we'll try to. Just depends on the timing this afternoon, but sometime this week for sure," Paige promised.

"Yay!" Lucy grabbed her bucket and ran off again with her friend.

Paige stared at her as she went, shaking her head slightly that she could be that excited. She tried to pick more berries, but her mind was elsewhere. With the woman who was frustrated and upset by spending time with her daughter.

At home later that afternoon Paige stood at the kitchen sink still thinking about the field trip, but trying to focus on the fun they had had instead of the unpleasantness. She was beginning to make preparation for dinner when her cell phone rang.

Her heart always skipped a beat when she got a call un-expectedly. She mentally made a checklist of where all her siblings were and then answered the phone, "Hello?"

"Hello, is this Paige Kelly?"

"Yes, it is," she said nervously.

"Paige, this is Sarah, Mr. Thompson's assistant at Shady Pines."

"Oh yes, hi." She relaxed a little since the call wasn't about any of her family.

"Mr. Thompson asked me to call and schedule a meeting with you. Can you come to his office first thing tomorrow morning? At eight thirty?"

"Ummm, yes, I can do that." Paige tried to hide the confusion and concern in her voice. "Is there anything I should know?"

"Just be here at eight thirty, we look forward to seeing you. Goodbye." Sarah said this very cheerily and hung up the phone.

"Bye," Paige said to no one. She couldn't keep the anxious thoughts from surfacing, *Why does Mr. Thompson want to meet with me? Did I do something wrong?* She clicked through her phone and found a text Shannon had sent a little while before. It read: *Mr. Pierce here "observing" in the restaurant today. Looking around and taking notes.* She gasped and brought her hand up to her mouth. *What if this has something to do with Mr. Pierce? Surely they can't fire me over running into someone in the hallway! Or what if he found something he didn't like in the restaurant because he's looking to get me in trouble?*

What could it be? she thought to herself. *What could it be?*

No answers came to mind, so she tried to put the thought away and not worry about tomorrow. But she couldn't quite let it go. She felt nervous and concerned and she knew she would until she found out what this was all about.

Chapter 8

T he alarm clock started beeping, but it wasn't necessary. Paige reached over and shut it off, she had been awake for an hour. She had hardly slept during the night. She would fall asleep and have one bad dream after another: Mr. Thompson firing her, looking for a new job, having to spend more money out of savings for monthly expenses. She just couldn't stop thinking about the meeting today and worrying. The Shady Pines Country Club had been her life for the past three years and she couldn't stand the thought that she had done something to mess that up or that she might not be there any more.

Paige sighed. *Nothing to do but get up and get going,* she thought. She quickly showered and dressed for work. She had grown up sharing a room with her sister and a bathroom with her others siblings. But after her parents died she moved to the master suite. It just made sense because the little kids were in the habit of coming to her parents' room if they woke during the night. So now she had all this space to herself, she had gotten used to it, but at times it still felt like a big, lonely room. Once she was ready for the day she began the task of waking up the rest of the household. She exited the master bedroom and slowly climbed the stairs. She entered her brother's room and flipped on the light switch, which earned a groan from the direction of the bed. "Wake up Shep, school." She stepped out of the doorway, just missing the pillow thrown in her direction. "Get up now, grumpy pants."

Leaving Shep's room she stepped next door to her old room where Zoey had taken up residence with Peyton. She walked first to Zoey's twin bed and brushed the hair back off her face as she spoke gently to the thirteen-year-old. "Wake up, Zoey, it's a school day." Zoey opened her eyes briefly and looked up at Paige. "Hop up, sweet girl, go wake up Peyton." She left Zoey to the unpleasant job of waking the sleeping beauty, better known as the sleeping dragon at this hour of the day.

Paige skipped over the next door that used to be Zoey's room. She entered Joe's room and tripped over a toy truck left out in the floor. She flipped on the lamp as she rubbed a sore toe. "Good morning, Joe. I've got your favorite cereal for breakfast, hop up and get dressed and come down to eat." She left Joe as he wiped his sleepy eyes and went to her last, but favorite wake up of the morning. She sat on the edge of Lucy's bed and patted her back. "Wake up Lucy, it's morning time." Lucy rolled from her sleep and climbed over into Paige's lap.

"What's today Paige?"

"Today is Tuesday."

"So we go to school today?"

"Yes, you do."

"Do you miss Mommy today, Paige?"

"Yes, Lucy, I miss Mommy today." Paige sighed over the

question that came every morning, but felt it was better to be real with her sister. "Now get dressed for school and come down, I'll fix hot chocolate before the bus, Okay?"

"Okay. Paige?"

"Yes, Lu?"

"I love you."

"I love you too, Lucy."

Paige left the room and looked in each of the upstairs bedrooms to check on her siblings before going downstairs. "Don't forget your paper today, Shep. Hurry up, Joe. Zoey, is Peyton up yet?"

"Yes, I'm up," came the growl from Peyton.

"Good morning, Sunshine."

"Whatever."

Paige laughed and went to the stairs. She reached the bottom and crossed the living room into the large kitchen. She entered the room that her mother had considered a sanctuary. On one side was a large, L-shaped counter space for chopping, mixing and preparing dishes. Connected to the counter was the extra wide stainless steel refrigerator next to the double oven that Paige's mother, Elaine, had insisted on when they designed the house. Elaine had loved cooking for her family and entertaining others in their home, and her husband, Peter, had wanted her to have the best space possible for that. On the other side of the kitchen was the large kitchen table where all of the Kelly's had once shared family dinners. It was now covered with laundry, homework projects, and paperwork. Paige headed to the coffee maker and felt grateful once again for the automatic timer on the machine. She poured a large cup and went about setting up breakfast. She set out five bowls and poured cereal and milk, then got out the hot chocolate mix and reached for the kettle. By the time her younger siblings entered the kitchen the drinks were hot and the spoons were placed beside the bowls on the counter.

"Thank you, Paige" said Joe as he climbed on the stool.

"You're welcome, Joe." Paige knew that eating cereal for breakfast had been an adjustment since her mom had always fixed a full breakfast, but Paige had never been able to do that. "Everybody eat up, the bus will be here soon."

The next few minutes were a bustle of eating, brushing teeth and grabbing backpacks. The younger two ran out to meet their bus first and Paige kissed each of them and sent them on with a "Have a good day." She turned back to where Peyton and Zoey were cleaning up the breakfast dishes and Shep was finishing eating.

"Thanks, you guys." Paige said, "So, you will all be home after school today right?"

"Yep," Peyton muttered.

"Mmhmm," agreed her brother.

"Alright, I'll see you then." Paige said. The three grabbed their things and headed out the door. Paige finished straightening up the kitchen and gathered her own bag before leaving for work.

She climbed in the car and sat for a moment taking a deep breath. On a day like today she almost felt as if she should pray. Her parents would have prayed. They would tell her that no matter what, God is in control and has a plan for her. They would be unshaken. But Paige wasn't sure she could pray at all anymore. She still believed in God and she still sat in church every Sunday with the rest of the family. But she wasn't sure that God was interested in the day to day details of her life. Instead of praying she simply turned the key and pulled out of the garage.

At the country club Paige explained about the meeting to Shannon and asked her to cover for her until she got back, assuming she came back.

"Geez, what do you think it's about?" Shannon twirled a piece of her hair, she looked worried too.

"I have no idea," Paige said. "I hope it's nothing bad."

"Oh, I'm sure it's not," Shannon tried to encourage her friend. "You are the perfect employee, seriously this place couldn't run without you."

"Thanks," Paige said. She bit her lower lip and tried to focus on the supply list in her hand.

The two went back to their tasks and worked in silence. Paige nervously checked her watch and saw that she should head upstairs in just a minute. She took another deep breath. "Shannon, I'm leaving," she called out.

Shannon popped her head back in the door from the restaurant to the kitchen, "Okay, see you when you get back." She paused. "Good luck."

"Thanks." Paige tried to smile. She walked down the hall towards the elevator, but ducked into the bathroom to quickly check her appearance. She looked in the mirror and lifted her hand to a stray hair that had come out of her bobby pin. She put it back in place then tugged on her apron to straighten it out. *Should I wear my apron to a meeting?* She thought. She pulled it off and looked at herself. The white collared shirt and black pants looked well enough, but she felt out of uniform. She put the apron back on and stared in the mirror again. She stood for several moments in indecision, even wondering if she should have worn something besides her uniform for the meeting anyway. Then she thought she should go back and ask Shannon what she thought, but a quick look at her watch told her there wasn't time for that, she was nearly late already. Ultimately she went with her full uniform and chose to wear the apron as she always did. At least it felt familiar.

She walked out and quickly made her way to the elevator and up to the second floor. She entered Mr. Thompson's office and Sarah greeted her. A few minutes later she was told she could go in. Paige tugged on her apron one more time and walked through the door. She felt like she had finally collected herself and was mentally ready to handle this meeting. But then she saw him.

Russell Pierce sat on the couch opposite Mr. Thompson. They both had coffee in their hands and were casually chatting, but they turned when Paige walked in. Mr. Thompson stood to greet her and Russell followed suit.

Suddenly Paige felt even more nervous and a little like she might be sick.

"Hello Paige, thank you for joining us," Mr. Thompson said as he reached to shake her hand.

"Hi, umm, sure, anytime," she managed.

"Hi, Miss Kelly." Russell tried to be polite and shake her hand.

Paige reached out her hand, but couldn't make eye contact. *Oh no! Oh no! What is going on?* she thought. She tried to pay attention as Mr. Thompson offered for her to take a seat so they could chat. *Get it together, Paige!* she shouted inwardly at herself. She took a seat and focused on Mr. Thompson.

"Well Paige, I'm sure you're wondering what this is all about, so we won't keep you in suspense." He gave her a big smile.

"Yes, sir."

"Mr. Pierce here," he gestured toward Russell, "spent some

time in the restaurant yesterday, just to get a feel for how the place runs and look for any ways that we could improve what we're doing there."

Paige looked at Russell who smiled at her, she quickly looked away. Mr. Thompson seemed to be waiting for a response from her. "Yes, sir, there's always room for improvement."

"I agree, but Mr. Pierce seems to think that things in the restaurant are running quite smoothly and here's the thing," he paused and leaned forward.

Paige held her breath and bit her bottom lip.

"He thinks that the reason for that is because of you."

Paige blinked and looked from Mr. Thompson to Russell and back. She wasn't sure what to say, so she sat silently.

"Russ, you want to explain a little more?"

"Sure." Russell cleared his throat. He avoided eye contact with Paige and folded his hands in his lap as he began to speak. "So, James showed me around and it seemed that everything I pointed out as a strength of the kitchen or dining room he would tell me it was your idea. The systems in place and the way everything runs was put in place by you."

Paige looked at the floor. "Yes, I was just trying to be helpful."

"Oh yes, we're very grateful for you taking the initiative. In fact, I was quite impressed."

Paige looked up and met his eyes just for a moment. She saw a flash of awe in his face, and something else, something she couldn't quite put her finger on. "Thank you," she said just above a whisper.

Mr. Thompson spoke up. "Yes, well, we're impressed with your work ethic and the ways you have gone above and beyond your responsibilities to make the restaurant a better place. And because of that we would like to offer you a promotion."

She could hardly believe what he was saying. "A promotion?" she asked.

"We would like to make you the restaurant manager."

"Really?" Paige asked, the shock showing on her face.

"Yes, we have seen that James's gifts are in the artistry of food, but not in the everyday tasks that keep things going. We would like for you to take over those responsibilities officially. This would mean that you would no longer serve in the dining room in a waitress capacity. It would also mean you would oversee food planning for our special events. But you would have full authority over restaurant decisions."

Paige didn't bother to tell them that she already helped with the plans for special events and that James asked her opinion about everything, "I see," she said.

"Now, I'm not exactly sure what your work schedule is like right now as a server, but we would like this position to be full-time. However, it will require some weekend hours, so you can have the freedom to manage your forty hours as you see fit each week. For example, if you will need to be here for a half-day on Saturday, you can work a half-day one day during the week. Or you can come in early and leave early. Just keep track, and make sure you take care of everything that needs to be done. Also, your pay would change from hourly to a salary, plus as a full-time employee you will be eligible for benefits and health insurance."

Paige nodded slowly. *A salary. That would be life changing. And insurance? And paid days off?* But there were things to consider. She had worked a few weekends during her time there, but never very regularly. She knew this was a change that would need to be discussed with her siblings. "Thank you so much, I really can't believe you're even offering this to me,

I'm very grateful. But could I take a little time to think about it? Maybe until tomorrow?

"Of course." Mr. Thompson smiled his big, famous smile. "Why don't you just plan to let us know by the end of the week."

"Oh, yes, I'm sure I can do that. I just need to think it over and talk to my….my family." she said.

"Yes, of course, that will be just fine. Thanks for coming in, Paige." Mr. Thompson stood and reached out to shake her hand. Russell stood as well.

Paige stood and took his hand. "Oh, yes, thank you." She smiled. She looked to Russell, not wanting to be rude, but trying not to make eye contact. He looked as if he couldn't decide if he should shake her hand or not, ultimately he simply smiled at her.

"Thanks Paige, it was nice to see you again." His voice showed the same awkwardness that she felt. He ran his fingers through his hair and folded his hands in front of him.

"Thank you, you too. Have a nice day," Paige turned and walked out of the office before her own voice could betray her too.

Only after she cleared the reception area, walked down the hall and the doors were closed on the elevator did she finally let out the breath she felt like she had been holding the entire time. She covered her face with her hands and laughed out loud. She couldn't hold it in, her laugh echoed in the elevator with a sound so unfamiliar she didn't recognize herself. "Unbelievable!" She said out loud. "Unbelievable!" The elevator bell dinged and she realized that if someone was waiting they might hear her. She composed herself and tugged on her apron. She was still relieved to find the hallway empty once the doors open and she walked as fast as she could to tell Shannon about the meeting.

A few minutes later she stood in the kitchen with Shannon and James, who had already been told of the new plan. Shannon stared at her friend, her jaw hung open and she paused with her hand twisting a stray piece of hair. "Seriously?" she finally said.

"Yes!" Paige exclaimed. "Can you believe that?" She looked at James who was grinning from ear to ear. "Did you know?" she asked.

"Yep, sure did." James smiled.

"This doesn't upset you does it? I know this is your place."

"No, no, I'm happy for you! I was surprised they were offering, but you deserve this. You already run this place." He gave her a quick hug.

Shannon chimed in too. "Definitely, I'm so happy for you." She came in for her own hug.

"Thanks guys. I just can't believe it. This is so huge for me." She cleared her throat to push back the tears that were threatening to come. All three of them shared one more celebratory hug, then they went back to their work. Paige couldn't hide her smile.

Paige was thankful for a busy morning to distract her. As she walked between the kitchen and the dining room her thoughts were filled with questions: How long would she keep working as a waitress before starting the new position? Would she need to replace herself? What would her siblings think? Would it change her hours very much? Could she still be home before the kids got off the bus? She felt like she should be making a list of everything, but she knew a lot would be determined by Peyton and Shep's reaction.

. . .

It was the middle of the afternoon when Russell entered the restaurant. Paige was wiping down the counter when he approached her. She seemed to be in a good mood and she smiled at him as he sat down at the counter.

"Good afternoon, Mr. Pierce, can I get you anything?"

He was glad that some of the awkwardness between them was fading. "Just a glass of water." He paused and glanced at the desserts behind the counter. "What kind of pie do you have today?"

"Chocolate meringue with whipped cream."

"Mmmm." Russell rubbed his hands together.

"And it's real whipped cream, handmade by James, not the canned stuff." Paige smiled.

"Alright, you talked me into it. A piece of pie too."

Paige cut a slice and brought it to him along with his water. "Enjoy!" she said. She went back to straightening the counter close by.

Russell noticed that her mood toward him seemed to have changed, so he took the opportunity to chat. "So how long have you worked here, Paige?"

"It was three years in November." Paige's smile dimmed a little, but she quickly moved on. "How long have you worked here?" she asked jokingly.

"All in all I guess, let's see, about five years."

Paige gave him a quizzical look. "Five years?"

"Yes, if you count all the summers."

Paige still looked confused.

"I started here when I was fourteen, and stayed on until I

left for college. Then during college I worked through the summers, three months each, so I figure four summers counts as a year, so five years total."

"Oh, wow. I had no idea," Paige said.

"Yeah, I guess you could say I basically grew up here. I've know Mr. Thompson since I started caddying for him. That's why I couldn't believe it when they offered me this job. Sometimes I still feel like a little kid walking these halls."

"Oh I understand. I feel like I grew up here too, not because I was in high school, but I guess this was just the place that I started becoming an adult."

"Really?" Russell didn't want to let on that he knew about her family, he wasn't sure she was going to let her guard down.

"Yes, well it was my first real job and…" her voice trailed off. She started working on cleaning up the back counter and fell silent.

"And?" Russell pushed.

Paige stood with her back to him. She sighed with a face that he couldn't see. "And that's when I started taking care of my siblings."

"Oh…" Russell paused for a long moment. "Yes, I guess that changed things for you."

"Yes," was all Paige said. She seemed to try to change the subject. "When I started here I didn't know a thing about a restaurant, except that we ate in them a lot, and I definitely didn't know anything about how a kitchen should be run. But I just started seeing things that could work better. I read books on restaurant kitchen management and even household kitchen organization and started looking for things to do. And James was always great about letting me try out new ideas. Really, he is a genius in the kitchen, I mean the food is all people talk about. I just wanted to help him out since the other details stressed him out so much."

"Now you can do what you've always done, but you'll be compensated and recognized for it," Russell said. "You really deserve this, Paige." He looked at her across the counter and caught her gaze. When their eyes met the connection was so strong he couldn't force himself to look away. Not that he wanted to anyway. She only let the contact last for a second, though.

"Thanks," she said. She looked uncomfortable and busied herself with something on the back counter.

He wanted to reach out to her, for her to not look away. He desperately tried to think of something to say. "You really do deserve it," he repeated, then before he thought he continued. "I mean after what has happened with your family and your parents, I just thought it would help you out." As soon as the words were out of his mouth he knew he had blown it. He saw her freeze with her back to him and then slowly turn. She was tense and the openness from the moment before was gone.

"What?" She looked at him with shock on her face. "What about my parents?"

He thought about trying to cover himself, to say he just assumed her parents were gone, for just a moment he almost did, but then he knew there was no use. "I'm sorry Paige, about your parents. I know they…they've been gone a few years. My mother told me."

"You mother?" Her face was hot now.

"Yes, my mom is Gladys Pierce."

Of course she knew who Gladys was. She and Jim were well known at the church, always serving in one way or another. "Oh," she said quietly.

"She didn't really know much about them, just that you take care of all of your brothers and sisters. I'm sorry." He didn't know what else to say.

"Well it's true, you don't have to be sorry for knowing it." She turned so she faced him straight on. "But what do you mean, *you* thought it would help me out?"

Russell knew he had really messed this conversation up, there was no backing out of it. "Oh, just that, umm, I'm sure financially it could help you. I'm sure it can't be easy. So I mentioned the idea to Bob."

Paige looked as if she couldn't stand the sight of him. She turned and walked back into the kitchen. Russell sat awkwardly on the stool wondering if she would come back. When she returned she looked like she had tried to compose herself, but her anger had only increased. "So, what is it, you think I'm some kind of charity case? You think I can't take care of my family on my own? We do just fine, thank you very much."

"No, no! I didn't mean that at all. Of course you take care of them, and it seems like you're doing a great job. But you deserve this job, you deserve to be paid for the job you already do. And even though it's not the reason I came up with the idea, it's a bonus that it will pay you more than you make now. Surely you can't complain about making more money." Russell looked at her as if the last part were a question.

She was running out of steam a little bit, but she wasn't giving in. "That's not the point, I won't take a job that is only offered to me out of pity. I won't do it. I'll go and tell Mr. Thompson right now that I've thought about it and I won't be accepting the position. With that she called out to James that she was leaving and walked straight out of the restaurant.

Russell started to chase after her, even got as far as the door. But then he stopped. *How did this happen?* he thought. He stood in the doorway and watched her walk down the hall. He ran his fingers through his hair and tried to think of how to fix it, but nothing came to mind.

. . .

Paige hurried to the elevator, went up to the second floor and quickly walked down the hall to Mr. Thompson's office. She was still angry and the emotion was making her feel more bold than usual. She entered the office and saw Sarah on the phone, but she interrupted. "Is Mr. Thompson in?"

Sarah held up her hand as she finished her call and hung up, "He's in, but I don't think he's available at the moment," she said politely.

"I need to speak to him right now, it's about the meeting we had this morning." Paige bit her lip and tried not to pace the office.

Sarah hesitated, but seeing the urgency in Paige's face she said "Alright, I'll see what I can do." She stood and knocked on her boss's door, she stepped in for a moment and when she came back out she told Paige, "He'll see you, but he has an appointment soon."

"Thank you," Paige rushed past her. She wanted to do this before she lost her nerve.

"Hello, Paige." Mr. Thompson crossed the office and motioned for her to the couch, "Won't you sit down?"

"No, thank you, sir. I don't want to take much of your time.

I just wanted to tell you that I won't be accepting the position in the restaurant." She crossed her arms in front of her and held her chin proudly in the air.

"Oh? Really? I'm very sorry to hear that." Mr. Thompson sat down on the couch, obviously surprised and confused. "Is there any reason you don't want the job?" he asked.

"I don't want any charity and I don't want to be given a job because of my family." Paige could only imagine what he thought of her and her family situation.

Mr. Thompson leaned back and rubbed his chin. He didn't say anything for a minute. "Paige, I can tell you're upset, please sit down."

The kindness in his voice calmed Paige a little and she reluctantly took a seat on the couch opposite him.

"I'm sorry that you feel like you've been offered this job for the wrong reasons, but I can assure you that the only reason I agreed to this offering is because of all the many things Mr. Pierce observed in the restaurant that are all credited to you. I admit that, at first, I didn't want to change anything. It seemed that if things are going well we should just leave them. But Mr. Pierce was able to convince me that you were doing a job that wasn't yours, and that you weren't being compensated for. I can admit now that I see that you've been doing the job all along. This is simply making that official."

Paige locked her gaze on the carpet and wished that she could melt into the floor. Of course the job was Mr. Pierce's idea. He was the one who thought she needed help.

"Now I don't know why anyone would look on it as charity to be paid for a job you've been doing anyway, in fact many people would demand back-pay for the past. I appreciate that you aren't doing that."

Paige looked up and met his eyes, but still didn't speak.

"Now Paige, we appreciate all that you have already done for us here. It was a step out for us to consider making this promotion from an hourly waitress to a salaried manager's position. Some people would say it's a little crazy. I really don't want to be letdown on this idea. But if you plan to turn down this promotion, I think you should really think about whether you want to continue to work here at all. If you can't accept something that is being offered to improve your situation, that seems quite ungrateful. I'm not sure that's the kind of person we need on our staff, and I would be very disappointed to find that you are that kind of person."

Paige cleared her throat to speak. "Yes, sir" was all she managed. She was clearly embarrassed.

"So can we count on you?" he asked.

"Yes, sir." She nodded quietly.

"Excellent!" he clapped his hands together. "We are thrilled to have you serve in this new position. I know there are plenty of details to go over and questions you might have. You can talk with Mr. Pierce about all of those, just talk to his assistant to set up a meeting." With that he stood and opened the door for her.

"Yes, sir. Thank you." Paige walked through the door. She thanked Sarah and slowly walked back down the hall to the elevator. As the doors closed she thought about how, just a few hours before she had stood in this spot elated about a new job with new possibilities.

Now all she could think about was having to face Russell Pierce again.

Chapter 9

*P*aige was exhausted once she got home. She was running a few minutes later than usual, after her encounter with Russell, and felt in a rush to get there before the twins arrived. She barely made it in the driveway before the bus pulled up.

"Hey Paige." Lucy ran to her and gave her a hug. "Can we make strawberry ice cream today?"

Joe was dragging behind, but when he heard dessert mentioned he picked up his pace, "Oh yeah, can we? Please, Paige?"

Paige was already walking towards the door to the house. "I don't know guys, I'm not sure today is a great day for it. I just got home and I've got a lot to do. What if we plan to do it this weekend? Then we'll have plenty of time to enjoy it."

"Aww, the weekend is forever away," Joe complained.

"Yeah, that's like four whole days, we want to do it today," Lucy agreed.

"Not today," Paige snapped at them, then took a deep breath when she looked at their faces. "Not today," she said more quietly. "I haven't been to the store for everything we need to make it, so it will have to wait. But I promise we will do it soon, the weekend if not before."

The twins looked like they still wanted to argue, but they moved on anyway. Paige rubbed her forehead, she didn't want the way she was feeling from work to affect her mood at home. She walked through the door and reminded them to get out any homework they needed to do. She walked to the kitchen and busied herself unloading the dishwasher and started preparing dinner. She wanted the meal ready to put in the oven so she could talk with her siblings before dinner. Shep, Peyton and Zoey all arrived home and did homework or went to their rooms.

After Paige had dinner in the oven she stood at the counter to gather her thoughts for a moment. She shut her eyes tight and took a deep breath. Then she walked to the stairs and called out, "Everybody, I need to see you all together in the living room for a little bit." It took several minutes for the older ones to come from their rooms and to tear Joe and Lucy away from playing, but once they were all settled around the living room Paige began.

"I have some important news about my job." Shep and Peyton immediately gave her a concerned look, she raised her hand to stop them from asking. "It's a good thing really, just different. I've been offered a promotion, they want me to move up from being a waitress to be the restaurant manager." She paused to see her siblings reactions.

"Wow, that's great Paige!" Peyton was the first to speak.

Shep seemed reluctant to make a comment without more detail. "So what will that mean?"

"I'm not sure exactly yet, but for one thing it means I'll be making a salary instead of being paid hourly, so it will be more money."

"Whohoo!" Peyton clapped.

"But it also means that my hours will be a little different. Sometimes I'll have to work later or go in earlier. They also want me to help with food for the special events, so that might sometimes mean that I'll need to work on a weekend."

"Oh," Peyton said.

"What happens when you work late and can't be home before Joe and Lucy?" Shep asked the obvious question.

"I've thought about that, and we might just have to take it on a case by case basis. But it will probably mean that I need some help from you and Peyton to make sure someone is here when they get off the bus."

"Hmm, great." Shep said sarcastically.

Paige sighed. She was afraid she would get this reaction.

"I can try, but I can't help it when I have practice," Peyton said immediately.

"I know," Paige said.

"And I have practice too, and other stuff that I do." Shep reminded her.

"Yes, I know." Paige gritted her teeth. "I am going to do my best to not disrupt your schedules, like I said, we'll just take it on a case by case basis. But listen, this is a good thing for us. It will mean more money for all of the 'other stuff' you like to do, and benefits for me at work. I didn't expect you to jump up and down that you might need to help out around here a little more, but I did hope you would at least be supportive since this is good for all of us." Paige raised her voice as she spoke.

"Sorry, Congratulations on your promotion." Shep said

halfheartedly.

"Yeah Paige, we're happy for you, really." Peyton spoke up.

"Paige?" Lucy asked.

"Yes, sweetie?"

"If you got a promotion, shouldn't we celebrate?"

"Thank you, Lu, yes we should."

"Then…" the girl smiled as sweetly as she could, "Don't you think we should celebrate with strawberry ice cream?"

Paige covered a smile. "Yes, and we will. This weekend," she said kindly.

Lucy looked disappointed.

"So is dinner ready yet?" Shep asked impatiently.

"We have a few more minutes, you can go, I'll call you when it's time to eat." They all dispersed back to their rooms. Paige sat in her chair and watched them go. She hadn't had high hopes that they would be excited, but she thought they would be at least a little happy. But she had to admit to herself that she wasn't thrilled with the way the job had come about. The whole thing was a big mix of emotions, and somehow she couldn't blame her siblings for feeling the same way.

But she wasn't going to let their bad attitudes completely ruin it for her or have a pity party. She stood and went to the kitchen and put some music on to pass the time until dinner. She let herself get lost in the words and rhythm as it played. She would worry about the job and all the change that was about to happen later.

Chapter 10

Sunday morning arrived with the promise of all day rain showers. Russell laid in bed listening to the rain against his bedroom window and thinking about the week that had flown by. After a long day on Tuesday, he had kept himself busy visiting various departments and taking notes, like he had done in the restaurant. And every morning he made sure he had his fill of coffee before leaving his apartment.

Bob had filled him in on his meeting with Paige. Russell had been afraid of his boss's reaction to the situation, but he seemed to not want any details.

"Russell, I believe Paige has the skills and abilities to take the position, but I need you to tell me now if you suggested this out of charity for her or for the betterment of the club." Bob had said.

"Sir, I had the best interest of the restaurant in mind. And as I have said multiple times, I don't see that there's any question that she has already been doing the job. I think it's for the betterment of the restaurant that she remain employed here

Chapter 10

and not figure out that she could go elsewhere and do better for herself." Russell replied.

"Very well," Bob said. And that was that.

Russell knew that Paige was supposed to meet with him to discuss the details of the position, but neither of them had initiated the appointment. He knew they couldn't continue to put it off, but he wasn't sure how to approach her again.

He lay in bed and shook his head, *If only I hadn't opened my big mouth,* he thought to himself for the hundredth time. *She was starting to open up, I just know it. Now she'll probably never speak to me unless absolutely necessary.* Since that day he had thought of dozens of other things he could have said to keep the conversation going. If only he had thought of one of them at the time.

The sound of his cell phone ringing interrupted his thoughts. He picked it up without looking at the screen and said "Hi, Mom."

"Good morning, son." Gladys' cheery voice rang out over the phone. "What are you up to?"

"Mom, you know I'm still in bed."

"Oh, did I wake you?" She didn't sound overly concerned.

"Nope, just lying here thinking…"

"Thinking about what? Coming to church with us this morning?"

"Mom…" he groaned. Gladys had continued to ask Russell to visit their church, but each week he came up with one reason or another why he couldn't. Some Sundays he was visiting other churches. He insisted to his parents that he wanted to find his own place to go to church, he just wanted to do this himself.

"Oh what? You're visiting churches anyway, why not just

visit ours? You don't know if you will like it unless you try it. That's all I'm asking, that you just try it. If it's not for you, I won't ask again."

"Hmmm, you promise?" Russell asked teasingly.

"I promise," Gladys replied.

"Just one time?" he said as he sat up in bed.

"Yes, just once."

"Hmmm." Russell let the silence hang between them, he could practically feel his mother's excitement through the phone. "Alright then, just this once."

"Yay!" Gladys shouted. "The service starts at 10:15, I'll meet you in the foyer at five after, don't be late. Oh and we'll do lunch afterward."

"Sounds good, I'll see you there." Russell hung up the phone and leaned his head back against the wall. He sighed. "What have I gotten myself into?" he said out loud. "Oh well, at least this will get her off my back. She'll keep her promise." He looked at the clock. If he got up now he could make it to his favorite bakery for breakfast before he had to be at the church.

He jumped up and got going. He was dressed and ready in thirty minutes and headed out the door with his Bible under his arm. The bakery was a few minutes drive on the way to the church. As he expected it was a busy morning, but he was in and out in a few minutes with his coffee and bagel. He ate as he drove the short five minutes to the church.

As he pulled in the parking lot he noted the total drive time of ten minutes from his apartment. He wasn't ready to really consider attending his parents' church, but if there was a pro and con list, the proximity would go on the pro side. He sat in his car for a moment, as the rain fell hard and heavy on his windshield. He whispered a quick prayer. "Lord, I admit that I haven't even considered attending this church as a real possibility. But if you have plans for me here I pray that you will keep me from being too stubborn to like it just because it's my parents' church." He paused and thought long and hard for a moment. "And Lord, I pray that You also won't allow me to change my mind just because of someone else who goes here." He wouldn't allow himself to admit that he might have agreed to come because of the possibility of seeing Paige. Deep down he thought that seeing her somewhere besides work might break the ice. "Amen" he said. He climbed from his car and ran to the door with his arm above his head to try to stay as dry as possible.

Russell entered the building and was greeted warmly by a volunteer holding the door open. "Good morning, come on in out of this rain."

"Good morning." Russell smiled back and walked past the man into the foyer.

The church building seemed traditional on the outside, a large, red brick building with big white wooden doors and a tall, white steeple. But the inside was more modern. The foyer echoed with the sounds of many voices, the noise ricocheted off the hardwood floors up to the high ceiling. In the middle of the foyer stood a large round table that held a red and yellow flower arrangement. The soft white walls held large prints of Bible verses written in calligraphy on canvases painted in bright colors . A staircase led to the balcony upstairs and downstairs the hallways split off on either side of the sanctuary.

Russell walked to the table and picked up a worship guide that listed the order of service for the day and a few church announcements. He glanced at his watch and saw that it was almost ten after. He looked around for his mother, but didn't see her. Just a moment later the double wooden doors into the sanctuary swung open and Gladys walked out. She was still talking over her shoulder to another woman who was following her.

"Yes, I'm thrilled to help with the shower, and we absolutely must have it at our house. The weather will be perfect for an indoor-outdoor event this time of year," Gladys said, "Excuse me though, Diane, we'll talk more about it later. I have to meet my son." She pointed to Russell and hurried over. "Hello, hello, I'm so glad you're here." She took her youngest son's arm and began introducing him to the few people still in the foyer.

Russell nodded and greeted each person with a smile. He was shaking hands with an older gentleman when he heard the entryway door and saw a group of people coming in from the rain.

She shook out her umbrella and then checked the two youngest children to see how wet they were before looking up. When she saw Russell, Paige froze mid-step.

Russell looked at the group in amazement. He saw two looking to be teenagers, one girl maybe nearing her teens, and two who must be in elementary school. He had tried many times over the past week, but still couldn't imagine what that was like.

"Russell? Russell?" His mother's voice caught him off guard.

"Oh, yes, hi." He managed. The couple he was meeting smiled and walked away saying they needed to find their seats.

His mother saw where his gaze went and pushed her son in that direction.

Paige had turned back to the kids, gathering their rain coats and trying to keep them from running off. But as Russell and Gladys walked towards them she straightened up and ran her fingers over her dress.

"Hello, Paige," Russell said warmly. For just a moment he forgot that things were supposed to be awkward between them because of his eagerness to meet her siblings. "This is my mother, Gladys Pierce. Mom this is Paige Kelly, we work together at the club."

"Hello, it's so nice to meet you." Gladys took her hand and smiled.

"It's nice to meet you, too." Paige gave her a small smile.

"And who are all these other handsome faces?"

The older Kellys looked embarrassed and the younger ones barely noticed. "These are my brothers and sisters, Shep, Peyton, Zoey, Joe and Lucy." Paige pointed to each one in turn.

"Hello, it's so nice to meet all of you," Gladys said. "We were just about to go take our seats, would you like to join us?" she asked.

"Oh." Paige looked uncomfortable. "We usually just sit in the back. The kids can be kind of distracting."

Gladys pressed on. "Oh that's alright, I bet they will do just fine. We would love for you to sit with us."

"Can we Paige? Can we?" Lucy asked, "We promise we'll be good, we can hear the music better in the front!"

Paige looked from Gladys with her eager eyes, to the twins waiting for an answer. Shep and Peyton seemed to be trying to avoid the entire conversation. Finally she looked to Russell, who hadn't said much.

As if on cue he spoke up. "Yes, please join us."

She seemed reluctant, but replied, "Alright, why not?"

"Wonderful!" Gladys beamed.

The two families became a small parade as they entered the sanctuary. Gladys led the way walking with her arm linked through Russell's and saying hello to people as she passed by. Paige followed them leading the twins and gently pushing them along the way, with Zoey, Peyton and Shep following behind. Russell felt as if everyone was watching them walk all the way down the aisle to the second row. Jim was already seated and he stood to be introduced.

Russell knew coming to a church where his parents were already known would draw attention to him as a newcomer, and then to add Paige and her family made it even more noticeable. Suddenly he felt badly for Paige, he hadn't meant to put her in an awkward situation. He didn't want the eyes of everyone in church on them as she sat next to him, so he quickly grabbed the seat on the outside of the pew next to his dad.

Paige sat next to Gladys and the rest of the kids filed into the row, spacing the older ones between the younger ones. They tried to settle in as the service began.

The worship leader walked on stage with his guitar and welcomed everyone. They sang a few worship songs, most of them updated versions of well-known hymns. The kids sang along to all the songs they knew. Paige stood quietly and simply read the words projected on the screen. The final song was "I Need Thee Every Hour". All the voices in the sanctuary blended together as the final chorus was sung a cappella.

After the worship songs ended the pastor greeted everyone and asked that they start in prayer. "Lord Jesus, we ask that you come and meet with us this morning. We are here to worship You and share in the fellowship of those who love you. Be with us now. Guide my words as I humbly seek to share Your word with Your people. Lord, draw us closer to You and in this time teach us more about Yourself. And for anyone who doesn't have a relationship with You, use this time to call them, prick their hearts with Your truth and lead them to follow You. In the name of Jesus I pray, Amen."

"I'm excited that today we're starting a new series on the book of 1st Thessalonians. We'll be going through the book a few verses at a time for the next several weeks. Today we'll start with chapter one, verses one through five. Please stand with me as we read these verses together." He paused while the congregation stood and found their places in their Bibles. Then he began to read, "Paul, Silvanus, and Timothy, To the church of the Thessalonians in God the Father and our Lord Jesus Christ: Grace to you and peace. We give thanks to God always for all of you, constantly mentioning you in our prayers, remembering before our God and Father your work of faith and labor of love and steadfastness of hope in our Lord Jesus Christ. For we know, brothers loved by God, that he has chosen you, because our gospel came to you not only in word, by also in power and in the Holy Spirit and with full conviction. You know what kind of men we proved to be among you for your sake." He paused again as he finished the scripture reading and motioned that the people could be seated.

"As Paul is writing this letter to the Thessalonians he starts out by encouraging to them. The Thessalonians are very new believers. Paul had been with them and shared the gospel, but was only with them a short time after their conversion before he needed to leave. So he writes this letter as a sort of follow up to his time with them. Paul tells them that he gives thanks for them and that he himself is encouraged when he remembers the way that the gospel has come to them and that they have been an example to other believers. So what is Paul's message to the church now? His message is to press on, to keep going. He says in verse three that he is thankful for their labor of love and steadfast hope. And that's what we're going to talk about today, being steadfast - enduring - in our walk with Christ in the hope that we have in Him."

"First of all what exactly is the hope that Paul is talking about? In chapter four, which we will look at in more detail in a few weeks, he writes about those who have fallen asleep - in other words, those who have died - and says 'For since we believe that Jesus died and rose again, even so, through Jesus, God will bring with him those who have fallen asleep.' He tells them this so they will not 'grieve as others do who have no hope.' So our first indication is to say that when we talk about hope we're talking about heaven. And that's right, we have a hope that there is more than this life. This isn't all there is for us. There's something for us beyond this earth and these bodies. And when we have lost someone if they are a believer we know we will see them again in heaven. So we have that hope. Hope of eternal life in Jesus."

"But we also have a hope here on earth. Hope that we can walk with God and live in a way that is honoring to him. Hope that he is working all things together for our good. Hope that no matter what we are never alone because our God is good and he is with us."

"It's interesting to see how Paul connects this hope with all three persons of the Trinity, the father, the son, and the holy spirit. In verse two Paul begins by saying, 'We give thanks to God...' for all of these things, for your labor of love and steadfast hope. It is because of God that these things happen.

In verse three he tells them that the hope itself is in our Lord Jesus Christ. Without Jesus there is no hope, there is no salvation and no gospel, the only hope we have is in him. And then in verse five he says 'our gospel came to you not only in word, but also in power and in the Holy Spirit with full conviction.' The Holy Spirit was sent after Jesus to be a helper, a convicter, and a communicator between us and the father. It is the Holy Spirit who empowers us to live in the hope that we have. So our hope is from God the Father, in Jesus Christ, the Son, and through the power of the Holy Spirit. We need all three to walk fully in this steadfast hope.

The other absolutely crucial thing that I want to point out in this section is verse four. Paul writes 'For we know, brothers loved by God, that he has chosen you.'" The pastor paused and let the words sink into the room. "He has chosen you. He chose you! God the Father, in heaven above, before the foundations of the world chose you. He looked out into the entire future of the world and he knew that you and I would be sinners, that we would break his perfect holy law and that we wouldn't be worthy of his glory and his presence in heaven. But he wanted us, he chose us. So he sent Jesus Christ, his own son to be born on earth, to live a perfect life and then to die on the cross for our sins. For your sins. And when we receive that gift of forgiveness, something that we don't deserve, he sends his Holy Spirit to live in us, to dwell with us and to empower us to walk in a manner worthy of the gospel that we believe. Why? Because he chose us. Because he chose you. And he did that to give us a steadfast hope. Hope in this life and hope for a future in heaven with him."

"If you don't have that hope in Jesus, I would like to encourage you to come to know him, to bring him your life, your sins, and your baggage and give it to him. He will take it and replace your lost, hopelessness with a full hope and full forgiveness. This morning we will have one more song, while the musicians play quietly I would like to challenge you to pray and to think on how you are walking in hope, or if you are walking in a hopeless way. Ask Jesus to give you hope and to fill you with joy. At the end of the song I will close us in prayer."

The musicians began to play and the room was filled with the song as around the church people bowed their heads in prayer. After a few moments the pastor began to pray. "Heavenly Father, thank you for this morning, thank you for being with us here and joining with us in our fellowship. Most of all, Lord, thank you for sending your son and for giving us a steadfast hope that we can walk in you. Be with us as we go and be glorified in us. Amen. Thanks for being here this morning, have a great Sunday!"

The room filled with noise once again as everyone began talking and gathering their families. Paige stood up and started trying to make a quick exit. She hurried the kids along getting out of the pew. She thanked Gladys for inviting them to sit with them. "Oh of course! They were all so well behaved, you're welcome to share our pew anytime."

"Thank you." Paige smiled. She looked at Russell as she passed by, but tried to avoid eye contact.

"It was good to see you," he said. "I'm sorry we haven't met yet to go over all the details at work."

"Oh, yes, that's alright, we'll get to it," she said. She looked around trying to gather her siblings.

"Sure, maybe tomorrow?"

"Sure, I'll umm, I'll call your assistant." Paige tried to walk away.

"Well it was good to see you." Russell winced inwardly as he repeated himself.

"Um, yeah, you too."

"Thanks for sitting with us. My mom just likes to make people feel welcomed."

"Oh, yeah, she's sweet. Have you been here on Sunday before?" Paige asked.

"No, this was the first time."

"I hope you enjoyed it."

"I did actually," Russell admitted, more to himself than to her. "The sermon was very good, and I liked the music a lot."

Russell was glad when his mom interrupted their lack of conversation. "Russell, honey, we're going to have lunch at the house. I've got a roast in the crock pot just waiting for us." She looked at Paige. "Paige we would *love* to have you join us for lunch. We've got plenty of food to go around and it would be wonderful to have you over." She raised her eyebrows in anticipation.

"Oh, thank you, but we can't." She looked at Russell and back at Gladys. "We have plans this afternoon."

"Alright, well another time then," Gladys said cheerily.

"Of course," Paige responded politely. "We should get going, come on everybody." Her teenage siblings walked with her and she tried to keep up with Joe and Lucy running around.

Russell watched them go and wondered at the feeling in his stomach, and at the strangest feeling that surprisingly he wished very much that Paige had said yes to his mother.

Chapter 11

*P*aige had felt eyes on her all through church and she felt them again as they walked out. Not only from the Pierces, but other church members who noticed her sitting with their family. As soon as they were out of earshot Peyton asked her sister, "What plans do we have?"

"We have plans to go home and eat sandwiches for lunch," she stated. She hurried them all to the car so she could get away as quickly as possible. Away from the Pierces, away from the looks, away from the church. But mostly away from the thoughts swirling in her head. Thoughts of sitting near the front with a family, of Sunday dinners after church, and of a woman who always made it her job to make new people feel welcome and very often invited people over to their home after church. A woman who Gladys Pierce made her miss and ache for all over again. Her mother.

After lunch had been eaten and the kitchen was clean, Paige sat alone in the living room. The rest of the family was enjoying their free time for the afternoon, and she was content to have a few minutes of quiet. Peyton came down the stairs and sat across from Paige on the couch.

"So, who's the guy?"

"What?" Paige pretended not to know what she was talking about.

"Oh come on, the guy?"

"Mr. Pierce? He's the new operations manager at work."

"Oh, I think he's more than a guy from work," Peyton teased.

"Oh no, I don't think so." Paige shook her head.

"Seriously? He stands in the church foyer like he's just waiting for you to come in, then they want us to sit with them, *and* they ask us over to their house? Sounds like his mom is a matchmaker or something."

"I don't know what she's thinking, but to me he's just a guy from work. In fact, he's basically my boss, so there's definitely nothing happening there." Paige gave Peyton a look that told her that was the end of the discussion.

Peyton changed the subject, "Do you know any more details about the new job yet?"

"No, I have to meet with…the boss to discuss them."

"Oh." Peyton understood. "Well Shep and I had a talk, if you have to work some extra afternoons or Saturdays, we'll do what we need to to help out."

"Thanks, Pey. I don't want to put any pressure on you guys, but I appreciate the offer, I'll work it all out."

"Well I'm sure you'll need us some, so just let me know what I can do."

"Thanks." Paige gave her sister a smile. The two sisters had always been close growing up, but things hadn't been easy and their relationship had often been strained the last few years. Peyton hadn't always been willing to help and she often resented Paige acting as a parent to her. But she had to do what needed to be done. "Have you finished your scholarship application?"

Peyton tried not to roll her eyes. "Yes," she said. Paige was always checking in on her through the college application process.

"And your cheerleading tryout paperwork?"

"Yep, mailed it in early."

"Better early than late."

"Hmm, yeah I guess so." The two sat in silence for a few moments, then Peyton bursted out, "Paige, what are you doing right now?"

"What?" Paige was surprised by the question.

"What are you doing right now?"

"Umm, well I just finished cleaning up the kitchen. I was going to make a list for the store and plan meals for the week."

"Okay, but like, what are you doing, like in life?" Peyton looked concerned.

"What kind of question is that? I'm doing what needs to be done, I'm taking care of things."

"Yes, but do you do anything just because you want to? Do you do anything for you?" Peyton asked with a sense of urgency.

Paige sat for a moment. "I guess there's not much time for that. I don't really think about it very much."

"Okay, but I'm going off to college soon, and then Shep won't be far behind me, and the younger kids are going to grow up too. So when are you going to live your life?"

"Peyton, don't give me this right now." Paige put her head in her hands, wanting to avoid the conversation.

"No, I'm serious. I know you gave up college at the time,

and you haven't dated since then, but do you think you ever will? You put your life on hold for a while, but that can't last forever."

"Maybe not forever, but now is not the time. I've got too much going on at home to worry about anything in the outside world."

"Why not now? What's going to make a few months from now or a few years from now better? You can't always use this as an excuse to push people away."

"Push people away? Who am I pushing away?" She felt defensive.

"Who are you letting get close?" Peyton asked.

That thought hung in the air, and Paige had no answer for her sister.

"I'm just thinking that you spend a lot of time worrying about my scholarship applications, and Shep's grades and the kids' activities, and when do you worry about you? Are you even happy?"

"Happy?" Paige asked, and wondered if she was. "I don't even *think* about being happy. I just think about making it from morning until night without losing somebody, and making it through the week with clean clothes and food on the table and getting everything done on time. Happy isn't even on my radar." She drew a quick breath as the words tumbled from her mouth.

"Paige," Peyton nearly whispered. "Oh Paige, you can't live like that. That's not a life."

Paige's emotions rose to the service at the sadness in her sister's voice. "It is my life. This is what I do. There's no choice."

Peyton looked Paige straight in the eyes. "Yes, there is a

choice. I can help more, the other kids can help more. You can't take on all the pressure and responsibility yourself. You have to get out of this house and have a life. You need to be happy, Paige. And you have to open yourself up to the possibility of things outside of this family. It's what they would have wanted."

Paige bristled at the mention of her parents. Paige could see that her sister was truly concerned for her, although she didn't know why this was all coming up just now, things had been this way for the past few years. She wanted to assure Peyton that she didn't need to worry, "It's alright Pey, I feel useful in the things I do. It might not always be exciting or fun, but I know that what I'm doing is needed. But I'll think about what you said, I promise."

"Well think hard. And don't push this guy away."

"This guy? Mr. Pierce? Peyton, seriously." Paige rolled her eyes. "There is nothing there. In fact, I think the whole thing is just because he found out about my family and he's being nice because he pities me."

"Or maybe he likes you."

Paige felt her stomach do a little flip flop. No one had even mentioned that a guy might like her in years. Just the sentence sounded like something from high school. "Oh he does not! Besides the fact that he's basically my boss, he's older than me, and he doesn't even know me. And I don't think he really wants to, any guy who knows my situation would probably run the other direction."

"Don't do that, Paige. Any guy would be lucky to have you, and someone who really cares about you would figure out how to put up with all of us."

"Yeah, but how would that work anyway? No offense,

but I'm the equivalent of a single mom with five kids...five! Nobody young enough to be interested in me is going to want to take on that kind of responsibility. Even if you don't count you and Shep, that's still a handful."

"You will never find out as long as you keep everyone you meet at arms length."

"Oh, I do not."

"Yes, you do. You won't even let someone get to know you. You have closed yourself off to anyone that might work their way into your heart." Peyton, stopped for a minute and spoke gently, "And I think we both know why."

Paige looked at Peyton's eyes, then she cleared her throat and looked away. "Anyway, like I said, I promise to think about all of...this. And I'll see if I can find me a guy to get hitched to as soon as possible," she winked, trying to lighten the mood. "Now, this grocery list isn't going to write itself, so either let me get back to it or tell me what you want to eat this week."

Peyton stood and walked over to give Paige a quick hug. "I'll eat whatever you make, you always take care of everything, so I'm not worried," she said and walked out of the room.

Paige wasn't sure if her sister meant just the meal plans or her entire life. She sat and thought to herself. If she was being honest she would say that she knew Peyton was right. She had put her own life on hold, but in some ways she felt like her life had always been on hold. As a college freshman she remembered how her family would tease her about studying too much and not having a lot of friends or going out all the time. She always felt like she needed to buckle down and learn while she was in school, and that there would be time for fun later. She also thought there would be time for boys later.

Suddenly she was hit with a memory. A conversation eerily

similar to the one she had just had with her sister. Except this time it was one of the last conversations she had with her mother. Paige had been home for the weekend, and on that Saturday morning she was sitting at the kitchen counter while her mother fixed breakfast for the family.

"So catch me up, sweetheart," Elaine Kelly had said as she pulled the egg carton from the refrigerator. "How is everything?"

Paige sipped her coffee before replying, "Everything is good. My classes are interesting and my first design project is due at the end of the month, I have to do a mock-up for redecorating my dorm room."

"That sounds fun."

"It really is. My roommate isn't all that interested though, I'm making her clean the room up so I can get before and after pictures."

"Mmhmm. So who else do you hang out with, besides your messy roommate?"

"Come on Mom, not you too. Why does everybody have to ask about my social life? You know my studies are important to me."

"Honey, I'm not trying to pick on you. I'm sincerely interested in your life and your friends."

"I have friends. Sometimes I go out with the college group from church and I have a lot of study group friends."

"I just want you to have a good time."

"I know Mom, and I do, I just put my school work first."

"Paige, I think it is very admirable that you work so hard in school, you definitely have the grades to prove that it's worth it. But I just want you to be happy too. I think you should work harder to meet people and make an effort to spend time away from your books. I know you think you have the rest of your life to have fun, but you need to have fun now too, otherwise, what's the reward of all that hard work?"

Paige thought about her mother's words. "Okay, I'll try."

"That's my girl," Elaine said. "Honey, listen to me. I know that you're smart and I'm so very proud of that. But I just want you to know that I pray for all of my children everyday. I believe when God's word says that He has a plan for you that He means it. He has a plan to give you a future and a hope. Lately God has been placing you heavily on my heart and telling me that he has something very special planned just for you, Paige. I don't know what it is yet, but I'm praying that He will prepare you for that time and I want you to know that whatever it is, you're going to be amazing."

Paige didn't know what to say, but gave her mother a smile and a quick, "Thanks, Mom."

She pulled herself back to the present, but her mother's words from that day stuck in her mind, "He has something very special planned just for you." Her mother had no way of knowing that just days later she would be in a car accident that would end her life and that her oldest daughter would take on the role of mother to the family left behind. *Well this certainly is special,* Paige thought, *I'm pretty sure this isn't what Mom had in mind. And I'm not even sure I want to believe that this is the hope and future that God planned for me.*

Like everything else in her life, Paige felt like if she wanted to "have a life", as Peyton put it, she would have to take care of it herself. But as usual, she would have to think about that later. She grabbed her paper and pen and started making her grocery list and pushed all other thoughts aside.

Chapter 12

*O*n Tuesday morning Russell checked his calendar to see if Paige had been added to his appointments for a meeting. Personally he had wanted to leave her alone on Monday, but professionally this needed to be taken care of. He picked up his phone and buzzed his assistant.

"Hello, Mr. Pierce."

"Hey Lauren, has Paige Kelly called to set up a time to meet with me?"

"No sir, I haven't heard from her."

"Alright, well I'm taking an early lunch today at ten-forty-five, but don't put anything else on my schedule this morning. I'm going to see if she can come by."

"I can do that for you. Would you like me to call the restaurant and set it up?"

Russell thought about that. *Yes, that would be easier* he thought, but then, *No, I want it to be more casual than that. But then again, would I worry about that for every employee?* He realized Lauren was still waiting for an answer. "Umm, yes…no…yes…no…" He sighed and made a decision. "Yes, thank you Lauren, that would be helpful. Just let me know what time. I would like it to be about nine-thirty if she can make that work."

"Yes, sir, I'll let you know."

Russell hung up the phone and let his face fall into his hands on his desk. "What is the matter with me?" he said aloud. "Am I back in high school?" He stood and paced back and forth in his office, trying to make sense of what was going on his head. He was still pacing when his office phone rang.

"Mr. Pierce, Miss Kelly will be here at nine-thirty," Lauren said.

"Great, thank you." He hung up and sat back down at his desk. He opened the document on his computer where he had typed a list of things to go over in his meeting with Paige. He read over it three times, and still couldn't remember what it said. He didn't know what to do with himself. He stood and went back to pacing.

. . .

Paige hung up the phone from talking to Lauren and starting wringing her hands together. She felt nervous, and then she felt embarrassed that she was nervous. She had wanted to stay mad, but after her talk with Mr. Thompson she had to believe that Mr. Pierce hadn't meant anything against her personally. She wished that she could just go back and not say anything to him about feeling sorry for her, or offering the job as charity. In fact, she wished she could go all the way back and not run into him in the hallway. She was a professional after all. She had been completely capable and confident in her work, and now here she was getting a major promotion and she felt like a teenager stumbling over herself in his presence. She had never been like that, even when she was a teenager. She tried to push her nerves aside, straightened her apron and walked out to the dining room where Shannon was waiting on the two members there for breakfast. She waited for her to come back to the counter and then spoke to her friend.

"I need you to cover the dining room for a little while this morning. I've got to go meet with Mr. Pierce," Paige said.

"Oh, couldn't put it off any longer, huh?" Shannon's eyes twinkled.

"Yeah, his assistant called and asked if I could come at nine-thirty. I had to say yes."

"Well good, you need to go. Don't you need to know about this job? I would be dying to get all the details."

"I don't know. I do want to know what is expected, especially since I already took it, but I just wish Mr. Thompson could have handled it."

"I don't see why you don't want to meet with him, he seems very nice, plus he is really cute."

"Shannon!"

"What?" she looked innocent enough.

"He's our boss." The shock still showed on her face.

"Well technically, *you* are my boss now. I don't really report to him. But even so, you can't even admit a teeny-tiny bit that you think he's cute too?"

Paige stared at her without responding.

"Come on Paige. It doesn't have to mean that you're chasing after him or planning a wedding. You can just say you think he's cute."

Paige hesitated. The truth might be worse than just saying he was cute. "Well, if I'm being totally honest…" she paused.

"Yeah? Come on!" Shannon encouraged.

"I would have to say that I haven't noticed how he looks."

"What?" Shannon nearly shouted. "You have got to be kidding me. Come on, Paige, are you blind?"

This was what she was afraid of. "I don't know, I just, I mean, I don't think, I just don't look."

Shannon just stared. "Seriously?" she asked.

"Well, yeah. I mean I'm just not interested in anything, so I don't really notice. But really, I can hardly look him in the eye after the way we met and then how I told him I wouldn't take the job, so I don't get a very good look anyway."

"Umm, okay, but still you should *notice*, Paige. You're alive, aren't you?"

Paige didn't have an answer for that.

"Girl, you've got to lighten up, live a little! Take a glance and notice that a guy is *super attractive*. You're twenty-two for goodness sake. What do you mean you're not interested in anything?"

Paige looked at the floor. "I just don't really have time to think about guys. But if I did, it definitely wouldn't be about my boss."

"You should make some time then. Cut yourself some slack. You work hard all the time. Nobody could ever accuse you of not taking care of things, but this is something you should take care of. Think about guys, Paige, please, think about guys. It's for your own good." Shannon smiled.

Paige smiled back at her friend. "Alright, I'll think about it."

"You'll think about guys? Or you'll think about thinking

about guys?"

"I'll think about thinking about it." Paige reached out and hugged Shannon. "But who needs guys when I've got a friend like you?"

"Umm, you do," Shannon teased. "You might have a friend, and you've basically got kids, but you need to find the guy too."

Paige smiled again and went back to the kitchen. *This is becoming quite a theme in my life.* She thought to herself. *I wonder if she and Peyton have been talking.* She busied herself with making some notes on upcoming menus and checked the re-order lists. For the time being she was still serving in the dining room, but she assumed that after her meeting with Mr. Pierce made things official that she would start looking to hire someone for her shifts. As much as she was happy to avoid the meeting, she was ready to get started with the real job and was already thinking of new ideas for the restaurant and kitchen. She had always been happy to help James out, but she hadn't wanted to push her boundaries too much and seem like she was taking over. But now that would be exactly what she was supposed to do, and with James's blessing on the position, she was excited to take it on.

Before she knew it the time had passed and it was nearly nine-thirty. She took off her apron, a decision she didn't question this time around, and picked up her notebook and pen. With a quick word to Shannon she headed out of the restaurant and down to Mr. Pierce's office.

Unlike Mr. Thompson's office, Mr. Pierce's office opened directly to the hall. His assistant's office was the next door over with it's own entrance. The door was slightly ajar, but Paige knocked and waited.

Chapter 12

"Come on in," Russell said, standing as Paige entered the office. "Hi Paige, it's nice to see you."

She took a glance around the office. It was a very plain room with the desk and chair facing towards the door, and two additional chairs facing the desk. There were several boxes against the wall and no decorations had been put up. "Hi, Mr. Pierce, nice to see you too." Paige forced herself to look him in the face and suddenly she wished that Shannon hadn't made all those comments about his appearance. She felt her heart do a flip-flop as their eyes met. She hadn't noticed before his deep brown eyes, or his strong jaw line. He reached out and shook her hand briefly and she took in his tall frame and strong arms. *No, no, no, don't do this to yourself Paige. Don't listen to Shannon. Just be professional.* She smiled politely.

"Please, call me Russell." He interrupted her thoughts.

"Oh, I don't know…" Paige started to say, but he interrupted her again, really this time.

"I insist. I much prefer it to 'Mr. Pierce', that makes me feel very old. I wish everyone could call me Russell, but anyway, you're in management now, so let's just go with that."

"Alright, I can try." Paige said.

"Please have a seat. Can I get you anything? Coffee? Water? Of course, I would probably have to go to the restaurant to get it, but I'm happy to." Russell smiled.

Paige couldn't help but smile back at him. "I'm fine thank you. I've already had two cups of coffee this morning."

"Oh really? So you're a caffeine addict too?" he asked.

She gave a little laugh. "I guess you could say that. It just seems necessary to life."

"I agree. I can't get by without my morning coffee. And my mid-morning coffee, and my afternoon coffee," he laughed.

"Yes, I'm the same way. Sometimes I try to remember to switch to decaf by dinner time," she admitted.

"Hmm, yes, I should think about that, might keep me from lying awake at night."

Paige gave a little laugh and breathed a little easier. She tried to relax and put away the awkwardness. She also tried not to picture him lying awake at night.

"I have to say that I'm glad you could come by today. I'm excited for you to get started and to see what you do with the restaurant, I'm expecting great things." He gave her an encouraging smile. "Now I'm sure you have questions, so let's jump right in."

"Well, yes, umm, I do. I guess first of all when do you want all of this to start?"

"Right away." Russell said emphatically.

"Oh, alright." Paige looked at him curiously.

"I know you will need to find someone to work your hours in the dining room, but really I don't see it as a huge transition beyond that. You're already doing so much, that it will just be easier when your waitressing responsibilities are lifted. I spoke with human resources and your new salary pay will start with your next paycheck."

"Oh, thank you," she said, sincerely surprised. "I don't know if I will have found someone by then."

Russell paused a moment. He folded his hands and placed them on his desk, then leaned forward and looked her directly in the eye. "Paige, I want to be very honest with you. I don't think you need to worry about that. I've said it already, but I'll say it again and again if I need to, you have been doing this job a long time. Please do not feel bad if you're paid for it while you're still spending some time in the dining room. If I could,

I would see to it that you were given back pay for all the time you should be paid for."

Paige looked away. "Oh that's alright. Really, I've always been happy to help. I never expected any of this."

"I know you didn't, and that's why I hope you will accept the salary as soon as possible and if nothing else, accept my apology that you have been overlooked for so long. I don't even know how that was possible."

She took a moment to take in what he was saying. She still found it hard to believe that she deserved the job, but she straightened herself in the chair and finally said, "Thank you. I'm grateful for the opportunity."

"Of course. So let's talk some details. As Mr. Thompson mentioned you will have some flexibility over your schedule because of the need for some later hours. Also, we don't really know what hours you will need with the ordering and planning and things. So it would be helpful if the first few weeks you could start to establish sort of a normal schedule that you can vary from as you need to. We have management meetings for all of the department heads on Mondays at noon, so plan to attend those."

"Oh, James usually attends those."

"Yes, but you will be taking over that responsibility."

"Oh, right." Paige wrote on her notebook.

"Also, we would like for you to take a larger role in our special events. Of course the restaurant handles the food preparation, but it's my understanding that our Event Coordinator, Karen, handles the planning part of the menu."

"Yes, that's right."

"I've noticed that we offer a few different packages and the guests just choose which one they want for the event, is that right?"

"Yes, it is."

"I would really like for you to take a look at those, possibly with James, and come up with some new packages. New ideas and selections, and possibly even more choices. And then I would like for you to be available to meet with people planning events to see what package fits their needs, or if they need a special menu. Is that something you could do?"

Paige imagined planning a menu from beginning to end with total freedom and a smile crossed her lips. "Yes, I think so."

"Wonderful, we'll coordinate with Karen so the two of you can meet and discuss what that will look like. Of course, that will also mean some amount of working nights and weekends to oversee events. Will that be alright for you?"

"Yes," was all Paige said.

"I only ask because I wasn't sure how that would work for your family."

Paige felt herself get defensive. "Yes, we will make it work."

Russell seemed to understand that she didn't want to discuss it. "Great. So what other questions do you have?"

"Who do I need to run ideas by?"

Russell seemed confused. "What do you mean?"

"Do I talk to you or Mr. Thompson about my ideas?"

"Your ideas?"

"Yes, for the restaurant." Paige didn't see why this was confusing.

"Paige, you're the manager. If you have an idea, you can go with it. You're in charge."

Paige looked like she was taking this in. "Really? Anything I want to do?"

"Yes. We trust you completely. Now if you're unsure or would like to talk through something that you're thinking about, I would be happy to listen and help you with it." Russell said this in a way that sounded more like a friend than a boss.

Paige still felt a little shocked. She knew she was becoming the manager, but the full weight of the responsibility, and the freedom, was just hitting her. She was in charge. She cleared her throat to push away the emotion she felt. "Okay, thank you."

"Of course, you're welcome. My door is always open. I hope you will let me know if there's anything you need or that I can help you with." Russell said earnestly.

Paige looked up and let her eyes meet his again. She felt as though his words meant more than just help with the new position or things that were work related. Strangely she felt herself wanting to open up to him. But only for a brief moment. She looked down at her lap and closed her notebook. "Is there anything else you need from me?"

"Oh, yes, actually." He shuffled some pages on his desk, looking for something. He pulled out a folder. "I need you to take these papers and sign the contract accepting the position and the salary amount that we discussed. This also includes all the details of your benefit package, sick days, vacation, etc., and the company health insurance plan that you're entitled to. Just take all of it and call H.R. if you have any questions. You can sign the signature pages and get them back sometime this week."

Paige reached out and took the folder. "Alright, I will. Thank you." She turned to go.

"Thanks for coming by, Paige, I'm looking forward to seeing you take on this job."

Paige turned and smiled, and walked out of the office without a word.

Chapter 13

*A*t ten-forty-five Russell met his dad and two brothers out in front of the club. He carried his golf clubs over his shoulder. It had been a long time since the four of them had played a round of golf together and Russell was looking forward to it. The other three men arrived together and met Russell at the entrance.

"Hey Son, how's your day going?" Jim Pierce gave Russell a quick embrace.

"Hey Dad, pretty good, or at least it was until these bozos showed up." He gestured at Jack and Sam.

"Oh yeah, we just figured it was time we came to check up on you, baby brother, make sure you can handle this place," Sam joked.

Russell expected the usual amount of teasing from his brothers. He only hoped they wouldn't embarrass him in front of the staff. "Mmhmm," he said. "I know that you're only here to use my employee discount."

"Aww, man, that hurts Russy, really it does." Jack held his

hand over his heart as if he had been wounded.

Russell rolled his eyes. "Come on guys, let's get going." The group walked through the clubhouse and came out through the men's locker room to the golf course. Once outside Russell saw that it was a great day for this. The sunshine was brilliant, and the spring temperatures made it perfect to be out enjoying the sport.

"So how do you like being back in town?" asked Jack. "Is Mom doing your laundry yet?"

"Nope, I actually have my own little laundry fairy who lives in the apartment. Although, to give some credit, I'm pretty sure mom taught the fairy how to fold the towels just right."

"Nice." Jack teed up for his first swing.

The men each took their turn and watched quietly. When they continued to walk the conversation picked back up. "What's new at work, Jack?" Russell asked.

"Not much, really. I meet with new clients on occasion, but for the most part I'm just servicing existing accounts. It's good steady work now, a lot better than when I first started out and had to work harder to find new clients all the time."

"Mmhmm, I know how that can be," Russell answered. "And Dad, how are you liking being semi-retired?"

Jim gave a small smile. "Well, I'm only as semi-retired as your mother will let me be. When I'm home from work she seems to find things for me to do, fixing something or taking a meal to someone, or visiting what she calls 'the old people'. So I'm still staying pretty busy."

"That's what keeps you alive, Pops," Sam jumped in. "Gotta keep moving."

"You've never had a problem with that, son." Jim smiled.

"So tell us about the girl," Jack said casually.

Russell stopped in his tracks. "What? Who? What girl?"

"Oh come on Russ, Mom told us about her. She works here right?" Sam looked around as if he might catch a glimpse of her walking by.

"Keep your voice down." Russell spoke strongly. "I don't need you to start a rumor."

"Well, it is? A rumor?" Jack asked.

"Boys," their father spoke up. "This is your brother's place of work, try to be civil."

"We will, if he spills already," said Sam.

"Look, I don't know what Mom told you…" he started, but Sam interrupted.

"She told us that there's a girl that works here at the club and that she goes to her church and that you can't take your eyes off her. Is that about right?" He looked at Jack.

"Yeah, and something about she has a big family?" Jack added.

"Alright, Alright, I'll tell you, just be a little quieter."

The four men continued walking down the path and the two older brothers made a motion of zipping their lips.

"Yes, she works here. And yes, she goes to Mom and Dad's church, but nothing is going on. I barely know her, and I'm pretty sure she would like to keep it that way." Russell rubbed his forehead, and his tone became serious. "Her parents died a few years ago, and she takes care of her younger siblings, all five of them. She's smart and creative and she's just been promoted to manage the restaurant. But that's really all I know about her. I wish there was something I could do to help her, but she seems pretty self-sufficient."

As Russell spoke his brothers lost their joking attitudes and listened intently.

"You care about her?" Jim asked.

Russell thought for a moment about how to answer that, he shrugged his shoulders. "I don't know. I just don't know. I can't stop thinking about her, and I've prayed about what God wants me to do here, at the club and in this town, and I keep thinking about her. I don't know. She seems like she has everything taken care of. She's organized and professional, and even with her brothers and sisters she seems like she's got it all under control. But I just feel like she needs someone to fall back on, someone she can depend on and trust. She must have lost so much and she shouldn't have to walk that road alone."

All the men had stopped walking and they drew in close as he spoke. Russell hadn't even realized how strong his feelings were in this. He just didn't know what to do.

"What has God told you?" said Jim.

"To help people."

"And to help her?"

"Yes, I think so."

"Then that's what you need to do." Jim made it sound so simple.

"But I don't even think she will let me. Every time she opens up just a little bit it's like I see a warning alarm go off and she shuts back down. She's so careful not to say too much, and anytime I say anything that even sounds like an offer for help she pushes it away so fast."

Jack spoke up. "But you're not responsible for her response, you still have to do what God has asked you to do. You have to keep trying."

"But how do I do that?"

"Just be there. Keep talking, keep asking. If she pushes you

116

away, push back in kindness. Just keep being there over and over again until God tells you something else," said Jack.

"And what if she never lets me in?"

"She will. How do you think I ever got Carrie to go out with me?" Jack smiled.

"Do you have any romantic feelings for her?" Jim asked.

Russell groaned, "Dad…"

"It's a legitimate question, Son."

"Well…I don't know, the first time I met her I literally trampled her, and then the next thing I know I'm basically her boss, and then I offer her a job that she says she won't take on pity, and now…well, I'm still her boss. I just have such strong feelings that I want to help her that I haven't really even thought about whether or not it's romantic."

"Son, having a strong desire to help and take care of a woman is a very romantic feeling."

Russell considered this.

"Wait just a minute," Sam said. "Go back to the part about trampling her?" He raised his eyebrows curiously.

Russell hung his head in his hands. "So my first day here, I was hurrying down the hall and she came around the corner carrying a big box. I didn't even see her and I ran into her and knocked her over. She fell in the floor, the box flew in the air and I nearly tripped over her."

Jack and Sam looked at each other, then burst out laughing. The serious moment was over as they started acting out the scene themselves.

"Oh, hello, I'm Russell, I run this country club now all by myself," Jack said as he pretended to walk the hall, waving as if he were in a parade.

Sam pretended to be a girl carrying a box and prancing

along. "La de da, la de da" he sang. "Ohhhhh nooooooo!" He spoke as if in slow motion and gasped as the two came close then ran into each other and fell to the ground. They rolled and laughed at each other.

Russell rolled his eyes and started to walk away from them. They continued their banter, but he ignored them.

Jim followed close behind and spoke to his youngest son. "Russ, Jack is right. You need to just keep doing what The Lord has asked you to do. And he's also right, Carrie wouldn't go out with him for two years."

"Really?"

"Yes, really, on both accounts. If you feel this strongly about it, then just try to be her friend and let her know she can trust you. That may be what she needs right now. You just don't know where it could lead."

"Thanks, Dad. I know you're right, I'll try, it's just hard. But I really want to help her in any way I can."

"I know you do. Just be careful, because if you don't have any romantic feelings for her then you could accidentally mislead her, then all trust will be lost. And romantic feelings doesn't mean pity or feeling sorry for her."

"Yeah, I get it." Russell told his dad, but deep down he knew he would really need to consider both of those things.

Chapter 14

*P*aige stood at the counter slowly sipping her third cup of coffee. It was just about time for lunch on Thursday and she had barely caught her breath all day. She had been waiting tables for breakfast and also interviewing for a new waitress and talking with James about some new menu ideas. She was still overwhelmed with the new job and felt like she wasn't sure which way was up. So it only made her more flustered when Russell walked in the door and made his way to the counter.

"Good afternoon," he said.

"Is it afternoon already?" She looked at the clock above the kitchen door.

"Well, no, I guess not quite." Russell stood with his hands in his pockets.

"Oh, phew, you scared me. I thought I must have lost an hour somewhere."

"Sorry about that, I guess I just got ahead of myself."

Paige looked at him, waiting for him to say more, when he

didn't she asked, "Is there something I can do for you, Mr. Pierce?"

"Nope, it's Russell. Remember?"

"Sorry, is there something I can do for you, Russell?"

"I just thought I would come in for lunch," he said casually.

"Oh right, well we'll be happy to have you. We're not very busy right now, so if you want you can have your pick of tables," Paige said, waving her hand as if showcasing the dining room.

"Actually I thought I would just sit here at the counter. And since you're not too busy I could keep you company."

Paige stopped and looked at him. She was quiet for a long moment. "Okay. Sure," she said finally.

Russell took a seat and Paige handed him a menu. "Just let me know what I can get you," she said.

"I might need a minute to decide. I haven't eaten here that many times since I've been back."

"That's alright, take your time."

"What's your favorite?"

Paige was surprised by his question. "You mean, what do I suggest?"

"No, I mean, what's your favorite? I mean, you've eaten here before, right?"

Paige blushed a little. "Of course, but usually I taste the specials when James asks me to. I don't order off the menu very often. But I do love the sandwiches for lunch. I never knew a sandwich could be that good until I had one here."

"Alright, sounds good. I'll have the club sandwich and a sweet tea."

"Great, I'll put that in for you."

Paige went to the kitchen and put in the order. Then she ducked back in the corner where she could see her reflection in a small mirror. She tucked a stray strand of hair back behind her ear and checked to make sure there was nothing in her teeth. She tried to calm the butterflies that had appeared in her stomach the moment she saw Russell. She didn't even know why she felt nervous, but she tried to calm her nerves before leaving the kitchen to face him again. She took him his glass of sweet tea and placed it on the counter and tried to act natural.

"Thanks," Russell said. "So how are things going?"

"Things? For the restaurant?" she asked.

"Yeah, sure." Russell took a sip of his tea.

"Pretty good I guess. Nothing really has changed a lot so far. I did some interviews today for a new waitress."

"Oh really? That was pretty quick."

"Yes, well, we always have a few applications on file from when people come in and ask if we're hiring. Plus one of our current waitresses had a friend who wanted to interview, so she came in today. I kind of feel like I should give priority to someone who already had an application in before her, but I did like her too."

"Hmm, yeah." Russell looked like he wanted to say more.

"What?"

"Nothing, just thinking about what you said."

"You think I should hire someone who put in an application first?"

"I think you should hire the person that you think will be best for the job."

Paige smiled and rolled her eyes just a little. "Well, obviously that's what I want to do. I'm just not really sure who that is."

"What kind of questions did you ask them?" Russell sounded sincerely interested.

Paige felt a little embarrassed. "That's part of the problem, I'm not sure I did a very good job. I've never interviewed anyone before."

"That's alright, I'm sure you did fine. Sometimes it's just about getting to know someone and getting a certain feeling about them."

Paige felt a little like she was starting to get a certain feeling about Russell. She tried to push that thought away. "I asked them if they had waitressing experience and why they wanted to work here."

"Those are great questions. What did they say?"

"One girl does have experience and said she wanted to work here because she hates the place that she works now."

"Mmmhmm."

"Another girl didn't have restaurant experience, but she has worked in customer service before. Right now she works in an office environment where she's in a cubicle. But she's looking for something with earlier hours and said she wants to be around people more."

"See, you learned something about them. That's helpful in knowing what kind of employee they will be."

"True," Paige said.

"Sometimes it's not just about if they can do the job, but if the job will be a good fit for them personally. If it's a good fit and they enjoy it, sometimes that makes them better at their job."

Paige smiled. "I hadn't thought about it that way. That's a great perspective." Their eyes met for a moment and the butterflies in her stomach kicked into high gear. "Let me go check on your sandwich," she said and turned to go back in the kitchen. She returned a moment later and set his lunch in front of him.

"Thank you."

"My pleasure," she said.

"So do you know now who you're going to hire?" he asked.

"You know what? I think I do." Paige sounded happy.

"Great, I'm glad I could help."

"Thanks," she said. "I really appreciate it."

"I didn't really do anything," he said.

"I guess it just helped to have someone to talk it out with."

"It usually does." He smiled. "You probably knew what you needed to do, just needed to think out loud. Glad I could be a sounding board. I'm happy to help anytime."

Paige looked in his eyes and felt certain that he meant it.

Chapter 15

*S*pring had arrived in full swing and the weeks were beginning to fly by at the club. It was a busy time of year for events, especially with wedding season quickly approaching, and the warmer weather bringing out all the golfers who had been away for the cold season.

Paige had begun working with Karen, the event planner, on the catering menus and it was taking up more of her time than she expected. One day she casually mentioned it to Russell who had started eating lunch at the counter in the restaurant every day. "I just didn't know it would be so time consuming," she said. She was growing used to seeing him everyday and the conversation flowed more easily now.

"But you like it?" Russell asked as he swallowed a bite.

"Oh yes, I really, really love it, it's probably one of my favorite parts of the job."

Russell noticed the way her eyes lit up as she talked about the different dishes and choosing the best dessert for each event. He thought for a moment before asking her, "So do you do any of the cooking? Or cook any fancy dishes at home?"

"Oh no, not really at home. I usually stick to basics after I spend all day in the kitchen. But here," she looked around as if someone might hear her, "James has shown me a few things, and sometimes he lets me help with a dessert or something. But other than that I don't really do any fancy cooking. I wish though."

"Is that what you wanted to study in school?"

Paige's eyes dimmed a bit. "Oh no, nothing like that." She looked away at a list on the clipboard she was carrying.

Russell wished that she was always as bright and open as she was once she got going on a topic that she was passionate about. But it was usually like this, moments of conversation that seemed comfortable and open and then just like that she would close off. As if she had just realized she was sharing too much. Sometimes he let it go, but other times, like now, he pushed on. "Oh, so what did you major in?"

Now she had that look, like it was something she would love to talk about, but she still hesitated. "Interior Design," she finally said.

He chewed another bite, then waved his fork in the air as he spoke. "Like decorating houses and stuff?"

"Kind of, but it's more than that."

"Like what?"

"Like understanding how the design of a place says something about it. The structure can determine the feel of a place and even the colors on the wall can create a mood when you walk in the room. I love the way you can plan out a room for the way you want people to feel when they're in it."

Russell felt his heart tug. *What would her life be like if she had been able to follow that path? What if she had given that her all?* he thought. He wanted to ask her to tell him more about school and if she thought she would ever go back, but he didn't push that boundary yet. He opted for a lighter discussion. "So have you ever decorated, say, a country club office?" he said, with a twinkle in his eye.

She smiled at him. "I can't say that I have. But if someone were to ask me for some suggestions, I would say to start by getting rid of the cardboard boxes and at least put some pictures on the wall."

"Hey, I've been a little busy."

"Are there still things in those boxes?"

"Um, well, yes," he admitted.

"Then either put them somewhere or get rid of them. They can't be too useful if they've been sitting in boxes this long."

"Hmm, good point. And I have been meaning to put some pictures up, but I don't really even know what to put. I've never really had an office before, or at least one where people came in to see me and that needed to look nice. Maybe I could convince someone to help me pick something out?" he dared.

"Mmmm, maybe," was all Paige would commit to. "Right now I've got menus to plan and supplies to order." She tapped her pen on her clipboard.

"Very well, I'll let you get back to it." He stood and wiped his hands on a napkin. He pushed the plate a bit and Paige picked it up off the counter.

"See ya later," she said and turned away.

He watched her go and wished that he could stay all afternoon at the counter. But instead he stood and left to return to his undecorated, box-filled office.

Once back in his office he did what he did every day after lunch, he sat at his desk and prayed. Mostly he prayed for

Paige, and today was no exception. *Lord, I feel so badly for her.*
She was just going along normally in life, following her dream and
going to school, and then in an instant her life changed and her
path was completely altered.

This was always my plan for her.

Russell heard the words and sat silently. *I hadn't thought*
about that.

My Son, I have always known what her path would be.

And this is the path for her?

It is.

Russell knew in that moment that he could not feel sorry for
Paige anymore. He was sad that she had lost her parents and
that things hadn't been easy for her, but he didn't need to be
sad without hope. In fact he was filled with hope because God
had a plan for her, her situation had never been a surprise to
him. Another thought gripped Russell.

Lord, am I a part of the plan you have for her?

Yes.

The word could have been spoken over a loudspeaker it was
so clear. Russell knew without a doubt that he needed to press
on in his friendship with Paige. He was glad that things were
easier between the two of them and grateful for the friendship
they were growing. But he knew he needed to push forward
more. The impulse was so strong that he started to rise from
his desk. But in that moment his phone rang.

"Hello?" he answered it.

"Russell, it's Paige."

He nearly collapsed in his chair. "Hey."

"I was wondering if I could come talk to you about an idea
for the restaurant. It's kind of a big deal, so I wanted to see
what you thought."

"Oh yeah, sure, I've got some time right now if that works."

"That's great. I'll be down in a minute," she paused for a second. "Do you want me to bring you some coffee?" she asked.

"Umm, yeah, that would be great, thanks."

"Okay, see you in a minute."

"Okay." Russell hung up the phone and sat frozen in his chair, wondering if he would be able to handle coffee. Even though he was sitting still he felt as if he heart was about to pound out of his chest from nervousness. Then as he thought about it he started to laugh. *Okay, Lord. I get it. You're funny you know. If that wasn't a clear sign I don't know what would be.* He breathed out hard. *Just help me here, I don't want to scare her away. Give me the words and help me not to seem too forward.*

That was all the time he had before there was a knock on his door and Paige came in. She carried two mugs of hot coffee.

"Hey, come on in, have a seat." Russell stood up and realized that he was talking too fast and tried to calm himself. He reached out for the coffee and sat back down at his desk.

"Thanks for letting me come by. I just started thinking about this idea, and I wanted to mention it to you before I got too far with it." Paige held her coffee mug close to her.

"No problem, I'm happy to help."

Paige set her coffee down on the desk and gestured excitedly with her hands as she spoke. "Okay, so here's the thing. You know breakfast is pretty slow, right? Just a handful of people in, and they usually just want coffee and a muffin or something."

"Yes, I remember noting that on the day I observed in the dining room."

"Right, so a couple of times we have talked about cutting

back the menu to be more like a continental breakfast, you know, muffins, pastries, etc., or a buffet with eggs and bacon or something."

"Mmhmm," Russell knew that had been mentioned before, but no one had ever been crazy about the idea.

"So, I was thinking, instead of cutting back and doing less. What if we went the other way and did more?"

Russell could see the excitement in her eyes, and even though he didn't know what she was talking about yet, he was getting excited too. "What do you mean?"

"What if we go all out? Do a gourmet breakfast special for different days of the week, belgian waffles, strawberries and cream crepes, cinnamon roll pancakes, specialty omelets. And we do a special announcement for the members, encourage them to start special celebration days here for breakfast. Come here for birthdays, anniversaries, special occasions. See if we can draw in a bigger crowd in the mornings. James has some amazing ideas and recipes, he's just never promoted them because of the small number of members at that time of day." She stopped for a breath and waited excitedly. "So? What do you think?"

Russell smiled at her. "I think it's a great idea."

"You do? Really?" She seemed to breathe a sigh of relief.

"Yes, I do. I never really liked the thought of cutting back and giving up. This is a great place for breakfast and we need something to draw more people in, not push them away. This is perfect. And the idea of promoting it as a special is great. We can put something in the club newsletter, put signs on all the tables in the restaurant and even do some advertising around the club." Here he held up his hands as if he could see the writing in the air, "Coming soon, brand new breakfast specials. Join us for all your special mornings. Make every morning special with our breakfast specials. The tastiest morning around."

Paige started to giggle at all his slogans. "Yes, exactly!"

"Definitely, I think this is a great idea. And honestly, even if it doesn't work, what do you have to lose?"

"That's exactly what I thought, it's not like we will drive people away by having a better breakfast. And if people just keep coming in and ordering the same stuff, then we can say we gave it a try. But I want to really give it a chance."

"Yes, I think you should. Why don't you meet with James and come up with some definite specials and decide which of my amazing slogans you want to use. You can also talk to Trent who handles the newsletter and promotional material to help you. Think about when you want it to start so you can work your timeline backwards to get everything done."

"Oh, that's a good idea. Work backwards. Yeah, that's good. Would you want to come to the meeting too? Maybe we can have James and Trent and me and you…" Paige let her voice trail off as she linked the two of them together.

"I'm happy to come if you need me to or if you think that would be helpful."

"Yes, I think so. You can work on your slogans before then." She smiled, teasing him.

He laughed. "Sounds good. Let me take a look at my calendar." He looked at his computer and clicked a few buttons. "My days this week are a little full. I'm still working my way around the various departments and I've got meetings about some details. What about next Tuesday, around ten-thirty?"

"James is usually prepping lunch by then, maybe after lunch, how about three?"

"Don't you usually leave by then?"

"Yes, but I think I can make arrangements on Tuesday, remember, I work a flexible schedule."

"Okay, sure, we'll say three. Just check with Trent and see if he's available then. "

"I'll email him."

"Great!" Russell typed the plan into the calendar on his computer. He cleared his throat, his nerves jumped back up into high gear as he said his next words. "You know, I've got another space in here where I see some free time."

Paige stopped writing on her own calendar. "Oh, okay, when?"

Russell looked her in the face. "Lunch on Saturday."

Paige looked confused. "Saturday? For the meeting?"

Russell could quickly see he was about to botch the whole thing. He knew he was going to have to be direct. "No, uhh, that's not what I meant. Paige, would you like to have lunch with me on Saturday?"

Shock registered on her face. She quickly looked down at her lap, flustered. "Oh, um, I, I, I don't think so." Paige stammered.

"Oh." Russell knew that pressing her to say yes could cause serious problems in the workplace, so he didn't say more.

She looked up to see the disappointment on his face.

"Can I ask, why?"

"I just, um, I have a lot going on. I have to take care of the kids on Saturday."

"Okay." Russell left it at that.

"Thanks for your help." Paige spoke quietly as she stood to go. She gathered her notes and took both of the coffee mugs from the desk. She looked as if she wanted to say something else, but instead she turned and walked out the door.

Russell leaned back in his chair and stared at the ceiling.

. . .

"Paige? Paige?" Shannon tried to get her friend's attention after she absentmindedly walked back in to the kitchen and placed two coffee mugs in the sink.

"Oh, hey Shannon, I'm sorry, did you say something?" Paige turned to face Shannon.

"Yeah, about four times. Are you alright?" She looked worried.

"I'm fine," Paige answered.

"You look pale, are you sick?"

"No, no, nothing like that." Paige stared off.

"What happened? Where were you?"

"Well, umm, I'm not sure."

"You're not sure where you were or what happened?"

"What happened. I went to meet with Russell about an idea for the restaurant. We were just talking and scheduling a meeting about it, and he….he…."

"He what?" Shannon eyes were wide with concern.

"He asked me out," Paige finally blurted.

Shannon gasped. "What? Paige are you serious?"

"Yeah."

"That's great!"

"Great?" Paige finally seemed to come around and stared at her friend with a shocked look.

"Yes, it's great! I've seen you two talking, and you always

look happy, this is so exciting!" Shannon hugged Paige.

"Wait a minute, I told him no."

"What? Paige…" Shannon groaned. "Why in the world did you do that?"

"Because…" Paige said.

When she didn't say more Shannon said, "Because what?"

"Because, because of my life." Paige shook her head.

"Your life? Paige, this is how you get a life. This is what I've been talking about. What did he ask you to do?"

"Go to lunch on Saturday."

"Well, that's easy. It's not a huge deal or a big commitment, it's just lunch. That can be casual, just go and then see what happens. Don't say no because you think you have to say no to something that's ten miles down the road."

Paige looked like she was thinking this over.

"Come on, Paige. Think about it for a minute. Are you saying no because you really don't want to go, or just because you think it's what you're supposed to do? Because if you want to go, even just a little bit, I definitely think you should. So…do you? Want to?"

Paige looked her in the eye and knew she had to admit the truth. "Okay, maybe just a little bit."

Shannon squealed. "Then go!" She shouted.

"Ugh! I can't!" Paige put her hand to her forehead and grimaced. "Even if I really wanted to say yes at this point, it's too late. I said no. He looked pretty disappointed."

"That's because he *likes* you." Shannon held her hands over her heart.

"It doesn't matter now anyway, he's not going to ask again."

"So call him, or walk back to his office. Tell him you changed your mind, tell him you had a momentary lapse in judgment.

Tell him you need lessons in social skills or that you're crazy or you have a hole in your head. Just say yes!"

"I can't, I just can't, I would be mortified."

"I will then. I'll just tell him for you." Shannon walked toward the phone.

"No!" Paige ran after her.

"I'll just say I'm your assistant calling to say you reconsidered the appointment on Saturday, and you're available now."

"Shannon!" The two were teasingly fighting over the phone when they both stopped at the sound in the doorway.

Paige looked.

Russell stood perfectly still in the doorway. She didn't know how long he had been there, but it was obvious he had heard enough to gather what was going on. He didn't speak for a few seconds and then quietly said, "You took my coffee, I didn't get a chance to drink it." He still stood perfectly still.

"I'm sorry." Paige stood in front of him now, she wasn't sure if she meant about the coffee or saying no.

"Did I hear right, that you've reconsidered?" Russell looked hopeful, but hesitant.

"Oh, we were just talking." Paige blushed, "But I really do have to take care of the kids on Saturday."

Russell had already come up with an answer for that excuse. "That's alright, what if you bring them with you? The weather should be perfect for a picnic at the park." Russell smiled.

"Oh, well, they do love the park."

"Is that a yes?" He raised his eyebrows and his eyes seemed to beg. Paige paused for a long moment, then said, "Umm, alright, yes."

Shannon threw her arms up in the air. Both Russell and Paige turned to look at her. She tried to cover it up, "Whohoo!

Look at that! It's time for me to clock out. I am soooooooo excited about getting off work!" She walked out of the kitchen, but turned so only Paige could see and gave her a big smile and two thumbs up.

"So….." Russell started to say, but wasn't sure what else to say.

"Um, you wanted coffee right?"

"Coffee, yes, coffee." He walked to the coffee maker and poured himself a cup. He turned back to her. "Okay, well, thanks…I mean, umm," he cleared his throat.

"Yeah, um, well alright." Paige babbled.

"I guess I'll see you then…I mean, before then, but then too…" Russell ran his fingers through his hair.

"Yeah, okay, see ya," Paige replied.

As he left the kitchen she stood and watched him go. She couldn't believe she had said yes and she knew she would spend the next couple of days debating with herself whether that had been the right thing to do or not.

Chapter 16

*O*n Saturday morning Paige stood in front of the bathroom mirror staring at herself. "What was I thinking?" she said to the girl in the mirror. "I can't do this!"

"Do what?" Peyton came walking into the bathroom to see what Paige was doing.

"Umm, nothing."

"Umm, not nothing," Peyton mimicked her. "What are you doing?"

"Just trying to think through my day," Paige fibbed.

"Oh yeah, what do you have going on? Laundry marathon?"

"I thought I would take the twins to the park."

"You're not going to Shep's game?"

"Not this time. It's a bit of drive. He said he didn't mind."

"What about Zoey?" Peyton herself was going to an all-day cheerleading competition.

"She's playing at a friend's house today."

"Mmhmm. So you want to take the twins to the park. And

why exactly can't you do that?"

Paige knew she couldn't keep things from her sister. "Okay, I'll tell you, but I don't want any comments."

Peyton looked at her sister and raised her eye brows. "Okay?"

"I'm going to the park, and taking the twins, and Russell Pierce is meeting me there for lunch."

"What? Really? When did this happen?" Peyton's eyes were wide with shock.

"He asked me on Wednesday."

"And you're just now telling me?"

"That's because at first I said no, and then Shannon talked me into saying yes, and so I had to tell him I changed my mind. Then it was awkward to see him at work the next couple of days. But I just didn't want you to think you were right about him. It's just lunch. I'm just having lunch with him and then that will be that."

"Oh really? That will be that?" Peyton said with tongue in cheek.

"Yes, I'm sure."

"Well good for you. But why are you saying you can't do this?"

"Look at me. I think I've totally forgotten how to put on nice makeup, and I don't have a clue what to wear on a lunch date to the park, with two kids." She groaned. "Seriously, did you hear how that just sounded? I'm going on a lunch date to the park with two kids." She leaned her elbows on the bathroom counter and let her face fall in her hands.

Peyton patted her back. "Oh come on now. I can help you find something to wear, and you don't need fancy makeup. And the kids thing? That's just real life. But Paige, I'm super proud of you."

Paige looked up. "Really?"

"Yes, you're doing it. You said yes and you're giving it a try. I'm so glad."

"Thanks Peyton, that means a lot, really."

"Just go and try to have fun and not worry that it's different. He knew about them when he asked you out. By the way, I would totally keep them for you today if I could."

"Oh I know, it was his idea though. Besides it will probably give me a distraction so I can focus on them if I need to."

"That's true, like a diversion if it's not going well." Peyton made a face. "Although I'm sure it will," she said quickly.

Paige sighed and walked out of the bathroom. She flopped down on the bed face first.

"Come on now, it will be alright. Let's go upstairs to my closet and we'll find you something to wear."

"Your closet?" Paige asked. "What's wrong with my closet?"

"You just said you don't have anything to wear. So come look at my stuff. Seriously, what are sisters for? We used to share clothes all the time." Peyton poked out her bottom lip.

"Oh, alright." Paige got up and let her sister drag her up the stairs.

After fifteen minutes of Peyton handing her things, and Paige saying no, she was finally dressed in a denim skirt that hit just above her knees, and a short sleeved navy blue top with white polka dots. She would slip on brown sandals later. She stood back to look at herself in the mirror.

"I love it!" Peyton said. "It says that you're casual enough to hang out at the park, but you made a little effort."

"Oh, good…I think," Paige replied.

"Now, let's see about your hair."

"My hair?"

"Yes, are you going to wear it down?"

"I was planning to just wear it as it is." Paige touched her long hair pulled up in a high ponytail.

"Hmm, okay, you can, but it might look nice down. Oh, but if it's windy you might want to pull it back, but if not down could work. Maybe you should just take a ponytail holder in case you decide to pull it back later." Peyton stressed over the decision.

Paige grabbed Peyton's hand. "It will be fine. Either way, I'll figure it out. Thank you."

Peyton relaxed. "I just want you to look nice. I'm so excited! We haven't done this in a long time."

"Get dressed?"

"Get you ready for a date!"

"Oh, yes, I know. Thanks Peyton, without you I might still be laying on the bed trying to decide on a fake disease that would make me too sick to go, but not sick enough that I couldn't take care of the kids."

"You'll be fine."

Paige looked at her watch. "You better get ready too, you need to go."

Peyton glanced at her watch too. "Yikes!" she said and ran for the shower.

Paige picked up some of the clothes that she had discarded on the bed and put them away. She walked down the stairs and through the living room where the twins were watching cartoons and into the kitchen. She went to the pantry and pulled out the cooler bag and all the essentials for preparing a picnic lunch. In a short time she had fixed sandwiches, packed a bag of potato chips and washed grapes. She put it all in the bag and tossed in a few water bottles and juice boxes. "Joe, Lucy, you need to go get dressed, we're going to the park for a picnic." The twins loved the park and they hooped and hollered as they ran for their rooms. Paige thought twice about the two of them picking out their own clothes and headed upstairs to approve outfits.

A short while later they were packed in the car, the cooler bag and a blanket in the back, and all ready to go. Paige checked the rearview mirror as she thought that Russell had probably never been on a date with two kids and a girl who drove a minivan to get there. He had offered to pick her up, but she thought it made more sense with the twins for them to just meet there. She didn't admit that she hoped this would feel more casual and less awkward.

When they pulled into the park Paige realized she hadn't thought about how packed it would be today. Once spring arrived everyone seemed to flock to outdoor activities to soak up the warm weather. She circled around twice before finding a parking spot. She gave Joe and Lucy last minute instructions. "Now, I want you to have fun today, but I also want you to behave. We'll find a spot and eat our lunch and when you're done, then you can go play. And you need to be polite to Mr. Russell that you'll meet soon. Okay?"

"Okay," they agreed in unison.

"Alright, let's go." They all three climbed from the van and the twins couldn't hide their excitement as they waited for Paige to gather the picnic supplies. "Hold hands while we cross the parking lot." They covered the distance through the cars as quickly as they could. The park was a beautiful part of the community. Once they were past the parking lot, a sidewalk led to a wooden bridge and on the other side was a playground with swings, monkey bars and slides, as well as a large field for playing. There were a few picnic tables, which were already filled with people, and a number of families sitting on the ground to eat. Past the play area was a paved walking trail that wound around a small lake.

Paige, Joe and Lucy crossed the bridge. Paige looked around and she was surprised at the burst of happiness that came over her when she saw Russell standing just at the other end. He was leaning against the railing wearing khaki shorts and a light blue polo shirt and tennis shoes. He had a pair of designer sunglasses pushed back on his head. When he saw Paige and the kids a big smile spread across his face and he turned to walk towards them.

"Hi," Russell said.

"Hey, how are you?"

"I'm good, how are you?"

"I'm fine." She already felt nervous now that they were actually here and immediately she directed her attention to the kids. "Guys, this is Mr. Russell, Russell, this is Joe and Lucy,"

"Yeah, we've met, remember? At the church." Russell said.

"Oh." Paige rolled her eyes. "That's right, I forgot."

"That's okay, hey guys, how's it going?" Joe and Lucy were distracted looking at the playground and mumbled some answers. Russell looked back at Paige and a look of confusion came over him. "What's all this?" he pointed at the cooler bag.

"Umm, lunch." Paige said, but it sounded more like a question. Only when he asked did it occur to her that he had asked her to lunch, which probably meant he hadn't expected her to bring it. She was just used to taking care of things herself.

"Oh, okay, I had planned to get something from the food trucks. I had heard that they are always here on Saturdays."

"Oh, yeah. I'm sorry. I just wanted to be prepared." She mentally kicked herself for not thinking. Of course, she didn't even know how to be on a date.

Russell jumped in to say, "Oh no, that's great, this is perfect. I'm sure that whatever you have is better than a greasy food truck." He seemed to be trying to put her at ease.

"Sandwiches?"

"Perfect, I like sandwiches."

Paige gave him a look that said she knew he was patronizing her.

"I tell you what, how about after lunch you let me get us all dessert?"

Paige gave a small smile. "Yes, that sounds good."

"Alright then, it's a plan. Let's go find a spot."

They fell into step as the four of them walked across the field to the picnic area. The kids ran on ahead excited to see some friends from school. "Can we go play, Paige?" Joe asked.

"After you eat," she responded.

They found a spot near a big oak tree and Russell took the blanket from Paige and began to spread it out. "So what have you been doing today?" he asked.

Paige sat on the blanket and started getting out the food, "Just our usual Saturday stuff, they like to watch cartoons in their PJs for as long as I'll let them."

"Oh yeah, I remember doing that as a kid. I loved Saturday mornings."

"Yeah me too, it seems like a very long time ago."

"Oh, not for me. I think I did it just last week." Russell smiled.

Paige smiled back. She handed Joe and Lucy their sandwiches and watched as they started eating them as fast as
possible. "Chew it up or you'll choke," she warned. She
reached in the bag and handed Russell a sandwich too, "I hope
turkey and cheese is alright."

"Oh yeah, it's my favorite."

"I thought I remembered that you ate a turkey sandwich one
day at the restaurant, so I was hoping."

Russell looked surprised that she remembered, but he simply
said, "Thank you."

"You're welcome," Paige replied, feeling like she might have
admitted she was paying attention to him.

"I'm done," Joe announced. "Can I go play now?"

"Me too," Lucy said around the last bite of her sandwich.
"Can we go?" she asked.

"Alright, yes, you can. But stay where I can see you and be
nice to the other kids." Paige raised her voice at the end since
the two of them were already running towards the playground.
They waved their hands in acknowledgement and Paige could
only watch them go.

Russell laughed. "I guess they're excited."

"Yes, they have a lot of energy, so they are pretty much
always excited when they can run around and climb on things."

"Do they come here a lot?" Russell started eating his
sandwich and reached for the bottle of water that Paige
offered.

"Probably not as much as they would like, but sometimes
we do. It's nice to give them an outlet, especially when the
older kids are off doing their own activities."

"Oh yeah? What activities are those?" Russell asked.

"Shep plays basketball and baseball, so there are always

games and tournaments. Peyton is a cheerleader so she cheers for whatever sport is going on, and she also goes to cheer competitions. Zoey doesn't compete yet, but she is taking cheer classes and she's stays busy with friends a lot too." Paige kept looking away to check on the kids as she spoke.

Russell watched her for a moment and let the silence hang. He seemed to be trying to take it all in. "That seems like a lot to keep up with," he said.

Paige turned to him and smiled. "Oh don't worry, I keep everything written down." She was trying to sound casual, but it was a true statement.

Russell voice was almost a whisper. "Paige," he waited until her eyes met his, "how do you do it?"

"Do what?"

A slow breath escaped his lips. "Everything."

She looked away.

"I mean it, how do you do everything, take care of your family, work, run a household, all of it? All by yourself."

She still wasn't looking at him and it seemed for a minute like she wasn't going to answer at all. Then she glanced back at him and for just a split second he thought she might cry. But then a look of resolve flashed across her face. Finally she took a long deep breath and spoke. "I just have to. So I do."

Again there was silence. Russell seemed unsure of what to say.

"I guess you want to know what happened," Paige said.

"Only if you want to tell me," Russell said, but he leaned forward in anticipation.

She sighed. "I don't really talk about it much. I guess I feel like the people who need to know already know and the rest can just fill in the blanks themselves. But we were a normal family, you know? I mean, maybe not totally normal, we're a little bit of a big family. Mom and Dad were both only children of only children, so no siblings, no cousins, no aunts or uncles. So they had always wanted a big family, and four seemed like a big family to most people, so they had four. And then Joe and Lucy were a complete surprise, but they were still thrilled, and we basically thought we had real life baby dolls around. And they were the perfect parents, the ones who go on the field trips and attend the PTA meetings and never miss a game or a recital. Dad was an attorney, well respected in the community, and mom stayed at home to take care of everything else. And they were the perfect couple too, they really loved each other and everybody knew it. They had a standing date night every other weekend. They had done that for as long as I could remember. Then my freshman year, I was away at school and they went out for their date night. They were out pretty late and they were coming home and a drunk driver came across their lane and hit them head on. It was a horrible accident. They both made it to the hospital, but their injuries were too much and they didn't make it long enough for me to get home from school." She paused for a moment as if the memory was sinking in.

"Everything was perfect. Of course they weren't really perfect, but they were to me, to us, to our family. And then they were just gone. Everything changed. And I just started putting one foot in front of the other. I just had to do what needed to be done. No one else could do it, so I had to."

"And so you quit school and went to work?" Russell asked gently.

"Yes, I felt like that was the best decision. I had to be at home with everybody, especially Joe and Lucy, they were so little."

"Did they have life insurance policies?"

"Yes, they did. But I just knew that if I started depending on that regularly it would be gone too quickly. So I paid off the house and the cars and gave us a monthly allowance for bills and the rest went into savings. I have some that I can pull from in an emergency, but most of it is put away for all of their college funds. I know that's what Dad would have wanted. He always wanted to take care of school for us."

Russell looked at her in awe. "That was pretty wise, especially when you were that young."

Paige shrugged.

"And that's how you ended up at the club?"

"Yes, I needed something where I could make decent money to pay some of the bills and for all the extras that come up. But without a college decree I didn't think I had many options. The restaurant offered a flexible schedule with the ability to work extra hours on occasion so I decided to take it. I never really intended to stay there long, it just happened. And then it was easy. It's fifteen minutes away, I'm usually home before the kids are off the bus, and it works."

Russell's look was full of sorrow. "But that's so much for one person to do."

Paige didn't want pity. "Of course, but a lot of people do it. Single parents, even moms who are married usually still do a lot of those things on their own."

"But surely there were people who offered to help, the church?"

"Oh, people offered. Wanted me to let them know what they could do. But how do you tell people how they can help after your parents are gone and you have five younger siblings that need to be taken care of? People brought meals for a while, and that was helpful. But nobody could help when Zoey wouldn't sleep alone anymore. Or when the twins cried because they had to ride the bus instead of being driven to school. Or when Peyton started having nightmares. Or when Shep wouldn't talk for days. So you just move on and start doing things yourself, and I've gotten pretty good at that. I wake kids up in the morning to go to school, I work, I fix dinner, I clean the house and do the laundry and I don't relax until everybody is safely in the house for the night. I don't know how I do it, but it has to be done, so I just do it." Paige was surprised at the relief she felt just by saying that out loud. It didn't change her situation, but knowing that somebody else just knew the whole story made her feel a little bit better. She hadn't ever planned to share all of that with him, but suddenly she felt like she didn't have to tiptoe in conversation with him, because he already knew.

Russell sat speechless for a few moments. He looked helpless, but the look in his eyes said he wished he could help. He reached out and touched her arm. "I'm so sorry Paige. You're so strong."

She looked at him and glanced down at his hand on her arm. She let her eyes linger there for a moment, but then she leaned away from him and started to clean up the picnic. "It's alright. This is just my life now." She felt like she had told him enough. She didn't want to share too much.

Russell stood up and started cleaning up too. "Here, let me help,"

"Oh, I've got it."

"No, really, you prepared the food and brought it, now you sit there and let me clean this up."

"But…"

"I mean it, you can't lift a finger to help or no dessert for you." He wagged his finger at her and gave her a wink. She looked as if it would be a difficult chore to sit and do nothing, but she smiled at him and sat back down on the blanket.

Just as Russell put the last items back in the cooler and carried the trash away, Joe and Lucy came running over to them. "Paige, the ice cream truck is here! Can we get some? Please, please," Lucy begged.

Paige looked at Russell. "Yes!" he said. "Ice cream it is. Whatever you want, it's my treat," he told the kids.

"Yay!" The kids shouted and ran off towards the truck.

"We better catch up with them," Paige said and started to stand.

Russell offered her his hand and pulled her to her feet. For just a moment they stood facing each other, her chin tilted to look up at his taller frame. For a moment it seemed like he might hug her, but then he dropped his gaze and started walking towards the kids. "What's your favorite ice cream?" he asked.

Paige fell into step beside him. "Chocolate chip. What's yours?"

"Coffee," he said.

"Of course," she smiled and they continued their walk to the truck.

Chapter 17

Monday morning Russell sat at his desk with his second cup of coffee for the day. Much of his thoughts still centered on Paige. He had spent a lot of time over the weekend in prayer about her, praying that God would open her heart to let people in, and to have the courage to let people help her. He had attended church with his parents again on Sunday. But Paige and her crew were already seated in the back when he got there and he only waved on his way in. After the service, they were gone before he made it back to the foyer.

As he sat thinking about Paige, his office phone rang. He set down his mug and answered, "Hello, this is Russell,"

"Hi Russell, this is Owen Reed, the pastor from Pine Haven Community Church."

"Oh hi, how are you?"

"I'm doing well, thanks, how are you?"

"I'm doing pretty good." Russell ran his finger through his hair, wondering what this call was about.

"Good, I'm glad. I noticed that you've been at our Sunday morning service a couple of times now with your parents, and I just wanted to call and introduce myself since we haven't had the chance to meet at church."

"Oh yes, my mom practically insisted that I visit the church."

The pastor laughed. "I'm sure she can be quite persuasive. I've known them a couple of years now, and your parents really are pillars in our church family, we're so blessed to have them."

"I know they really love being involved there."

"Listen, I was wondering if you might be available to have lunch together? I know you're not set on our church, but I would really like to just talk and get to know you and be of any help that I can in getting settled in the community."

"Sure, I would like that a lot."

"Excellent, are you available any time this week?"

Russell clicked over to his calendar on the computer. "Actually my week is kind of full. We usually have a lunch meeting on Mondays for our management team, but this week it got pushed to Tuesday, then the rest of my week is filled up. Unless you could do today?"

"Actually, yeah, I could do today. That would be great."

"Okay, sounds good."

"I've heard wonderful things about the restaurant there at the club, would you like for me to meet you there?"

"Oh no," Russell said, almost too quickly. "I mean, it is very good, and you should definitely try it sometime if you haven't, but I would love to get off campus, you know, stretch my legs a little." *And talk without the chance of being overheard,* he thought.

"Alright, that's fine. How about The Depot, about 12:15, is that alright?"

"Sure, that's fine, I'll see you then."

"Thanks Russell, I'm looking forward to it."

Russell hung up the phone and immediately prayed, *Lord, bless the time at lunch with Pastor Owen, please let me be able to speak freely about the way I feel and prepare him now with wisdom for me.*

I have prepared a way for you.

He breathed a heavy sigh. *Thank you, Lord.*

He went on about his work, trying to keep his mind on the tasks at hand rather than the lunch meeting. This wasn't hard since he had a lot of work to do, and the morning flew by. As he gathered his phone and keys to leave, he suddenly felt strange that he wouldn't see Paige at lunch. He hadn't really talked to her since Saturday and now he was afraid she would think he was avoiding her by not eating in the restaurant. He hurried out of his office and walked straight to the restaurant.

Paige stood behind the counter with her clipboard, checking things off her list. She looked up and smiled when she saw him. "Hello Sir, welcome, we have procured your usual seat for you." She gestured toward the seat at the bar and he saw that she had put out the "Reserved" sign on the counter, even though no one was seated on any of the stools.

He smiled at her joke, and his heart tugged a little that she was being playful with him, and that he had to tell her he wasn't staying. He was so glad he had made the decision to stop by. "Thank you, I'm so honored to have a permanent spot here."

"Oh yes, nothing but the best for our most loyal guest."

"I'm so sorry, but I might just be losing my status today."

"Oh?" She lowered her clipboard and her smile faded.

"Yes, I'm sorry, I'm not staying for lunch. I just came by to say hi, I've got a lunch meeting off campus."

"Oh." Paige actually looked disappointed. "That's alright." She recovered quickly. "Just don't expect this kind of royal treatment again."

Russell laughed. "Of course not, but I'll try to make up for it stopping by for coffee and dessert this afternoon. Do you think that might put me back in good graces?"

"Hmm, we'll see."

"Okay, well, I've got to run."

"Alright, see ya." Paige went back to the kitchen.

Russell turned to go, and now he was genuinely sad that he couldn't stay and talk with her over lunch. He hadn't realized how much she had looked forward to that time. And obviously he had too. He would definitely come by this afternoon. Besides, they needed to discuss some details for their meeting the next day about the breakfast plan. With that thought on his mind he left the club happy to have an excuse to see her later.

The Depot was a well-known and well-loved restaurant in town. A few miles from the country club in a strip of shops on Main Street in the middle of town, it was filled with pictures of trains and railroad memorabilia. They were known for having the best burgers in town. Russell parked on the street out front and went in to find Pastor Owen waiting for him. The place was already starting to fill up for lunch, so Owen had grabbed a table early. Russell approached and greeted him.

"Hi, Pastor Owen,"

The pastor stood to shake hands with him. "Hey Russell, so good to see you. And please, just Owen. I'm not much for titles." He was dressed in a button-down collared shirt and khaki pants.

"Me either, I'm still trying to get used to being called 'Mr. Pierce' at work."

"Oh yes, I'm sure that takes some getting used to."

"Yes, it does. Have you ordered yet?"

"No, just wanted to go ahead and get a table."

Russell nodded. "It can get pretty packed in here, glad you got here early. So we don't lose the table, why don't you stay here and I'll go order for us. What would you like? And please, it's my treat."

"Oh that's really not necessary," Owen started to say.

"You don't know what I want to ask you yet." Russell smiled.

Owen smiled back with a curious look. "Alright then, I'll have a cheeseburger with everything, and water to drink."

"And fries? You have to have fries."

"Absolutely, fries are a must at The Depot."

"Alright, I'll be right back."

Russell went to the counter and placed their orders. He returned to the table with a stand holding a number for their order. He was glad they had come to a place where they would mostly be left alone once their food arrived. "Should just be a few minutes," he told Owen.

"Okay, thank you. So tell me about yourself. Like I said, I've known your parents for a few years, so I've heard your name mentioned, and I've met your brothers, but that's all I know."

"For starters, don't believe anything my brothers say about me. They can be pretty tough on a guy."

Owen laughed.

"And also, probably don't believe too much of what my mom says about me either. She's way to generous to her baby boy." He smiled. "But really, I feel like I'm still getting started with being an adult. I grew up here my whole life, and went off to college to study business. After I graduated I was fortunate to get a job right away in sales, and I really loved it for a while. I traveled, basically did what I wanted, had a lot of fun, made good money, that sort of thing. And even though I never expected to be back here, I'm really glad to be home, settling in here in a town that I feel like I'll stay in for quite a while. Plus I love golf, so that's really all they had to say was included in the job to get me to come."

"I hear all the Pierce men are golfers."

"That's right, Dad started us all out young just so he would have an excuse to spend all day out on the course or at the driving range. Do you play?"

"Not as much as I would like, but yes, I do."

"You'll have to come out and play with us sometime. I can get you in. I kind of know a guy."

Owen laughed. "Thanks, I'll have to take you up on that."

"Please do. So what about you? How long have you been at Pine Haven Community Church?"

"Phew, let's see, I guess it's about eight years now. I came on as an assistant pastor after seminary, and then they offered me the role of senior pastor when the former pastor retired. So I've basically been here since I finished school."

"But you're not from here originally?"

"No, I'm from Wisconsin. I came down here for school, and the church offered me an internship while I was getting my degree, and then I stuck around."

"So you liked the south, huh?"

"Oh yes. You know they say, once you come down here you don't go back. And it's true. The people are nice, the weather is warmer, and the bonus for me is that I met my wife." He smiled.

"Oh that's definitely a plus."

"So yes, I like it here a lot."

Russell was glad they seemed to be getting along well and so easily. It made what he wanted to ask the man easier. He felt his heart start to beat a little faster as he prepared to ask his next question. "So you knew the Kelly family?"

"Paige and the kids? Yeah, I've known them for years."

"But, I mean, you knew her parents…before?"

Owen's eyes grew sad. "Oh, yes, I did. Wonderful people. They were very involved." He looked thoughtful as he continued, "Elaine helped host many events over the years and served so many people with meals, she was a woman who gave everything she had. And Peter was so respected not only at church, but also in the community. Most people don't even know the number of hours he spent using his office to help others without being paid. It was a privilege to know them."

"Yes, I've only heard good things."

"Paige works at the country club, right?"

"Yes, she does."

"Do you have much interaction with her there?"

"Actually, yes I do. She was recently promoted to be the manager of the restaurant. So technically she's her own boss, but I oversee all operations, so her area falls under my responsibility too. I'm not exactly her boss, but we work together a good bit."

"I see. That's great for her. She hasn't had an easy time of it, so I'm sure a promotion like that helps her tremendously."

"Yes. Did you know her well then? At the time of the accident I mean?"

"I did, she was away at college, but I had been there since

she was in high school, so I knew her a bit. I helped her plan the funeral and did the service. It was such a tough time. I remember trying to talk with her a few times, and my wife went to the house once a week for a month or so. But she seemed so determined to handle everything herself. She had always been a fun, energetic girl, but when her parents died it quite frankly seemed to take the life out of her. I think about her from time to time. Her family was always so involved, but it wasn't just their actions that mattered, they truly loved being involved in whatever The Lord led them to do and they served from the heart. Since they've been gone, Paige seems more like she's just going through the motions of going to church and checking it off her list. I've tried to reach out, but she's very closed off. An event like that can be detrimental to a person's faith."

Russell knew exactly what he meant. "Yes, I agree." He stared at his hands, lost in his own thoughts.

Owen looked at him, and only then did it dawn on it. "Russell, are you and Paige...are you close?"

"I don't know if I would say we're close, but we're definitely becoming good friends."

"Are you hoping for more?"

Russell half laughed, half sighed. "Have you ever had God so heavily place someone on your heart that you can't stop thinking about them?"

"Yes, I have."

"And have you ever thought that He was totally crazy for it?"

Owen smiled. "Yes, several times."

"He has shown me that He wants me to help her, and I have the strongest desire to just take care of her, for her to not worry as much as she does, and to not have to carry such a heavy load. But like you said, she's closed off, and she seems to just go through the motions of life. Every time she starts to open up to me it's like something switches off and she realizes she's letting me in and she runs from it. I don't know how to approach her, and I definitely don't think she will let me help her."

"Are these romantic feelings?"

"Honestly, I don't know. They didn't start out that way, but I think they are beginning to turn into that." Russell put his face in his hands. "I just don't know what to do or how to approach it."

"You want my advice?"

"Yes, please, anything."

Owen sat thoughtfully for a moment, "Keep praying."

"Keep praying?"

"Yes, you said The Lord showed you that He wanted you to help her, so keep talking to Him and asking Him what He wants you to do next."

Russell had to admit to himself that he hadn't been doing much asking lately. "I guess I can do that."

"And don't give up. In fact, I think you should be bold. If He wants you to help her then be bold about helping her, and if He shows you that He wants you to pursue her romantically, be bold about your feelings."

Russell nodded. "I guess I've got nothing to lose."

"Absolutely. And with God on your side you've got everything to gain."

Russell smiled. He felt a confidence about the situation that he hadn't before now. "Thank you, Owen, you don't know how much that helps."

"I'm glad. Just be her friend. See if she opens up to you, then see what happens."

They continued talking while they finished their meals and then parted ways, promising to do this again soon. As Russell left the restaurant he felt encouraged, and as Owen had said, he felt bold. He only hoped that his boldness would last. And that he wouldn't frighten away the girl he was starting to really care for.

Chapter 18

*P*aige walked down the hall of the country club writing notes on her clipboard, ideas about the new breakfast menu that she wanted to remember for the meeting the next day. She realized she wasn't paying attention to where she was going and looked up just as she almost walked into a decorative side table. She laughed as she thought about another time walking with something in front of her face had caused an accident. She stood at the table and finished writing her notes. A minute later she looked out the window facing the driveway to the club, she just happened to see Russell pulling in on his way back from his lunch. Her heart skipped a beat when she recognized him. The feeling was so strange, she placed her hand over her heart, and she couldn't help but smile.

What is going on with me? she thought. *I wasn't expecting this.* She tried to think about what her feelings really were for Russell. She had to admit that they were starting to develop a friendship, and she had even surprised herself by opening up to him. *Is that what I want?* she wondered. She thought about how her feelings might be starting to grow. Then she thought about the kids, and the house, and her work.

And her parents.

She shook her head and picked up her clipboard with a sense of finality. "No," she said out loud. "I won't do that." She looked around to make sure no one was hearing her. "I won't do this to him, and I won't do it to myself. I have to let him know there's no future there." With that she walked straight back to the restaurant and tried to push thoughts of Russell Pierce out of her mind.

Once back in the kitchen, Shannon came to say hello. She had an early class that day so she was working the afternoon shift and had just arrived at work. "So?" Shannon's eyes lit up excitedly. "Tell me about Saturday!"

So much for not thinking about it, Paige thought, "There's really not much to tell," she said. "We went to the park and ate sandwiches, the kids ran around, then we had ice cream and left."

Shannon stared at her. "That's it? No conversation?"

"Of course we had conversation. It would be rude not to."

"So what did you talk about?"

"Oh, just usual stuff, you know, what's your favorite ice cream, what are your hobbies, what's it like to raise your younger siblings?"

Shannon's eyes were wide. "He asked you that?"

"Yeah, basically."

"And what did you say?"

"I said that, yeah, it's tough, but I just do it. People do it, and I just make it work."

"Hmm, I guess that's true. So what did he say?"

"Oh you know, he feels bad for me."

"Oh Paige, he's just being nice," Shannon said since Paige was always defensive about people pitying her.

"I know. It's fine."

"So do you think he'll ask you out again?"

"Umm, no, I don't think so." Actually, that wasn't true at all. Paige thought that he definitely would ask her out again. She just had no intention of saying yes.

"Why not?"

"I just don't think there's a future there."

"Oh Paige, come on. Why not?"

"You know why."

"Girl, when are you going to stop making excuses? It's always the kids, or work, or that a guy wouldn't want to walk into that life. You've got to get past all that and move on with your life as it is. Don't you want to plan anything for the future?"

"I'm planning a lot for the future!" Paige tried not to yell, but her anger was rising, "I plan for the kids school, and for Peyton and Shep to go to college, and I plan for everybody to eat and be clothed and make it through the day alive."

"But what about you, Paige? You used to have plans for you. You were going to school, and surely you thought about being married one day? What about plans for you?"

Paige didn't have an answer for her friend. She looked away for a moment, and finally she spoke. "I don't know, okay? I don't have plans for me. Maybe someday, but right now I have a lot of other people to worry about. And yes, I had plans, lots of plans, and in one moment they went out the window, so what's the point?" She blinked quickly to push away the tears that tried to surface.

Shannon teared up too. "I know Paige, I'm so sorry. And I know you're right, it seems like all your plans are gone, but that doesn't mean you stop living. You know that's not what your parents would have wanted for you. They would still want you to make plans."

Paige wiped her eyes quickly since other staff members were beginning to come in for the afternoon. "Well, yes. But I don't have time to think about that right now. I've got a restaurant to run." She patted her clipboard and tried to smile. She patted Shannon on the shoulder and walked past on the way to her desk.

Paige sat down at her desk and tried to focus on the menu. She had created a little office space in the back corner of the kitchen. It was out of the way enough that she could think to herself, but close enough that she could talk to James when she needed to. She had a small desk where she set up the laptop computer the club had given her, and a stack of clipboards, one for each area of the job that she kept notes for: kitchen, event catering, ideas for the new breakfast. She made a few notes on the clipboard for upcoming menus, but her thoughts were elsewhere.

After about thirty minutes Shannon came back to her desk. "Hey, just wanted to tell you, Russell just came in for coffee."

Paige looked up at her. "Did you tell him I was back here?"

"No, but I'm sure he wants to see you."

She looked at her watch. "Look, tell him I'm not here. Tell him that I'm coming in early tomorrow so I left early today."

"I'm not going to lie to him."

"It's not a lie." Paige stood and quickly grabbed her bag and keys. "I'm gone. I'll be here early tomorrow."

Shannon gave her friend a look that said she knew she was

running away.

"Bye, I'll see you in the morning." Paige hurried out the back door before Shannon could argue with her. She made her way to the employee parking lot and nearly ran to her car. Once she climbed behind the wheel she let the emotions she had been holding at bay come on full force. The tears flowed quickly.

She cried for the loss of her parents, for the loss of her future. She cried that even though she might want to just the tiniest bit, she knew she couldn't open herself up to the possibility of anything happening with Russell. "I can't get attached to him," she said to the empty space in the car. "I can't let him get to me." Then she sobbed a loud uncontrollable sob, and when she caught her breath she barely whispered, "I can't lose someone else."

Chapter 19

*P*aige had just finished loading the dishwasher and wiping down the counter when her cell phone rang. She called out to remind Joe, Lucy and Zoey that they could only watch one show on TV then she grabbed the phone and answered it. "Hello?" She didn't recognize the number.

"Hey Paige, it's Russell."

She stopped dead in her tracks. "Oh, hey." She glanced in on the kids and then headed into her bedroom for some privacy. "How are you?"

"Oh, I'm fine, just a little disappointed that's all."

She tried to think if there was something at work that she forgot to do, she had left in a rush, maybe something slipped her mind. "Did I miss something at the club?"

"Oh no, nothing like that. I'm just disappointed that I didn't get to talk to you today. I must have just missed you this afternoon."

"Yeah, I wanted to get home before the kids. I'll be there early tomorrow to make up for it."

Chapter 19

"I'm not worried about that Paige. I don't keep track of your hours."

She knew he was trying to say that this was a personal call, not professional. She still tried to keep him at a distance. "Did you need something?"

"Nope, not for work. I just wanted to talk to you. How was the rest of your weekend?"

"It was fine."

"Good, did the kids have a good day at school? Joe said they had a some kind of outdoor day coming up."

"Oh yeah, field day. It's on Friday."

"I always loved that, signals that the end of the school year is coming. Plus the weather is so great outside. Makes me want to just move my office out on the course."

"You would have to move it right back in during the spring rains."

"Hmm, that's true. You certainly have an eye for details, I should probably keep you around to keep me from making illogical decisions." He was teasing her.

"Yep, that's me, Miss Logic." Her tone was dry.

He changed the subject. "What are you up to tonight?"

"Just the usual. Dinner, watching the kids, a little bit of laundry."

"Sounds exciting."

"Oh you know it."

"What if I come by and take you out for ice cream?"

"I can't leave." She sounded like she couldn't believe he would suggest something like that. "The kids can't stay home by themselves."

"Shep and Peyton aren't home?"

"No, they both had things tonight."

"Things?" he asked.

"Yes, things, they're not here." She didn't offer more details.

"What about if I pick up ice cream and bring it to you?" The sound of his smile came through the phone line. He was determined.

Paige sighed. She had hoped she could push him away without actually telling him that's what she was doing. "I don't think so."

"Oh? Why not? I know you like ice cream, and you just told me all you have to do is laundry. Believe it or not, I know how to fold clothes."

Paige almost laughed at the thought of him folding the kids socks and underwear. She couldn't help but joke back with him. "I don't think laundry and ice cream go together."

"Oh yeah, you're probably right, everything would probably get sticky. Which would defeat the purpose of just having washed them. Alright then, I'll come over and bring ice cream for me to eat while you fold the laundry."

"Hmm, what a great offer."

"So what do you say?"

"Russell…" she trailed off, not really sure what to say next.

When she didn't continue he said, "Yes, Paige?

She squeezed her eyes shut and tried to say it. "I can't do this."

"Do what?"

"This. With you. I can't."

Russell paused. "OK, well that's not really a complete sentence, but what do you mean? What do you think I'm asking for?"

"Oh come on, don't make me spell it out."

"I need you to be clear."

"I can't...I can't....I can't be in a relationship with you."

Russell paused again, wanting to be bold, but not wanting to frighten her away. "Paige, I'm not asking you for any kind of commitment. I want to spend some time with you because I always enjoy talking to you. I want to get to know you, because I don't really know you that well. I would really like to be your friend. Are you really saying you can't be my friend?"

Paige didn't have an answer. "Of course, we can be friends, I just don't want you to think I can be anything more."

"I'm not worried about the future Paige. I like you, I like your family, at least what I know of them now."

"Oh yeah? Wait until you do their laundry."

Russell laughed. "Okay." He grew serious again. "Come on, Paige, let me be your friend. Let me be your family's friend. Can you do that?"

Paige took a long, deep breath. "I guess."

"Excellent." Paige could hear his smile over the phone. "I would sure hate for you to miss out on having me as a friend, I'm a pretty good one."

She smiled, despite herself. "Oh I'm sure you are. You're the kind of friend that talks people into things, aren't you?"

"Only things that are good for them."

"Oh really? For example?"

"Well, for example, like eating ice cream. You know it's made of milk, milk is good for you.

Paige gave a little laugh. "I guess I'll just have to take your word for it." She sensed that he wanted to ask again to come over, but he didn't. Instead they talked for another half hour, laughing and joking, no more serious conversation. But then Paige needed to go.

"Oh I forgot, I told the kids they could only watch one TV

show, but it's probably led onto the next show by now. I better check on them," she said.

"Alright, I guess I'll see you tomorrow," Russell said.

"Yes, I'll be there."

"See you then. Goodnight, Paige."

"Goodnight." Paige ended the call and sat on the edge of the bed for a few moments. She thought about the phone call and the way she had laughed. She had caught sight of herself in the mirror once during the conversation and she couldn't help but see that she looked very happy. The look surprised her, she almost didn't recognize herself, laughing and smiling. She stood to leave and said to herself, "I can be a friend." She thought about that for a second, trying to decide if she believed herself or not. "I can do that," she said with finality and walked from the room.

Back in the living room, Peyton had come home and joined the younger kids on the couch. "Oh hey, you're home early," Paige said.

"Yeah, I was supposed to meet my group for our group presentation that's due next week, but everybody bailed. Don't worry we rescheduled for Thursday and if nobody shows up I'll do the whole thing myself."

"Oh, alright. Did you eat? There's still some leftovers in the fridge."

"Good, I'm starving." Peyton stood and the two walked to the kitchen.

Paige realized that she was still letting the kids watch TV. "I know I let you go past your time already, when this episode is over turn it off, got it?"

The three mumbled in answer.

In the kitchen Peyton had already found the leftover dish

and was reheating it in the microwave. "Hey Paige, have you ever thought about doing freezer meals?"

"What? Like frozen dinners from the store?" Paige was confused.

"No, no. Part of our group project is planning like a household budget, and I'm in charge of the food part. So I was looking online about ways to save money on food and I came across this blog about having a big cooking day where you plan all your meals for the month, or maybe just the week, and then you put all of them in the freezer. Then every night you just pull something out and stick it in the oven."

"Oh really?"

"Yeah, so I was thinking. We should do that," Peyton said.

"We should?" Paige put plenty of emphasis on the "we" part.

"Yeah, it could be fun. You and I could do it together, and even Zoey could help. And then dinner would be super easy for you."

"Mmhmm. I'll look into that. So you just do all the cooking at once?"

"Yeah!" Peyton sounded so excited about the idea. "And then you have the rest of the month free!" Paige looked at her sister, "And what would I do with all that free time?"

"Well, sometimes you might have to work later, and then I could just put something in the oven. I mean, even Shep could do that. And it could just give you some down time."

"Mmhmm."

"And you know," Peyton tried to sound nonchalant, "If there's any body you want to spend some extra time with, it might free you up for that."

"Like who?"

"Like, umm, maybe a cute country club manager." Peyton

169

gave a sly grin.

"Mmhmm, I knew there had to be some ulterior motive."

"Ulterior motive? What are you talking about? How is it an ulterior motive for me if you're the one who gets to spend time with a guy?"

"I'm not sure, but it still feels like it."

Peyton smiled. "That's just because you're not used to letting anybody do anything nice for you."

Paige knew her sister was half-joking, but the statement hit her hard. Was that true? Did she really not let anybody do anything nice for her? She walked over and gave Peyton a quick hug. "Okay, send me the website and I'll look at it and we'll give it a try."

"Yay!" Peyton clapped her hands together.

"OK, Miss Cheerleader. Oh, I think I hear the end of that TV show, I've got to get them away from the screen. We'll talk more later." Paige hurried off to check on the kids. But Peyton's words stayed with her more than Peyton must have thought they would. Had she really become so self-sufficient that people needed to beg to help her? Paige wasn't sure if it was true, but she determined in her mind to start paying attention and find out.

Chapter 20

*T*uesday morning Paige walked into the restaurant at six thirty. She had laid out breakfast for everyone with specific instructions for getting ready for school, then left Peyton in charge until the bus came. She needed to make up some time from the day before, but she also had plenty to do. She wanted to have everything ready for the meeting that afternoon before she had to go to the lunch meeting for the management team. She no longer wore her waitressing outfit to work, and today she wore a light purple collared shirt and a pair of khaki dress pants with grey flats. As usual she wore her hair back in a high ponytail to keep it out of her way. She entered the restaurant through the back door. She had her own key now so she could come and go early or late. Once inside she was headed straight to start the coffee maker, when she noticed that the light in the dining room was on. She glanced at the counter and saw that the coffee maker was also on. Cautiously she set down her keys and bag on her desk and crept towards the door to the dining room, unsure of who or what she would find.

There sat Russell, in his usual seat at the bar, with two fresh cups of coffee. He hadn't noticed her yet and he was leaning over the counter reading his Bible. She stood staring at him for a moment, until he looked up and saw her in the doorway.

"Good morning." He smiled. "I've got coffee."

She started to walk to the counter and reached out for the mug he offered her.

"Nope, not on that side. Come around here and sit." He patted the stool next to him.

She hesitated, but gave in and walked around and took a seat. The coffee was the perfect temperature.

"How did you know what time I would be here?"

"I didn't. I just got here at six since I was pretty sure you wouldn't be here before that."

"And is this something a 'friend' does?"

"Oh absolutely. A friend can get to work early and make coffee for a friend."

"I didn't know you knew how to make coffee back there."

"I asked Shannon about the procedure when I was here yesterday. You never know when a skill like that can come in handy."

"Mmhmm." Paige sipped her coffee and tried to think of what to say next.

"So, busy day today?" Russell beat her to it.

"Actually, yes. I've still got to finalize some menus for upcoming events, then the management meeting at lunch and the meeting this afternoon with James and Trent. So yes, it should be pretty full. You?"

"Yep, pretty much the same, I have to go to those meeting too."

"Right, right."

"But I like busy days, makes me feel productive. Plus the day goes by quickly too. I hate just sitting around in my office watching the clock." He leaned his elbows on the counter and bumped the Bible. When he noticed it there he closed it and moved it to the side.

"What were you reading?" She gestured towards the book.

"Oh, a few Psalms. I like to pray through them to start my day."

"Oh, that's nice." Paige didn't say more.

"Do you read much? The Bible I mean," Russell asked.

Paige seemed uncomfortable. "Not really, I mean I believe it, and we go to church and hear it. I just don't really have a lot of time for it."

"I can understand that. I used to feel the same way." Russell spoke gently. "But I've realized that I really do have time, I just have to be intentional about it, and when I make the time it's really life giving for me. I feel more ready for the day when I've spent some time in the word."

Paige stared at her coffee mug. She had always gone to church, her parents had taken her since she was an infant. But she hadn't really known people her own age who spent time reading the Bible every day. Sure in high school the youth pastor had always told them they should, but most of her friends didn't and she had never wanted to find the time for it. And after her parents death she didn't really see the point. Of course she wanted to go to heaven, but in the meantime she was mostly concerned with getting done what she needed to do everyday.

Russell interrupted her thoughts. "Do you have a Bible?" he asked.

"Oh of course, my parents bought it for me in high school." She smiled as she thought. "I think it's a neon pink, teen study Bible."

"Oh, so you like pink, huh?"

"Not so much now, but back then, yes, I was all about bright colors."

"Oh yeah? So what were you like in high school? A cheerleader?"

"Oh no, not at all, Peyton is the cheerleader."

"An athlete?"

"Kind of, I played volleyball, but it was just for fun. I never wanted to play in college or anything."

"So what were you involved in?"

"Mostly academic stuff. I was on the yearbook staff and vice president of the student council."

"Mmhmm, were you also a 'Mathlete'?" he teased.

She reached out and pushed his shoulder feigning offense. "No, I was just a regular nerd, not a super nerd."

"Mmhmm." His eyes twinkled at her.

"What about you? Mr. Popularity? Most likely to run a country club someday?"

Russell laughed. "Mostly I was a dumb jock, basketball in the winter, golf in the spring. But I wasn't really a stand-out, just a member of the team."

"I bet you weren't dumb though."

"Okay, you caught me. No, not really. I was on the honor roll."

"Aha! So you're a nerd too."

"Mostly because my parents expected it. A lot of guys on the basketball team would barely make the grades to try out. But at the Pierce house we had our own minimum GPA to be able to play sports."

"I see. Sounds like a good idea."

"You know, it really was. Of course I didn't like it at the time, but it makes sense. It made me learn to work hard in both areas. If I wanted to play I had to work hard at studying, and then, because I had had to work to earn the right to play it made me want to be a better player so it was worth the effort."

"They sound like great parents."

"Oh yeah, I appreciate them using that as a tool. It's definitely something I want to do with my own kids someday."

They both fell quiet for a minute at his mention of kids in the future.

Russell broke the silence speaking again. "Oh yeah, speaking of my parents. Every year my family has this big party on Memorial Day. We started it when my brothers and I were little to celebrate the end of the school year and the official start of summer. Anyway, my parents still do it and invite all of us and neighbors and friends from church, and I wanted to invite you and your family."

"Oh, well…umm…that sounds nice, I'll have to see…"

Russell didn't give her the opportunity to say no or make an excuse. "You can bring everybody, or if the older kids have something, just bring whoever can come. You don't already have plans do you?"

"Well, no, we don't."

"Great! Then you'll come?"

"Um, okay, sure." Paige racked through her brain thinking if this would work. She decided that she would think about it later. She slid down off of her stool. "Well, Mr. Honor Roll, I need to get to work if I'm going to get everything done this morning."

"Yeah, me too, this was nice."

Paige looked at him and honestly agreed. "Yes, yes it was. Thanks for making the coffee."

"Anytime," he said. "See you later." He stood and gathered his things and the two went to their separate workspaces.

Paige walked to her desk and turned on her computer. She sat and looked over her notes for the upcoming menu and tried to focus, but suddenly all she could think about was what she would wear to a Memorial Day party. *Woah, I sound like Peyton,* she thought to herself. But she knew that she couldn't deny that she actually wanted to go to the party. After all, Russell would be there and she was beginning to see that she genuinely enjoyed spending time with him.

. . .

That afternoon Paige and James left the restaurant together to go to the small conference room for their meeting. James carried a small tray of desserts and Paige had a stack of cups and a carafe of coffee. When they got to the conference room Russell and Trent were already seated at the table.

"Ahh, yes," Russell said when he saw them. "It's always nice to have meetings with the restaurant staff, they bring food." He smiled. He stood to walk over and took the coffee from Paige and set it on the table.

"Thank you," Paige said. She sat down at the table and pulled the bag from her shoulder that held her clipboard and pen. "Are we ready to get started?"

"We are if you are, it's your meeting," Russell said.

"Oh yes, well, alright then. Trent, do you know James?"

The two men stood and shook hands. "Oh yes, I've eaten his food plenty of times. Some of the best meals I've ever eaten."

"Thank you," James said.

"I don't want to take up too much of anyone's time, so let's jump right in," said Paige.

Russell, James and Trent listened intently while she spoke. Russell couldn't help but notice how her eyes lit up. "I think you all know that we are starting a new breakfast to help promote the restaurant and bring in more members during the morning hours. James already has some great ideas about specials for the menu, so the biggest thing I want to talk about today is preparing to get it started and planning how to promote it and let all the members know it's coming. But James, would you like to quickly tell us about your menu ideas?"

"Oh yes. I want to start out by continuing to offer some of the basic things we always have, especially since that will give an idea how much of the specials people are ordering versus the new specials. So you can still order eggs, bacon, bagels, et cetera. But then, just like we do for lunch, we will have a daily special. I'm thinking crepes with choices of fruit, topped with chocolate and cream, specialty omelets, cinnamon roll pancakes, country breakfast bowls, blueberry croissant puffs..." James trailed off. "You get the point, delicious specialty breakfasts, something out of the ordinary."

Trent spoke up. "Man, I wasn't going to eat one of the desserts you brought, but now that my mouth is watering I'm going to need one." He laughed.

"Of course, please do." James pushed the tray towards him.

"Thanks, James," Paige said. "So that kind of gives you an

idea. We have planned out a full list of a different special every day for two weeks so we can reevaluate and see which ones were popular before planning further. Which brings me to my next point. We would like to set a date for starting and we want to introduce it right as summer begins so it's happening at a fresh season and time for the club. Plus summer is a time when a lot of people are vacationing or have friends and relatives visiting from out of town, so we want to encourage them to bring their guests here for a special breakfast, and to eat here before they head out for a round of golf or a game of tennis."

"That sounds perfect," Russell said around his bite of chocolate pie. "So what's the exact date?"

"June first, the Monday after Memorial day." She smiled both at the excitement of starting the breakfast specials and the fact that she had something to look forward to on Memorial Day.

"So that's just three weeks from yesterday, right?" Russell asked.

"Yes, that gives us time to plan the menus and add everything to our upcoming order lists."

"Okay, and Trent, how would that look for you?" Russell looked at him and they all chuckled as they waited for him to finish the bite he was chewing.

"That should be fine. The member newsletter goes out two weeks from today, so I still have time to add that promotion, and we can put out signs as early as next week."

"That will be perfect. I would also like to do signs for the tables in the restaurant," said Paige.

"Okay, that's no problem," Trent said and made a note on his pad.

"But I'm totally drawing a blank on what to say in the promotions. Someone suggested 'Make all your mornings special with our new breakfast'." She grinned at Russell. "But I'm just not sure how to capture what we're trying to say."

Trent stared at his pad thinking. "Hmm." He drew something on the page. "What if we start promoting it as a summer special? Saying it's available for a limited time? Because, let's be honest, if it doesn't work out it will go away, right? And then if it works well we can promote again as 'Back by popular demand' or 'Here to stay, by popular demand'."

Paige thought about this and looked at Russell, "Well, it's my hope that we will keep it, so is it dishonest to promote it that way?"

Russell looked thoughtful for a moment. "We did say we would start it on a trial basis, right?"

"Right," Paige said.

"Okay, so let's officially say that we're offering breakfast specials during the summer months, June through August, and then we will reevaluate at that time. Does that seem fair?"

"Yes, I think so." Paige nodded, feeling comfortable with that decision. That gave her a deadline for giving it a try.

"So I think we are safe to say breakfast specials available for a limited time, and if we see that they are popular and people will still want to order them, we can make a new decision at that point." Russell concluded.

"Okay, cool," Trent said. "Then I think we should make the promo materials very summery, bright colors and call them 'New Summer Breakfast Specials'. James if you can pick one or two of the specials that might be the most visually appealing, maybe something with some of the summer fruits like blueberries or strawberries, I can work those into the graphic. Then all we will need to do is add the starting date and a note of what time breakfast is served, and I think we'll have something good."

"Sound great," Paige said.

"And it will work for posters, signs on the tables and a note in the newsletter. I can even add a banner on the website too."

"Oh thank you, that's a great idea."

"Trent, can you send the graphic to all of us once you've got it designed? I would love to see it," Russell asked.

"Oh sure, I should have it by tomorrow or Thursday, that way we can make any necessary changes and send it to the printer by Friday, then we should have posters and table signs by Tuesday or Wednesday."

"That's perfect. Thanks for your help," said Russell.

"Yes, thank you Trent," Paige added. "Alright, are there any other details I'm not thinking of?" she asked.

"Will you need to do any additional training for your servers? And will you need to bring in more servers for breakfast to cover the larger number of members that we hope will be coming in?" Russell wondered.

"Yes, and yes. I've already spoken to some of our current staff to see if any of them might be available to add working breakfast to their schedule. The good news is, most of them have more availability in the summer, plus we are already hiring and training new people in the summer, so if we need to add more to breakfast that shouldn't be a problem. As far as training, our current staff already deals with lunch and dinner specials, so this won't be a big change for them. But I have developed a summer contest for them, as an incentive to push the new specials we will have a server scoreboard. I won't go into the details, but it should be fun for them."

"That's great," Russell said. "It sounds like you've got everything covered, thank you for all your hard work on this Paige."

Paige blushed slightly. "Of course, I'm excited to see how it goes." Their eyes met and she could see that he was impressed with what she had done. "Well alright, that's it then. Thank you everybody for being here and for all your help. Please let me know if you have more questions or if you think of anything I've missed."

The group broke up quickly, James gathered the empty tray and the coffee and headed to the kitchen, Trent gathered his things and left too. Paige and Russell stood up, but remained at the table talking.

"You know it really is amazing," Russell said.

"What? The food James makes?" Paige asked, knowing that wasn't the answer.

"No, the fact that you were overlooked for so long when it is so clear how perfect you are for this job."

Chapter 21

⁕

"Peyton? Shep? Are you guys coming?" The weeks had flown by for Paige with all the work in the restaurant. She couldn't believe it, but she felt like she had blinked and it was Memorial Day weekend. Now the younger kids were loaded in the van and she was just waiting for her teenaged siblings. Dressed in khaki shorts with a teal sleeveless top and brown strappy sandals, she checked the contents of the back of the van one last time to make sure they had everything. She brought changes of clothes and beach towels for the kids in case they got wet or dirty, and sunscreen for everybody. She also had a few fold out chairs just in case. She had asked Russell if she could bring anything and he continued to insist that she didn't need to. Finally he broke down and told her that his mom said if she really wanted to bring something she could make a dessert. So she had put together a four-layered-dessert with a piecrust, chocolate pudding, cake and whipped cream.

Finally Peyton and Shep came out and climbed into the van.

Shep crawled over the little kids to get to the back seat and Peyton took the front seat next to Paige. "Sorry," she said.

"Alright, let's go."

The drive to the Pierce's house was full of the kids talking and arguing over which radio station to play, and Peyton and Zoey discussing an upcoming concert they were hoping to attend. Paige said very little. Despite the fact that she had been, and still was, excited about going to the party today, today she was very nervous. She kept trying to remind herself that she and Russell were just friends, and that she had been invited to his family's house as a friend. But she felt as though there would be pressure to admit they were more. Before she knew it they were in the driveway and it was too late to back out. They all piled out of the van and walked toward the door. Paige carried the dessert. Just before she knocked she reminded them all to be polite and asked the kids not to be too loud. Then she turned and raised her hand to knock, but just then the door opened.

"Hello!" Gladys opened the door and welcomed them. "Come in! Come in! We're so glad you could join us today. Oh Paige, this looks delicious!"

"Oh thank you."

"Now, remind me of everyone's names again," she said.

Paige pointed to each one in turn. "Peyton, Shep, Zoey, Joe and Lucy." Each of them smiled politely as they had been told.

"Peyton, Shep, Zoey, Joe and Lucy," Gladys repeated. "I'll do my best to remember. Alright, here let me take that." She reached out for the dish and took it. "And please feel free to make yourselves at home. Let's walk through here and I'll introduce you."

The group followed Gladys from the foyer and into the

living room. Several people were gathered around sitting on the chairs and couches, and more people were outside in the yard. All in all there were about fifty people gathered. The sound of all the voices talking at once blended into a loud hum throughout the house.

"Paige this is my daughter-in-law Carrie, she's my son Jack's wife. Carrie this is Paige, she's the friend of Russell's who manages the restaurant at the club."

"Oh yes, hi! It's so nice to meet you." Carrie stood and reached for Paige's hand.

"And these are her siblings." Gladys looked excited to practice her newly memorized names. "Peyton, Shep, Zoey, Joe and Lucy." She pointed.

"Nice to meet y'all."

"I need to take this dessert that Paige made and set it in the kitchen. Can you show Paige around and introduce her? And show the kids where they can play?"

"Of course."

"Thanks, Carrie. Paige, we'll catch up later, alright?"

"Sure, sounds good." Paige turned back and tried not to look too uncomfortable.

"I can show you around, but you guys," she looked at Joe and Lucy, "are welcome to go outside and play with the kids, right through that door."

The twins looked up at Paige waiting for permission. "It's alright, you can go. Just behave," she told them. That was all they needed to hear and they were off.

Carrie looked at the rest of them. "There are some pre-lunch snacks outside too, and water and lemonade in the kitchen. Please make yourselves at home."

"Thank you." Peyton was the first to speak up. "Want to

go get something to eat?" she asked Zoey. The younger girl nodded and they walked off with Shep following them.

"I think that takes care of everybody." Carrie smiled. "And I really do want to talk since I've heard so much about you, but I think I'll be in trouble if I introduce you around without taking you to see a certain someone." She smiled as if she was holding a secret that Paige wanted to know.

Paige smiled back and only hoped that her face wasn't red.

Carrie smiled even bigger at Paige. "Russell's outside, come on." She led the way through the living room and out the French doors that led to the patio. They were greeted by the smell of meat cooking, and the air had a tint of smoke from the grill. At the edge of the patio a large, lush, green lawn stretched way out to a tall wooden fence. Kids were running around the yard kicking balls and playing with large bubble wands. A number of adults stood or sat in lawn chairs throughout the yard, some holding plates of appetizers and cups of lemonade or soft drinks. Just to the side of the yard was a paved spot with a basketball goal.

A group of men were standing just on the edge of the basketball court and Russell was with them. He wore a dark green t-shirt, grey basketball shorts and tennis shoes. When he saw Paige he stopped mid-conversation to greet her. "Hey!" He exited the circle and jogged over to her and Carrie. He approached her and wrapped her in a hug.

Paige was taken aback. He had never hugged her before. She noticed the smell of his laundry detergent mixed with a little bit of sweat, but the hug didn't last long and when he pulled away she felt her cheeks turn red again, but she smiled at him, "Hey."

"I'm so glad you guys could come. Have you met everybody?"

"Just Carrie." Paige gestured towards his sister-in-law and then pushed both of her hands into her back pockets.

"Well then, come on, let me introduce you to some people."

Paige followed him over to the group of men who were still talking, but most of their gazes had followed Russell while he went to Paige.

"Hey guys, I want y'all to meet Paige. Paige Kelly, these are my brothers, Jack and Sam."

Each of them reached out to shake her hand. "Hey, nice to meet you," Jack said.

"Nice to meet you too," said Paige.

"I'm sure you've heard a lot about us," Sam said.

She looked at Russell and laughed. "Umm, maybe a little."

"Probably most of it isn't true, just so you know." Sam winked.

"OK, I'll remember that," Paige said.

"Yeah." Russell gave Sam a look. "Anyway, these are our friends Mike and Dave,"

Paige waved. "Hi," she said.

"So we were thinking about playing some three-on-three basketball, but we need one more guy. Is Shep here? Will he play?"

"Oh yeah, he's here, and I'm sure he will." Paige looked around trying to find her brother and saw him standing near the drink table. "Oh there he is. Hey Shep, come here." He walked over. "You remember Russell, right?"

"Yeah, hey," Shep said.

"They want to know if you'll play basketball so the teams will be even,"

"Oh sure." That seemed to put Shep at ease. He hadn't really wanted to come today, but he would play basketball with anybody, anywhere, anytime.

"Great." Russell did some quick introductions of all the guys and then they started off to the court to pick teams. As the others walked away Russell hung back a second to say to Paige. "Will you be alright?"

"Oh, yeah." She was surprised he asked. "I can watch, or I might go see if I can help in the kitchen."

Russell smiled at her. "Oh you don't have to do that, but if you want to go in I'm sure my mom would love your company. Or you can stay and watch me dominate out here." He twirled the basketball on one finger.

Paige laughed. "I'll be fine, either way."

"Okay." He stopped and held the ball still. "By the way, you look really nice today."

Paige blushed again. "Thank you." Peyton had helped her out again and loaned her something from her closet. "Now go on."

With one last grin at her, Russell jogged away to join the game.

Paige stood and watched for a few minutes as they started playing. She glanced around to make sure she could lay eyes on each of the other kids. Peyton and Zoey were sitting together on a long foldout lawn chair, eating and talking with each other. Joe and Lucy were in the thick of it with all of the other kids.

Paige watched a few points as the teams of three dribbled the ball up and down the half-court of concrete. After each point Russell would look over to see her. A few minutes went by and after one more point Russell looked at her again, she smiled and waved, then motioned that she was going in the house. He waved back and kept playing.

She walked into the kitchen and glanced around at all the food on the counters and the table. She saw Gladys standing in the door to the pantry, so she walked over and waited until she came out. "Oh hey Paige, how's everything going?" Over her clothes, Gladys had put on a ruffled, flower print apron.

"Great! The kids are all playing or talking, and Shep is playing basketball with the guys."

"Oh, that's wonderful,"

"Can I help with anything?"

"Oh I think I've just about got it covered here, but I'm going to chop up these vegetables to go on the grill. I would love it if you just sat here at the counter so we can talk."

"I can do that."

Gladys set up her cutting board and a dish to put the vegetables in and went to work while she spoke. "So Russell told me you're starting a new breakfast menu at the club?"

"Yes we are, it's been a lot of work and a lot of fun. We're very excited to get it started. It opens a week from today."

"That's great, maybe Russell can get us in for breakfast one day soon."

"Oh yes, you'll have to come by and let me know what you think."

"Of course. So how has the transition been for you, working as the manager?"

Paige had to think for a minute. "You know, it's really been good. I thought it would feel really different, and in some ways it does, but I guess in a lot of ways I was already doing a lot of the job." She laughed quietly to herself. "I guess Russell was right."

"Right about what?" Gladys asked.

"Well, he said I was already doing the job and that's why

he recommended the promotion for me. At first I thought it was just because he felt sorry for me." Paige realized she had said more than she meant to, she tried to cover quickly, "But I guess he was right after all, about the job."

"Mmhmm, I see." Gladys looked at Paige as if she was trying to decide whether or not to push the question of why Russell would feel sorry for her. Ultimately she must have decided not to because she changed the subject. "Your hair is really lovely, have you always worn it long like that?"

Paige twisted the end of her ponytail and thought to when she wore her hair down more and kept it trimmed and fixed all of the time. "Oh, no, not always, but it's definitely been long for a while."

"I just don't think I've ever seen you with it down."

"Oh yeah, it's just easier to pull it back, especially working in the restaurant."

"Oh yes, I'm sure it is,"

There was a quiet lull as the mumbled voices outside mixed with the sound of Gladys chopping vegetables. Then she stopped, laid down the knife and leaned on the counter as she looked Paige in the eye.

"So Paige, just between us girls, tell me, what's going on with you and Russell?"

Paige looked away, and chewed her bottom lip. She was sure these questions would come eventually. She had tried to prepare herself for them, but sitting here she didn't know what to say. "Nothing really, we're friends." She knew the words didn't sound believable, even to her.

"Oh really?" Gladys gave her a look that only a mother can give.

Paige felt like a child without an answer to an adult's

question. So she shrugged her shoulders. "Yes," was all she could say.

"Well, if that's true then it's really too bad. Because I like you." She winked at Paige and excused herself to take the vegetables out to Jim at the grill.

Paige sat at the counter in the quiet. Everyone else had gone outside. Just then Carrie came down the stairs from feeding baby Caroline and putting her down for a nap.

"Phew!" she said. "Caroline is asleep and Luke is outside playing with his cousins, so I can take a short break." She smiled and sat down on the stool next to Paige. "So I heard Gladys go outside, did she ask you about Russell?"

"Umm, yes, she did. So don't you start too." Paige tried not to sound embarrassed.

Carrie laughed. "Listen, I've been around this family for quite a while now, so it's no surprise."

"Yeah, I guess I should have expected it. But really we're just friends. Between you and me, I think he wants more, but I've told him that's not happening."

"Oh really?" Carrie asked.

"Yes," Paige said with certainty.

"So why is that?"

"Well," Paige paused to take a deep breath. She tried to think of how to explain without going into too much detail. But suddenly she felt like she could really talk to this woman that she had only just met. "My family situation is obviously very different."

"Yes, Russell told us about your parents. Well, he told Jack and Jack told me. I'm so sorry for your loss, I can't imagine what that must have been like."

"Thank you. It was quite a shock for a while, but now we're

settled in, you know? We're used to things the way they are now, and I don't really want to rock the boat. Plus I just don't think a relationship is a good idea for me right now, and I don't think a guy would really want to take on all the baggage that I come with."

Carrie looked thoughtful before speaking again. "Don't you think a guy who is interested in you deserved the chance to decide for himself if he wants to take that on?"

Paige didn't have an answer.

"And so what does that mean for you? You need to wait until the kids go off to college to have a relationship? How old will that make you? Like thirty-five?"

Paige mumbled, and the answer was more for herself than Carrie. "Something like that."

"Paige, you can't do that. I'm not saying you have to date Russell, and honestly you don't have to be in a rush to dive into a relationship and get married, but your plan can't just be to put it off forever. If the right person comes along you just have to be open."

"Maybe I'm just never going to get married. Maybe this is what I'm supposed to do."

"You're right. Maybe it is. And if you're happy and serving your family in this way is joyful for you, then that's good. And if you never meet someone who you want to spend your life with then you have been a part of a wonderful family and raised kids. But if you're just doing this because you think you should and you're actually pushing away someone that could potentially be the person for you, then that's wrong. That's not what God wants for you."

"I guess I never thought about it that way." Paige was genuinely trying to take it in and think about what Carrie was saying.

"I don't want to lecture you or tell you a bunch of things you already know, but I have to tell you about my own story. I knew Jack all through college and I had even been to his parent's house for a gathering like this one a few times. But I was so determined that I didn't want to get bogged down in a relationship. I wanted to be single and graduate and start my career. I wanted to be a pediatric doctor and take care of kids. So I shied away from any kind of serious attention from guys. I had plans. But Jack wouldn't quit asking. So I finally went out with him, just to shut him up. But I had fun, so when he asked again I said yes. And we had fun again. So we kept going out and the next thing I knew we were a couple. Once I realized that, I broke up with him immediately. I didn't want anything interfering with my plans, so I didn't see him or talk to him or take any of his phone calls. And then something would happen and I would think, 'I can't wait to tell Jack' or I would see something funny on TV and think about how Jack would laugh at that. Just a hundred tiny things throughout the day that made me think of him. I started to miss him so much and so one night I sat down and thought really hard about my life. Did I really want to achieve all my goals and then not have someone to share it with? I knew I didn't, and I knew that Jack was the first person that I wanted to tell everything to for forever."

Paige sat enraptured in the story, she could see herself in it. Not in the same way, but she could imagine herself sending the twins off for the last time and then standing in an empty house. Was that really what she was working towards?

She wasn't sure what else to say. "I guess you're pretty happy you made that choice."

"I wouldn't change a thing. I have the best life, and it's something that I could never have planned or even thought of. God had a plan and purpose for me, and this is it. And He had the perfect partner for me in Jack. I'm so glad I get to spend my life with him. And this family? I'll tell you this about the Pierces, yes they're loud and fun and goofy, and all up in your business, so they're gonna ask you questions you don't want to answer. But they're also the real deal. Real people who really love each other and take care of each other. And they take care of other people too."

"Yes, I think I can see that."

"I'm not telling you what to do. Even though after being around them for so long I have a little bit of Pierce in me, and I would really like to tell you that Russell is a great catch and you better grab him up before someone else does. But really I just hope you will think about what you want. Sometimes you just have to open yourself up to a possibility to see what will happen."

"Thanks for telling me your story. I promise I'll think about what you said." Paige smiled.

"Good, because seriously, Russell is a great catch." Carrie winked at her. "Just kidding. Come on, let's move outside and see what's going on." The two stood and walked out the door together. Someone had turned on a sprinkler and the kids were running around getting soaked in the yard. Paige caught sight of Joe and Lucy and was glad she had brought them a change of clothes.

The basketball game had wrapped up and Jack walked over to his wife and gave her a big hug, rubbing his sweaty face on her cheek. "Ewww," Carrie squealed. But it was a playful squeal and she kissed her husband. "So who won?"

"We did," all the men said.

Russell walked over and stood next to Paige. "I scored the winning goal."

"Psshh, whatever," Sam spoke loudly. "More like you got lucky with a granny shot."

Russell playfully pushed his brother. "You're just jealous. Hey Dad, is it time to eat yet?"

Jim Pierce stood by the grill and help up his hand with five fingers spread out. Jack, Sam, and Russell all three put two fingers to their mouths and whistled loudly. All the kids stopped running and the adults stopped talking to listen up. "Five minutes to lunch," the brothers shouted in unison. At that announcement parents went to gather kids to wash their hands and faces off and everyone began to set up chairs where they would eat.

Russell spoke to Paige. "I'll get Joe and Lucy, and then we'll set up chairs there by the fence, is that alright?"

Paige was taken aback at his instruction. "Oh, okay, sure, sounds good."

"Be right back."

As she watched him walk away she thought about Carrie's words. "Don't you think a guy who is interested in you deserves the chance to decide for himself if he wants to take that on?" *Is that what he's doing?* she wondered. *Is he trying to show me that he can handle the family part?*

"Do you want me to help get the kids food?" Peyton interrupted her thoughts.

"Um, no I think I've got it. Russell's getting them now," Paige said.

Peyton gave her a questioning look.

"You two can get your own food, and you can sit with us if

you want, or not, whatever you want to do."

Shep walked up to join them, but Peyton spoke. "Come on Shep, Zoey, let's eat over at the tables and leave Paige and her 'friend' alone." She smiled as the three of them walked away.

Paige started to call after them, to tell them to come back and to absolutely not leave her alone, but Jim stood near the door and raised his hand. It seemed to be the signal for everyone to quiet down. As everyone took notice of him standing there, the adults stopped talking and did their best to quiet the children. Gladys came out to stand next to her husband and the two of them joined hands. "Everyone, let's pray," Jim said.

All across the yard couples joined hands and held kids, Jim waited while everyone settled in. Joe and Lucy ran to Paige and huddled close. Russell was shortly behind them and walked over and stood beside Paige. As everyone bowed their heads and closed their eyes he put his arm around her and rested his hand on her shoulder. It was already quiet enough to hear a pin drop, but now all Paige could hear was the sound of her heart beating. She stood perfectly still and tried not to breathe loudly.

"Dear Jesus," Jim prayed, "Thank you for the gift of so many friends and family members that are here with us today. Thank you for this beautiful day and for the chance to celebrate and fellowship together. Thank you for the food you have provided. I pray that you will bless the food to nourish our bodies and may our time together be glorifying to you. May we walk in a manner worthy of the gospel of Jesus Christ. In His name we pray, Amen."

The sound of "amen"s echoed across the yard. Russell dropped his hand from Paige's shoulder just before everyone opened their eyes.

Jim's voice boomed, "Alright everybody, let's eat!"

All the voices started back up again as kids started running around and parents gave instructions. Gladys began trying to point everyone to the starting point for a food line.

"Come on, let's get some food." Russell led the way for Paige, Joe and Lucy as they headed into the kitchen and began to maneuver the line.

Paige followed a few steps behind and couldn't help but watch Russell as he helped the kids start to fill their plates while balancing his own. She knew if she didn't watch herself she would start to fall for him. And if she did she would fall fast.

. . .

Afternoon was turning to evening and most of the crowd had left for home. All of the Pierce family members still remained and the kids were running around the backyard catching fireflies in big glass jars. Paige and Russell sat next to each other in lawn chairs near the edge of the patio. The other adults were either inside or playing with the kids.

"I feel like I should go help your mom clean up," Paige said.

"Oh she wouldn't let you anyway." Russell leaned his head back in his chair, looking totally relaxed. "She would say 'It's your first time here and you're a guest, guests don't help clean up. But next time you come you won't be a guest anymore and you can help then.' It's a house rule, one time here, you're a guest, the next time you're family."

"What makes you think I'll be coming back here again?" Paige asked teasingly.

"Oh I think you'll be back. We're the kind of people who get under your skin and you just can't get rid of us."

"Yes, I'm learning that."

"Really though, did you have a good time?" Russell looked her in the eyes and saw that she looked happy.

"Oh yes, your family really is great. I might be a guest today, but they made me feel very welcomed. I talked to Carrie for a while."

"Oh yeah? Did she tell you any embarrassing stories about me?"

"Oh yes, all kinds."

"She's heard them all by now, so I wouldn't be surprised."

"No, really, she's very sweet. She seems to think you're pretty great too."

"I will take that compliment for sure. Oh, I almost forgot." Russell stood up quickly, "Come on, I've got something for you."

"For me? What is it?"

"You'll have to come and see."

"I should watch the kids…" Paige glanced over and her eyes searched the yard for Joe and Lucy.

"Oh they're fine, and Peyton is just over there, if they need something they will find her."

"Okay," Paige said cautiously.

"Come on." Russell walked towards the door and she followed him inside and across the living room to the stairs. Upstairs he walked to the second door and opened it. "Don't judge me by the decor, but this used to be my room." He walked through and stood by the dresser. It was still decorated like a high schooler's bedroom with band posters and basketball trophies lining the walls. "In fact, if my mom had gotten her way it still would be, she actually wanted me to move back in here when I came back to town." He laughed.

Paige stood in the doorway and leaned against the frame. "You wanted to show me your room from when you were a teenager?"

"No," he said. "I wanted to give you this." He reached to the top of the dresser and picked up a rectangular box, "I just put it up here so it would be out of the way during the party."

Paige hesitated in the doorway, so he walked to her and handed her the box. Cautiously she took it with both hands and slowly lifted the lid. Inside was a leather bound Bible with her name engraved in gold lettering. She drew in a quick breath. "Oh, you didn't have to do that," she whispered.

"You said the one you have is neon pink and designed for a teenager, but you're not a teenager anymore. I thought you might like to have a grown-up Bible." He smiled.

"It's beautiful," she said. "Thank you."

"You're welcome, I hope it'll be an encouragement to you."

"Thanks." Paige could barely speak. No one had given her a gift that meant this much to her since her parents. Without thinking or talking herself out of it she set the box down and hugged him. It wasn't a long hug, but one that showed him she was grateful.

"Thank you, Paige."

"For what?"

"For letting me be your friend." He looked her directly into her eyes and tried to hold her gaze.

"I'm still surprised that you want to be my friend." She looked at the floor, but he moved to look her in the face again.

"You need to get used to it, because I'm not going anywhere."

"Is that so?"

"Yes, it is so."

"Even after Joe sprayed you with the ketchup and Lucy cried because the boys wouldn't let her play tag with them?"

"Even still."

"What about when our conversation gets interrupted in a few minutes because Peyton wants to know if she can go somewhere with a boy or Shep has put another dent in the car?"

"What do I need to do to show you that none of that is going to scare me away? I'm here Paige, right here. I know that those things might happen, but that's part of your life. And if that's part of your life then I'll get used to it, because I want to be a part of your life."

"You mean you want us to be friends, right?"

"Friends, yes. Paige, I want us to be very best friends." His gaze was intense as he looked straight into her eyes. She couldn't break eye contact with him for a second. He seemed so serious, so unwavering that she couldn't argue.

"I think I might be okay with that," she finally said.

He smiled at her. "Okay, good."

She smiled back.

Russell took a deep breath and smiled at her. "Alright, I'm going to ask you something now, and your first response is going to be to say 'no', but fight that urge for just a second and try to say 'yes.'"

"Hmm, I'll see what I can do," Paige teased him.

"I'll take that." He took a deep breath and paused for effect, then he said, "Paige, will you please go to dinner with me on Friday night?"

She paused too, squinting her eyes and pretending to fight an urge in her mind, then finally she looked at him and said, "Okay."

"Well, it's not a yes, but I'll take that too." He smiled.

She smiled back. She picked up the Bible and closed the box and then walked back down the hall.

He watched her go and let her get a head start on him down the stairs. He wasn't sure exactly what had made a change in her, but he knew it was a start. And in his heart he knew it was the start of something very great.

Chapter 22

R ussell put on his watch and checked himself in the mirror one more time. He had told Paige they were going somewhere nice so she should dress up. He wore dark khaki dress pants, a blue striped collared shirt and a gray blazer. As he went to pick up his keys his phone rang.

"Hey, Mom," he answered.

"Hi Russell, how are you?"

"I'm great Mom. I'm heading out the door to go pick up Paige." He had already told her they were going to dinner, in fact she had recommended the restaurant where they were going.

"Oh good, I'm glad I caught you. I've been praying for you today."

"Oh, thanks, I appreciate it."

"I've been praying for her too, Russell. I'm concerned for her."

"I know Mom, I have been too. I told you ever since I met her I have just wanted to help her."

"I know son, and I'm thankful that you have that desire, but I just want you to think about how you help her. I talked to her the other day at the house. She is in such a struggle. I can see the pain and heaviness in her eyes, it's still there. Losing her parents, taking on such a huge responsibility. She has struggled and she's still struggling. I don't think she has leaned on anyone for help, not even Jesus."

"I know," he sad sadly. "She's very independent. She doesn't want anyone to think she can't do it by herself. I want to help her let go of that, show her that people can help and it doesn't make her incapable."

"Yes, but even if she let's you in, you can't bear all her burdens for her. Only Jesus can do that. Point her back to him."

"You're right Mom, thanks. I think I needed to hear that. I will keep that in mind and keep praying for her."

"Good. I know you have the best intentions."

"You taught me well then I guess," he laughed.

"We tried." He could hear the smile in her voice. "Alright then, I'll let you go, have fun!"

"Thanks, Mom. I'll talk to you later." They said goodbye and when Russell hung up he felt a heaviness again, knowing he couldn't take all her pain away was hard. "Lord, guide me in how to help, let me show her the way to You." He didn't hear an answer, but his heart was filled with peace and joy. He hurried out the door.

When he arrived at the Kelly's house and walked to the door, he could hear the sound of voices inside. He knocked and Peyton opened the door. "Hey, come on in," she said. "Paige will be down in a minute, sorry the kids are wild right now."

"Oh, that's alright." He stepped through the foyer into the living room and stood near the wall watching as Joe and Lucy jumped on a stack of pillows they had piled on the floor. Then he heard the sound of footsteps coming down the stairs. He turned to see and his breath caught in his throat at the sight.

Paige was dressed in a sleeveless, navy blue, knee-length dress. The neckline was high and the bodice was ruffled cascading down to a flowing skirt. She carried a small clasp purse and wore silver high heels with thin straps. The ensemble was completed with dangling silver earrings and a single bracelet. Her hair hung around her shoulders in soft curls. She came down the stairs and stood before Russell. All she said was "Hi."

In that moment, with one look, Russell knew he was a goner. He couldn't think about his desire to help her or about God placing a burden on his heart anymore. All he saw was a beautiful woman who he knew he was about to fall hard for.

He couldn't speak for a full five seconds, but then he cleared his throat and said the only clear thought in his mind. "You look beautiful."

Paige brushed a hair behind her ear to hide her blush. "Thank you. You look nice too," she said.

"I like your hair down. I've never seen it like that." Russell was unaware of anyone else in the room.

"I haven't worn it like this in a very long time," she said. At that moment the noise of the kids reminded them that there were other people there. Paige turned her attention to them and spoke. "Guys listen, now Peyton is in charge tonight, mind her. She's got pizza ready for you to eat and then you can watch a movie and then it's bedtime. No arguing."

"I've got it." Peyton started to push her towards the door. "Go. Don't worry about us."

"Alright, I have my phone if you need me."

"Okay, but I won't. Just have fun."

"Alright, bye," Paige said. Russell opened the door and ushered her out. They walked down the sidewalk and Russell walked to her side of the car to open her door. During the car ride they made small talk. The drive wound around a curvy road up the side of a mountain into a wooded path leading to the restaurant. The place was a well-known spot, and as they headed down the path Paige realized where they were going.

"Really? Are we eating here?" She was surprised.

"Yep, I told you I wanted to take you somewhere nice." Russell smiled at her shock.

"I know, but I didn't expect this."

Russell pulled into the circle drive in front of the restaurant known as The View, it was the fanciest restaurant in town. A valet opened Paige's door for her to step out. Russell handed over the keys and walked around to join Paige. He spoke as they walked toward the door. "I just want you to relax and enjoy dinner, no kids, no clean up, no stress."

She smiled and seemed a little nervous. "I'll try."

They entered the restaurant and the hostess seated them immediately, since Russell had made a reservation. They were led through the dining room out to the covered deck and seated at a table near the railing. Their view overlooked the ridge below the mountain and the breathtaking sunset served as a backdrop.

"Well, what do you think?" Russell asked as they took their seats.

"It's amazing," Paige nearly whispered.

"I'm glad you like it, the food is also supposed to be spectacular, so I hope you're hungry."

Paige smiled and started to look at her menu. She had only

started scanning when Russell said, "Order whatever you want, and I insist we get an appetizer and dessert, I plan to leave here totally stuffed."

Paige giggled, her nerves were beginning to fall away as she let herself relax and enjoy the company of the man she was finally calling her friend. She didn't know what was coming, but for once she chose not to worry about it and just have a good time.

They chatted as they ate the bread the server brought to the table and ordered a crab cake appetizer. The server told them the specials for the night and they each chose one instead of ordering off the menu. "James says, always order the special at dinner," Paige had said earlier in the car. The server thanked them and took their menus and left them to talk.

"So, you know all about my family, and even though I've met them now, I don't really know that much about yours. Tell me about them," Paige said.

"So growing up as the youngest of three brothers is a bit challenging. I was the little kid to them when they were paired off, so I also became the brunt of the jokes and the punching bag. So sometimes it's hard for me to take them seriously, but my brothers are really great guys. Jack went to school at Auburn and he works as a financial advisor at a firm in town, he met Carrie while they were in school and they got married after graduation. He's the more serious one, most of the time, works hard, provides for his family, pretty straightforward guy. And of course they have Luke, who's four, and baby Caroline."

"Yes, I talked with Carrie a little at the party,"

"Salt of the earth, she's the sweetest person. She's really been the sister that I never had."

"And what about Sam?"

Russell chuckled. "Sam is kind of a loose cannon, but he's got a great heart. He lives to entertain anybody and everybody and he's usually the center of attention wherever he goes. He went to school and did alright, and he had a couple of different jobs at first, but he's been at the technology company for a long time now. But Izzy, his wife, just rolls with the punches. She's great too, they are a very fun family. And they have the four boys."

"I don't think I met her at your parents."

"No, one of the kids was sick so she stayed home and Sam brought the others."

"Oh, gotcha. And how did they meet?"

"High school. One thing Sam has always been committed to is Izzy. Once they started dating he never looked at another girl. They were together all through high school and got married their freshman year of college. A lot of people couldn't handle that, but they have made it work."

"And what does your dad do?"

"He's semi-retired, but he does financial advising, the same as Jack does, in the same firm. In fact he's already passed on a lot of his clients to Jack, and eventually he'll fully retire and leave the rest of his business to him too."

"Oh, that's nice."

"You said your dad was an attorney right?"

"Yes, he was. And he spent most of his career here. After he graduated from law school he started out in a big firm in a bigger city, but he and my mom decided they wanted a small town life, so they moved here and stayed."

"Did your mom work?"

"She did when they were first married, but after I was born

206

she stayed home. She was the center of the family, you know? Always there, doing work, but just taking care of everybody. Plus she was involved with church and always hosting events and having people over to the house. I guess she was kind of like your mom, maybe a little more in the background, she didn't like to be in front very much, but she definitely cared for people the way your mom does."

Their food arrived and there was a pause in their conversation.

"Can I get you anything else?" the server asked.

"I think we're fine, thank you." Russell said. Once she walked away he asked, "Should we pray?"

"Oh yes, alright," Paige said.

To Russell it seemed the most natural thing in the world to reach out and take her hand as he closed his eyes and bowed his head. "Dear Father, thank you for tonight, thank you for this time to spend together. Please bless this food and bless our conversation tonight. Amen." When he looked up he saw that Paige's eyes were open and locked on their hands touching. He thought that if he didn't need his hand to eat he would have kept holding her hand all night, but she released it as soon as he finished praying and tucked it in her lap.

For a moment they ate in silence as they both took their first bites. Russell broke the silence, "Tell me about when you went to college."

"Well, it was very short, I only made it through half of the fall semester, but it was great, I really loved it. They try to encourage freshmen to take basic classes their first semester, like math, history, and things like that. But I didn't listen to that at all. I took several classes in my major and just jumped right into it. I figured I had to take the basic classes anyway and so I would at some point, but I wanted to find out right away if I really was going to like my major."

"And you did?"

"Oh yes, I could have talked all day about room design, color coordination, fabric choices, furniture layout. Like I said, I only made it through half of the semester, but I enjoyed the classes and projects so much."

"Do you ever think about going back to school?" Russell asked.

"Sometimes, and maybe someday I will, but right now it's just not possible."

"Did you ever look in to getting your degree online?"

"Hmm, no I never really thought about it, I guess I've never had the time."

"I bet you could make it work, especially with a flexible schedule at work."

"Yeah, maybe. But I really like what I'm doing now, and my plate's pretty full with the restaurant and all the events that we have going on right now. But who knows, maybe someday."

Russell didn't push the point. "Were you involved with any other activities in college, a sorority or sports?"

"No, nothing like that. I kind of thought that I would focus on my studies the first semester and then the second semester I would try to get more involved. But obviously that didn't happen. What about you, what was your college experience like?"

"I was a business major, so I took a lot of general business classes. It's pretty boring stuff, nothing exciting like fabric color arrangement." He smiled. "But it interested me, so it was good. I kept up with my work, but I was always hanging out with friends or going to a football game, or basketball or baseball or something. We found stuff to keep us busy all the time. I wouldn't go back now, but it really was the time of my life."

"That sounds fun. Do you keep up with friends from college?"

"A few, we're spread around the country, and nobody grew up in town, but we try to get all of us together once or twice a year."

"That's nice."

"So you say, 'maybe someday', for a lot of things, and I know you like working in the restaurant, especially now that you get to run the place, but what do you see yourself doing in the future? Say five years down the road?"

Paige took in a deep breath and blew it out. "I don't know really. I guess I kind of feel like I've just put my life on hold. In five years I guess Peyton will be graduating college, and Shep will be in college, and Zoey about to start. But the twins will be in middle school, so I'll still be at home with them I guess. It's weird, you know, if I had stayed in school I would be graduating this year. My life would just be starting off with a career and who knows what else. But now that's not really in the picture."

"But Paige, you did just start a new career. You're not a waitress anymore, you're in management at a very successful country club. Not that I want you to leave, but after working in a position like that, you will have more opportunity than you think."

"I hadn't thought about that."

Russell took a breath before continuing, "And, as your friend, I have to tell you, I think it's time for you to stop putting your life on hold."

Paige shook her head. "People keep telling me that, but I just don't think anyone understands."

"Explain it to me. I'm all ears."

"I can't just run off and leave my family. They need me. If I don't do everything I do, who is going to do it? Peyton will leave for college in the fall and Shep isn't great about watching the kids, and Zoey is still is a kid too. And they still need a parent too."

"I'm not saying you need to leave them, I'm saying you have to work to find ways to be there for them and have a life too. When was the last time you left Joe and Lucy with a friend or babysitter and had a whole day to yourself."

Paige stared it him without saying a work.

"Have you ever done that?"

"Well…"

"Paige, really? You've never taken a Saturday for yourself?"

"Sometimes if I've worked on Saturday they've stayed with a friend or Peyton has watched them or something. Or I've gone to run errands for a while by myself."

"See? That's what I mean, there's a way you could let someone watch them so you could do something for yourself, or you could make time to study for an online class, or, I don't know, you could go to dinner with a handsome guy who thinks you're amazing for all the things you do and the way you're totally committed to your family."

"I know, I know, you're right. It just takes a lot of effort and I've never been good at thinking about it enough to plan something."

"I think you should start."

Paige laughed. "Okay, tell you what, tomorrow morning you take Joe and Lucy and maybe even Zoey, and I'll just go shopping and then take a nice long nap."

"Okay, what time?"

She looked at him wide-eyed. "I'm just kidding."

"I'm not. What time?"

"You don't want to do that."

"I absolutely do.

Paige just looked at him. "Why?"

"I want to help. I want to give you some breathing room. I want you to feel like you're not alone."

Paige looked away as she blinked away the tears that were trying to surface.

"Paige? Do you feel alone?"

She cleared her throat trying to gain control of her voice. She shook her head as if she couldn't admit to that awful truth.

The waiter came to the table and poured more water in their glasses. "Would you like to see a dessert menu?"

"Yes, thank you." Russell spoke somewhat abruptly, but he hoped she would leave them be for a minute. When she was gone he spoke gently. "Paige, I know that your life hasn't been what you've expected, and it's been hard to shoulder the burden you've carried. But you need to know that you're not alone. God has never left you alone."

"Oh please don't give me the 'God has a plan for you' speech, I've heard it. If this is His plan then fine. I've been doing alright for the past few years, but in my opinion this really isn't his best for me. Best would have been if my parents hadn't died. Best would have been that I finished school and started a career. Best would have been having children when I was older and married and able to do it with a husband and a dad, not alone as a single twenty-year-old."

He reached for her hand again. "Paige, I'm so so sorry. Ever since I met you I have spent so much time thinking about you and wishing that I could fix this for you. But I can't. I can't bring your parents back and I can't wave a magic wand and make your life easier. But I wouldn't be a good friend if I didn't tell you that this definitely is God's plan, and that He has a purpose. Would you be as close to your siblings if you had been away at school for the past four years?"

She composed herself. "No, I guess not."

"You would have missed Peyton's prom and Shep's baseball games and Zoey's cheerleading classes and Joe and Lucy's school plays. But you haven't missed any of that. You've been there for them. And even though it doesn't seem best, it's been for good. And maybe now God is ready for you to have someone to walk through life with."

She looked at him and stared into his eyes, her own eyes asking if he was saying what she thought he was.

He thought about his mom's advice and wanted to push her in the right direction. "But maybe He can't give you any of that until you come back to Him and trust that He knows what He's doing and that, like everybody says, He has a plan for you."

"Maybe," Paige said half-heartedly. "Anyway, that's enough serious talk, what sounds good for dessert?"

Russell sighed, half disappointed that they weren't continuing the line of conversation, but half relieved that she seemed to bounce back to herself and want to talk about something happy.

They began looking over the dessert menu, she teased him that of course he would want coffee with it, and he pointed out all the items that included chocolate. They had just about settled on two desserts that they could both share when Paige's phone rang.

She laughed. "I knew Peyton would call. I bet she can't get the twins to turn the TV off. Hey Peyton," she answered, still laughing.

Russell watched as her laughter died away and her face became ashen. She listened for a minute and then barely pulled the phone away from her face to tell him, "We have to go...now."

Chapter 23

"*T*ell me exactly what Peyton said," Russell told Paige. He had left the table to get their server and pay the bill. Then he hurried both of them to the car when the valet brought it around.

"She said that Lucy had been complaining that her tummy hurt. She didn't think it was a big deal, but then she started throwing up. Then she started crying and saying that her tummy was hurting really bad, so Peyton took her temperature and it was one-hundred and four." Paige gripped the seat where she sat, she looked pale.

"It's okay, we'll be there soon."

They arrived at the house quickly and Paige jumped out of the car and ran to the house. Russell was right behind her. Once inside they went straight to the living room where Peyton sat on the couch with Lucy. "I'm so sorry." Peyton looked distressed. "I just didn't know what to do."

"It's alright, you did the right thing," Paige assured her. "Lucy, can I see about you, please?"

The little girl rolled over from where she laid and held on to her right side. "Paige, my tummy really, really hurts."

"I know, I'm sorry. Can you stand up?"

"Uh uh, it hurts."

"I know it does, but I need you to try."

Lucy stood up but couldn't make herself straighten up all the way.

"Now, point to where it hurts."

Lucy pointed to the lower right of her abdomen.

"Thank you, come here you can sit with me." She gathered the little girl in her arms and stroked her head.

"Paige." Russell sat down beside her.

She turned to face him, expecting him to say he was leaving. She would tell him she would call him later after she took care of Lucy.

Instead he looked like he was settling in to help with the situation. "I think this looks like appendicitis."

Her eyes grew wide. "Really?"

"Yes, Jack had it when he was younger. I don't remember all the details, but I know it's the right side that hurts and that he had a high fever and cried because of the pain."

Paige held Lucy a little tighter as the girl started to cry, but she tried not to press on her side. "Do you think I should take her to the emergency room?"

"I think that would be best. Better safe than sorry."

"Okay." She turned to Peyton. "Can you stay here? Is Joe asleep?"

"Yes, he's fine, I'll stay, we'll be fine."

"Thanks." Paige felt numb going through the motions of taking care of everything.

"Come on," Russell said. "I'll drive."

"Oh no, you don't have to do that. I can take her. You should go. I'll call you later when I know something."

"No way, I'm going. Want me to carry her? She looks a little heavy for you."

Paige looked down at her sister. "Lu, we're going to take you to the doctor so they can look at your tummy and see what's wrong. Do you want me to carry you to the car or do you want Russell to carry you."

"Russell," she said.

Paige looked at him. "Alright, I guess you win." She gently handed her off to him, secretly glad to be relieved. "But I'm sitting in the back with her, you can't stop me."

"No arguments," he said as he turned toward the door.

Paige turned back to hug Peyton. "It will be alright, I'll call you as soon as we know anything. Try not to worry."

Peyton's eyes filled with tears. "Okay."

Paige followed Russell to the car and they settled Lucy in the back seat, then Paige climbed in and sat in the seat beside her, as promised.

During the drive to the hospital Paige let every terrible possibility run through her mind. Russell tried to distract her, but there wasn't much he could say.

When they arrived at the hospital Russell pulled up to the emergency entrance and let Paige and Lucy out while he went to park the car. Paige was sitting in a chair with Lucy in her lap when he walked into the waiting room.

"I don't feel good," Lucy cried.

"I know, sweetie. I'm so sorry. When we see the doctor hopefully they will make you feel better." Russell took a seat beside Paige. "Hey," she said. She felt herself start to lean into him, until a nurse came out and called Lucy's name. "Alright, here we go." The three of them stood and followed the nurse through the door and into the triage area. Beds lined the wall and were separated by curtains. Paige was thankful it seemed like a quiet night with only a couple of people in the E.R. They were shown to one of the beds and Paige set Lucy down. She stood holding her hand and Russell stood on the other side of the bed while the nurse asked a few questions.

When she was finished collecting information she said, "The doctor will be here in just a minute," and then pulled the curtain closed and walked away.

Paige dreaded the waiting, so she was glad when it really was only a couple of minutes before a doctor pulled back the curtain and greeted them. "Hi there, Lucy, are you not feeling well?"

"Uh uh." Lucy held onto her side as she tried to sit up.

"Hi everybody, I'm Dr. Hooper,"

Paige reached out her hand. "Hi, I'm Paige."

"Let's take a look here. Lucy can you lay on your back for me?"

"Okay." Lucy complied.

"And it looks like she's had a fever and some vomiting?"

"Yes," Paige answered. "Her temperature was one hundred and four last time we checked."

The doctor pressed gently on Lucy abdomen and had her try to sit up and stand. Then he let her lay back down on the bed. "I'm sorry to say I think it might be appendicitis."

Paige felt as if she might be sick. "So that means surgery?"

"We will do a few tests to confirm, we'll run a blood test and do a CT scan. But if it proves that I'm correct, then yes, it will mean surgery."

Paige gripped the side of the bed tightly. She felt a little lightheaded.

"They'll come and get a blood sample and then take her down to CT. Mom and Dad you guys can walk with her down the hall…"

"Oh, we're not…ummm, I'm her sister, but I'm her legal guardian."

"Oh alright, well you can walk with her to the scan, but I'm going to have someone bring you the permission forms to sign so we're all ready to go once we get the test results. We won't want to waste any time."

"Okay, thank you."

"Alright, we'll see you in a few minutes."

Paige looked at Russell as soon as the doctor was gone. He tried to give her a reassuring look.

All within a few minutes a nurse came and took Lucy's blood, prepped her for the scan and was ready to wheel her down the hall. All three of them went to the radiology area and Paige and Russell sat in the chairs in the hallway while they took Lucy in. "Paige, I'm scared." It was the first time Lucy had expressed anything other than pain.

"I know sweetie, it will be alright, just like having your picture taken while you lay down, okay? I'll be right here waiting for you."

"Okay."

While they waited another nurse came and sat with Paige to fill out the necessary paper work and get all the needed signatures. Paige wanted to argue in hopes that they wouldn't need the surgery, but she knew they wouldn't want to put it off any longer if the tests confirmed the doctor's suspicions.

After Lucy came out of the scan they were taken back to a room in the E.R. Lucy laid in the bed and almost drifted off to sleep. They had put in an IV with some pain medication so she was starting to feel a little better. Paige and Russell sat trying to pass the time. Paige felt like hours were going by even though it was only about thirty minutes. The doctor came back in and Paige nearly jumped from her chair to stand at Lucy's side. Russell was right behind her.

Dr. Hooper spoke. "I'm sorry, but I was right, it's appendicitis. It needs to come out immediately."

Paige took a deep breath and held it for a second. Lucy was just barely awake and groggy. "Okay," Paige said. "Okay," more to herself than anyone else.

"Did you sign all the paperwork already?"

"Yes,"

"Alright then, someone will be here in a few minutes to take her down to surgery. A nurse can show you the way to the waiting room and I'll come out to let you know how everything goes. Try not to worry, this is all very routine."

"Okay, thank you," Paige said.

"Paige." Lucy was waking up. "Are they going to make my tummy better?"

"Yes, Lu, but they're going to do something called surgery so they can take the boo boo out. They are going to take you down the hall and you'll just take a little nap while they make it better, alright?"

"Can you stay with me?"

Paige braced herself and tried not to cry. "I'll stay with you as long as I can, but I can't go in the room with you. Just like the scan where they took your picture, remember? But I promise I will be waiting for you and I'll be here when you wake up. And you can just sleep all the way through it."

"Okay." Lucy yawned and laid back down on the bed.

A nurse came in and said hello as she checked her clipboard. "Alright, we have Lucy, here right?"

"Yes," Paige answered.

"And it looks like we're going to take out your appendix." The nurse spoke a little too cheerily.

"Looks like it," Paige agreed.

"Okay, we're going to take her down now," the nurse said as another orderly came in to help wheel the bed.

"Can I walk with her?" Paige asked.

"You can to the door, then only O.R. staff is allowed past that point."

"Okay," Paige said. She stood back as they prepared the bed and then began to push Lucy out of the room. She walked through the door and held onto the side of the bed as they walked down the hall. It was a short walk and Lucy was already falling asleep again.

"This is it." The nurse had lowered her voice and sounded more compassionate now. "The waiting room is just down that hall through the double doors." She pointed.

"Alright." She leaned over and kissed Lucy on the head. "I love you Lucy. I'll see you when you wake up." Then she stepped back away from the bed and watched as they pushed the little girl past the doors and down the halls until she couldn't see her anymore.

Paige took three steps in the direction of the waiting room where the nurse had pointed, but she couldn't go any further. She put her hand on the wall and covered her face with her other hand as she finally let the tears come. She gasped for breath as she let out a long sob. In an instant Russell was there, he gently put his hand on her back and when she turned to face him he took her in his arms and let her lean into him.

For a few minutes they stood there while Paige let herself cry and sob. He held her tightly, her high heels making her head rest just on his shoulder. As she began to catch her breath and wipe her eyes she pushed back and he looked at her face. He reached to her cheek and brushed away a piece of hair. Then he stooped to look her in the eyes. "She's going to be just fine. I know this is scary, but it's going to be alright."

She sniffled and tried to regain her composure. "I know, I know."

"Come on, let's go sit down."

She let him lead her down the hall to the empty waiting where they took a seat in the corner.

The emotional exhaustion was starting to set in for them and they sat silently for a little while. Paige called Peyton and updated her on the situation, she tried to sound calm. Once she was off the phone she leaned back to relax for a minute, but then she sat up and said, "What if we hadn't come? What if I just thought it was a stomach bug and sent her back to bed?" Her voice was filled with panic.

Russell tried to calm her. "But we did come. There's no reason to worry about the what ifs."

"But I didn't even think of appendicitis until you said it. If you hadn't been there then I probably wouldn't have brought her."

"But I was there, and I recognized it immediately because my brother had it around her age. Do you think any of that is a coincidence?"

"I don't know."

"I do. It's just like we were saying earlier, that God has a plan and a purpose. No I'm not glad that Lucy is experiencing this, but I'm glad that I was there, and I'm even glad that Jack had it because it helped me know that we needed to get her to the hospital."

"Yeah, I guess that's true."

"Paige, you're doing an amazing job with these kids. I've told you before, but I really want to tell you all the time how impressed I am with the way you handle everything. And honestly, I think you would have figured it out and you would have known that you needed to bring her. But sometimes God just wants to put people in your life to help you when you need it. I'm just thankful that tonight I got to be one of those people."

She leaned her head into her hand as she began to tear up again. Without hesitation Russell reached over and took her other hand and held it tightly in his. Paige felt too tired to resist so she let her hand remain in his and they let a comfortable silence fall between them. It was getting to be pretty late and Paige could feel her eyes starting to feel heavy.

Before too long the waiting room door opened and the doctor walked in. Paige stood quickly and dropped Russell's hand. He gave them the news before he even reached them. "She did fine, everything went smoothly."

"Oh, thank you." Paige felt the relief sweep over her.

"It hadn't burst, so we got it out with no problem. She'll have a little scar on her belly, but she should recover just fine."

"Alright, can I see her?"

"Yes, they're moving her to recovery soon, so I'll walk you down to the room now and she'll be there soon."

"Oh, thank you."

"You're welcome, Paige. I'm so sorry, I remembered after I left that the name sounded familiar, your father was Peter Kelly, wasn't he?"

"Oh, yes sir."

"I knew him on a professional level and I remember the night of the accident. I'm so sorry for your loss."

"Thanks."

"If you need anything while you're here, please be sure to ask for me personally and I'll see to it."

"Oh, alright, thank you."

"Come on, I'll show you to her room."

As they walked down the hallway Paige reached for her phone and texted Peyton the good news. They arrived in the room before Lucy did and Dr. Hooper showed them in and gave Paige some information on what to expect for the next few days while Lucy would stay in the hospital. Then he said goodbye and that Lucy should be there soon.

Within a few minutes Lucy was wheeled in on her bed, she was sleeping but the nurse with her said she had already come to and asked for her big sister. "She'll probably sleep for a while, but I'll be in and out to check on her. Just push the button by the bed if you need anything."

When the nurse left Paige stood beside Lucy's bed and kissed her on the forehead, she pulled a chair up so she could sit close while she slept.

Russell sat in the other chair in the room and watched Paige as she cared for her sister. He adjusted his position in the seat and the noise surprised Paige. She had forgotten he was there for a moment.

"Oh Russell, I'm so sorry about all of this. You should go home, really. I think we're fine now."

"Don't be sorry one bit. I already told you how glad I am that I was there. Even though this wasn't exactly the way I expected our dinner to end."

Her face went pale. "Oh my goodness, that seems like ages ago that we were sitting at the restaurant. I'm so sorry."

"Hey, I said don't be sorry. Besides, this just means that you owe me, so you have to let me take you out again." He winked.

Paige blushed. "Deal. But really, go, get some rest."

"No way. I have lots more to do."

"You do?"

"You bet. Didn't the doctor say you would be here for a few days?"

"Yeah, I think two or three."

"Then, you're going to need supplies…and some clothes."

Paige looked down, realizing that she was still in her dress and heels. "Oh, yes, I guess so. But I can take care of it."

"No, you can't, I can, and I am, no arguments."

Paige hesitated, but realized she didn't have much choice. "Okay, fine."

"Call Peyton and tell her what to get together for you and I'll go by your house and pick it up.

"Oh, alright, that's a good idea."

"Will you be alright while I'm gone?"

"I'm sure I will. She's asleep. I can get the nurse if I need anything and I plan to just sit here and watch her breathe."

Russell smiled. "Sounds good. Call Peyton. I'll be back as soon as I can." He started to go but turned back as if a thought had occurred to him. "Will Peyton and Shep be alright at home with the other kids?"

Paige thought for a moment. "I think so."

"Have they stayed at home by themselves for this long before?"

"Well, no. I've never left them overnight."

Russell winced just briefly, but recovered quickly. "That's

alright, they'll be okay. Peyton can handle it. It's just Zoey and Joe."

"Right, they should be fine." Paige bit her bottom lip.

"Don't worry, I'm sorry, I shouldn't have brought it up."

"No, it's fine. I'm calling Peyton so I'll talk with her and make sure everything's alright."

"That sounds good. Alright, I'm going." Russell turned and gave Paige a hug, one she didn't resist, before he turned and walked from the room.

Paige sank back down in the chair and stared at Lucy. The day had not ended the way she expected either. In many ways she wanted to just lay her head down on the bed and cry. But she kept thinking about what Russell had said, maybe he was right. Maybe this was all part of God's plan, maybe he did have a purpose after all. There was one thing for sure she knew she could agree with Russell on. She was glad he had been there with her.

Chapter 24

⁂

Russell woke suddenly and immediately felt the crick in his neck. He sat up and rubbed the back of his neck while taking in his surroundings. It took a moment for him to remember what had happened and why he woke up in a chair in a hospital room.

When he had arrived back at the hospital late the night before he found Paige asleep in the chair next to Lucy's bed. He hadn't wanted to disturb her, but he didn't want to leave her alone either. He had taken a seat, only planning to stay until she woke up and he could let her know to call him if she needed anything. But he must have fallen asleep himself because here he was and he could see the sun streaming in through the window. He looked to the bed and saw that Lucy was sound asleep, but Paige wasn't in sight. He heard a noise in the bathroom and noticed that the bag he had brought for her wasn't in the room. Just then he heard the sound of a hairdryer. He leaned back in the chair and let his head fall back against the wall.

In a few minutes Paige emerged wearing jeans and a fitted T-shirt and flip-flops. Her hair was pulled back in a ponytail. "Oh hey," she said when she saw Russell. "I tried not to wake you up."

"Oh no you didn't. I'm sorry, I didn't mean to stay all night, I guess I just fell asleep."

"That's alright, I did too. I'm just sorry you slept in that chair. It looks terribly uncomfortable."

"Hmm, yeah, probably not my best sleeping decision ever, but I'll live."

"Thanks for bringing me my stuff last night."

"You're welcome. I can bring you more if you need anything."

Paige laughed. "I think Peyton packed me enough for a month, so I'm good."

"Alright, but let me know if you change your mind."

Just then there was a knock on the door. Paige had gotten used to nurses coming and going every few hours to check on Lucy, so she casually said, "Come in."

Gladys Pierce quietly peeked around the door.

"Mom?" Russell stood up quickly.

"Russell? I didn't know you were still here." Gladys was surprised to see her son.

"I didn't mean to be. I just fell asleep in the chair and…well, I just woke up." He ran his fingers through his hair.

Gladys noticed Lucy still sleeping and lowered her voice. "Hi Paige, I just wanted to come by and check on you. I brought breakfast." She held up a bag from the bagel and coffee shop.

"Oh thank you. You really didn't have to do that."

"I know, but I know it can be hard to get something for yourself when you want to stay with your little one."

"Yes, it is, thank you." Paige remembered that Gladys must know what it felt like to sit in the hospital with your child after an appendectomy.

"You're welcome. Russell I might have enough for you,"

"That's okay, Mom. I should probably run home and shower."

"Hmm, yes, that's probably a good idea," she said as she looked him over.

"Gee thanks, why don't you just say that I look awful."

"I didn't say that, you just look a little…tired. You should try to get some rest."

"Hmm, okay." He hugged his mother then went to Paige and gave her a hug as well. It was a long hug that showed some of the closeness they had shared through this ordeal. When he pulled back he looked her in the eye. "Let me know how Lucy is when she wakes up, and call me if you need anything at all, and even if you don't I'll be back later on."

Paige opened her mouth to protest.

"Uh Uh." He held up his hand. "Don't tell me not to come. I'll see you later. In fact, unless someone else beats me to it I'll plan on bringing you lunch after while."

Paige sighed as if she was resigned to the idea. "Alright, but like your mom said, try to get some rest first."

He smiled, realizing that she was trying to take care of him too. "I will."

. . .

Once Russell was gone from the hospital room Gladys looked

at Paige and gave her a knowing smile.

Paige tried to ignore it and said, "So I guess Russell called you and told you about Lucy?"

"Yes, he called me last night on his way to your house. We've been praying for her and for you. I'm so sorry you had to go through that." She began getting out bagels from the bag and setting them on the small table in the corner.

"Thank you, it was pretty scary, but I'm so thankful Russell was there and recognized the signs so we didn't waste any time."

"I'm surprised he even remembers Jack having his appendix out, since he was so little. But I'm glad too that he was there with you."

"Yes." Paige absentmindedly twirled her ponytail, drifting away in her thoughts to the night before. She could still remember the feel of his hand on hers and the way he held her in the hallway when she cried.

"Well, listen, I don't want you to worry about a thing while you're here. Did they say how long she will stay?"

"Two to three days."

"That's alright. Everything will be just fine. I've already spoken to Peyton and I will help make sure that the kids are taken care of and that the meals are provided for."

"Oh no! The meals!"

"I know, don't worry, I promise we won't let anybody starve."

"Oh no, it's not that. Peyton had wanted to do this big freezer meal cooking plan, so we were going to do it today. We shopped Thursday and she and I were going to cook together. Now everything will probably go bad before we can get it prepared." Paige covered her face with her hands.

"Oh Paige, I'm so sorry. I'm sure that would have been fun

for you to do together. But please don't worry. We'll take care of the food, it won't go to waste."

Paige shook her head. Of course that wasn't the most important thing to be thinking about at a time like this. It was just another reminder that things don't go as planned and sometimes everything in her life seemed doomed. Then a thought occurred to her. "Wait, did you say you've already talked to Peyton this morning? I can't remember the last time she was up this early on a Saturday."

Gladys laughed, glad that she could see a little humor in the situation. "Yes, but this is a special circumstance. She said she would call you but didn't want to disturb you if you were sleeping since she knew you had been up late last night. But she and the other kids are anxious to know if they can come see Lucy. They've all been worried."

"Oh yes, of course. I'll call her right now. I just didn't think she would even be up yet. Of course they can come."

"Alright, well I won't stay, I just wanted to make sure you had something to eat. But here's my number." She handed Paige a card. "Please let me know if there's anything I can do, but try not to worry."

"Thank you, this really is above and beyond, and any help with the kids will be huge. I've been a little worried about leaving them at home alone. Peyton can handle it I'm sure, it's just that she never has before."

"I promise to check in with them, or if it would make you feel better I would be happy to even go and stay at the house for a few days, or have them come stay with me?"

"That's very generous, and I appreciate it. But Peyton probably needs to do this, to step up a little. But I'll keep that in mind just in case."

"Absolutely, call me any time day or night and I can be there in a few minutes."

"Thank you."

"You're welcome." She hugged Paige. Her eyes twinkled a little as she said, "I know you said you and Russell are just friends, but as far as I'm concerned, you're our people now. We love you and your family already, Paige, it would be our pleasure to help you."

Paige felt exhausted from the night before, from the lack of sleep and the emotional roller coaster. Maybe that was why she felt her eyes fill with tears and why she gave in to the heartfelt second hug that Gladys gave her. She pulled back and wiped her eyes, "Thank you, that means a lot," she said.

Gladys squeezed her hand and said, "Of course, sweetie. Now enjoy the coffee and bagels, they're from Russell's favorite breakfast cafe." She winked and walked to the door.

Once the door shut behind her Paige sank in the chair beside Lucy and tried to push back the tears. Lucy stirred at the sound of the door. She had slept most of the night, but she shifted often as if she was uncomfortable and more than once she had awoken crying in pain. Paige stood back up and went to the table to the coffee Gladys had brought. She stood sipping the hot beverage and staring out the window.

Why would she want to take us in and help when she barely knows us? As soon as the question popped into her mind she thought again that her own mother would have done the same thing.

I have provided for you, Paige.

The words were so clear that Paige almost looked around to see where they had come from. She had heard this voice before, but it had been years ago.

I have a plan and a purpose.

Paige turned from the window. *How can I believe that?* she thought.

There was no response.

I want to believe that everything will be alright, that this is all "for good", but how can I? Everything was supposed to work out differently. My parents weren't supposed to be gone so soon, this wasn't the life I was supposed to live.

But it is. My plan never changed.

This was too much for Paige. After her parents death she had always continued to go to church and take the kids. She put on a good face and did what she was supposed to do. But she had put distance between herself and God. She knew that if something needed to be taken care of that she would have to do it herself. God hadn't taken care of her parents, so why would he take care of her and her siblings? People kept saying that this was God's plan, but could she believe that now after everything that had happened? Even now that Russell had walked into her life and wanted to be a part of it? She wasn't sure. She felt like God had already let her down and she didn't know how she could trust Him again. Or anyone else for that matter.

She walked away from the window and picked up her phone to call Peyton, she needed to talk to her sister and make some plans for the next few days. She needed to figure out what to do for herself and her family.

Chapter 25

Paige sat on the recliner in their family room with a book open on her lap, but she wasn't reading. Lucy was lying on the couch asleep. She had been released from the hospital on Monday, but they had told them she was still in the recovery process. She was moving around and getting back to normal, but she still seemed tired that afternoon so she had watched a movie until she fell asleep. Paige sat thinking about the past few days and how things how gone. Russell had been at the hospital with her off and on Saturday and Sunday, then on Monday Gladys came to sit with Lucy for a while so that Paige could go in to the restaurant for the first day of the summer breakfast specials. Since then she felt like she had been rushing back and forth from work and the house and the hospital until Lucy came home.

Now it was Thursday and she was trying to think through what needed to be done the rest of the week at home and at work. But she couldn't focus on anything. She felt like her mind was going a million different directions and she couldn't think clearly about any one of them. She put down the book in her lap and reached for her work bag on the floor beside the chair. She reached in trying to find her clipboard, but instead her hand grabbed something else. She pulled it out and stared at the Bible that Russell had given her. She hadn't opened it, but she had put it in her bag one day and never taken it out.

She laid it on her lap and stared at the closed cover, seeing once again her name written on the front. She tried to remember where it was Russell said he read that gave him encouragement in the mornings. Psalms? That was it wasn't it? She opened up the Bible remembering something she had heard at Bible camp once about letting your Bible fall open to the middle and you would find Psalms. Sure enough, there it was right in the middle, the Bible had opened right to Psalm 46. She figured that was as good of a place as any, so she read.

"God is our refuge and strength, a very present help in trouble.

Therefore we will not fear though the earth gives way, though the mountains be moved into the heart of the sea, though its waters roar and foam, though the mountains tremble at its swellings. Selah.

There is a river whose streams make glad the city of God, the holy habitation of the Most High.

God is in the midst of her; she shall not be moved; God will help her when morning dawns.

The nations rage, the kingdoms totter; he utters his voice, the earth melts.

The Lord of hosts is with us; the God of Jacob is our fortress. Selah.

Come, behold the works of the Lord, how he has brought desolations on the earth.

He makes wars cease to the end of the earth; he breaks the bow and shatters the spear; he burns the chariots with fire.

Be still, and know that I am God.

I will be exalted among the nations, I will be exalted in the earth!

The Lord of hosts is with us; the God of Jacob is our fortress. Selah."

Paige read the words and sat as she let them sink in. It had been so long since she actually read the Bible on her own that she wasn't even sure how to do it. But those words struck a chord, "God is our refuge," "Help in trouble," "God will help her when morning dawns." Paige thought about all the things she tried to handle on her own, things for her family, taking care of the house, doing things at work. She didn't like asking people for help, then it would look like she couldn't take care of herself and her family, and she was certainly capable of that. *But God wants to help me?* she wondered. *Is that true?*

Be still, and know that I am God.

Paige looked back down at the words on the page, but she felt as if she could hear them in a small whisper. Maybe He did want to help her. But be still? She couldn't remember the last time she had been still. She was always moving, going, planning, thinking about what she should be doing right now and what she would need to do next. *Be still?* The question hung in her mind. *How can I be still when there is so much to do?*

I will help you.

There it was again, the small whisper. If she thought it had been a long time since she had read her Bible, it had been just as long or longer since she had sat and prayed. But here, in the quietness of the house, she felt an urging inside of her to reach out and to talk to someone, even if that meant someone she wasn't sure she was ready to trust.

"Well, I guess it won't hurt." She cleared her throat, and closed her eyes as she began, "Dear Lord…Jesus, I don't really know how to pray anymore. I used to pray when I was younger, maybe when I was just a child,"

Pray like that.

"These last few years haven't been easy, and I know I haven't talked to You a lot since then. Honestly, I wasn't sure I wanted to. It's been hard to think about trusting You when everyone was telling me You had a plan for my parents to die and leave us. But if it's true what this Psalm says, that we should not fear even though the earth gives way because You're with us. Are you with me God?"

I have never left you.

The words were as clear as anything she had ever heard and tears began to roll down her face.

"But why did You let this happen? Why did my parents have to die?"

My plan is perfect.

"This wasn't supposed to be my life."

Would you really want it to be different?

She stopped to think about what her life would be like if her parents hadn't died. She would have just graduated from college and would probably be starting her first job. Maybe she would be in a serious relationship, or getting married. But like Russell reminded her she would have missed out on a lot of important events for Shep and Peyton, Zoey and the twins. And she had a career right now, managing the restaurant, planning events. And her life was busy, but it was filled with purpose in caring for her family. And if her life wasn't the way it was, would she have met Russell? Was it possible that this was what God had always planned for her?

For the first time she felt like maybe she actually wanted to believe that. *But I just can't.* She thought to herself. She shook her head and closed the Bible. "I just can't believe that You planned for my parents to die and then keep trusting You with my life."

I'm still here, I will never forsake you.

The words were still there, but Paige didn't want to listen anymore, maybe someday she could begin to understand, but now now. She started to get up from her chair when her cell phone rang. She looked at the screen and saw that it was Russell. For a second she considered not answering it, but it was work hours and he might have a question about the restaurant.

"Hello?" She stood and took the call into her room so she wouldn't disturb Lucy.

"Hey," Russell sounded cheery, "What are you up to?"

"Not much." She didn't elaborate.

"Oh, well then, if you're not busy, you really should come in and get some work done, we could use you around here."

"Is something wrong? Do I need to come?" Paige felt panicked.

"No, I'm just kidding."

"Oh." Paige let the silence hang.

"Although I certainly wouldn't mind seeing you. I've missed you."

"It's only been two days." Paige wasn't about to admit the truth, that she missed him too.

"I know, but I've gotten pretty used to seeing you, so two days seems like a long time."

"I'm sure you'll survive it."

"How about I come by the house tonight?"

"Um, I don't know. I'm still trying to get everything settled around here."

"I can help, what do you need? For me to fold laundry?"

Paige could hear the laughter in his voice and smiled to herself, but didn't give in. "Very funny. No, I just have things to catch up on."

"I can bring ice cream..." he offered.

"Not tonight, Russell."

"Alright." He decided to let her be. "How's Lucy?"

"She's doing better. She still says her tummy hurts sometimes, but she's up and moving around for the most part. She's taking a nap right now. She's been asking if she can go back to day camp tomorrow. I think she's actually a little bored. But I'm still thinking one more day off and then she'll have the weekend before she goes back. I'll feel more comfortable with it by then."

"Yeah, I can understand that. But either way, I'm sure she'll be alright. You could always let her go and if she's not feeling well you could go get her, couldn't you?"

"I hadn't thought about that, but yeah I guess so."

"You're still off tomorrow?"

"Planning to be, but I might come in if she goes to school. I'm so sorry that I've missed this week with the new breakfast and everything."

"That's alright, I've been by and checked in with James throughout the week. He says you took care of everything and that you've been available on the phone if he needed you. I actually wanted to be the one to call and tell you what a success breakfast has been, but he said he already told you."

Paige could feel herself blush even on the phone. "Yes, he

said the dining room has been filled every morning. And the contest I set up for the servers is practically ridiculous since every guest is ordering the special. But we'll see how it goes as the newness wears off over the next few weeks."

"Right, but I don't think that's something we'll have to worry about. I don't want to count my chickens yet, but it's going so well, Paige. Really, you should be very proud."

Paige did feel proud. It was the first time in her job that she had seen an idea from conception to practice and it was an exciting thing to see. "Thank you," she said. "Well, I better go, Lucy will probably wake up soon and I need to see about dinner. I'll talk to you later."

"Alright, have a good night, bye Paige."

"Bye." Paige sat on the couch again, staring off once more. She started thinking about dinner options when her phone rang again. She thought it must be Russell calling back, but she didn't recognize the number. "Hello?"

"Hi Paige, it's Carrie Pierce."

"Oh hey Carrie, how are you?"

"I'm doing fine, how is everything with you? I heard about Lucy, poor thing."

"Yes, it's been kind of a rough week, but we're doing alright. Lucy is recovering well, in fact I was just telling Russell that she's begging to go back to day camp tomorrow, probably getting bored with me."

"Are you going to let her go?"

"I'm not sure, I'm still thinking about it.

"Well, I don't want to push you to send her back if she's not ready, but I have a proposition for you."

"Oh?"

"If you decide to send her, will you still be off work

tomorrow?"

"I'm not sure, I might go in."

"Okay, obviously that's fine, but let me tell you what I was thinking. Tomorrow both of my kids go to mother's day out for a few hours, and I was wondering, if you're off work, would you like to do something with me? We could do a little shopping and get lunch, you know have a little girl time. What do you think?"

Paige wasn't sure what to think. She hadn't done something like that in a very long time. "Well, that sounds fun. I'm just not sure about Lucy."

"I have an idea about that too, if you send her to camp it would be no problem, but I'm thinking that if she stays home I know a certain someone who would be willing to come and sit with her for a while. Might even be fun for her to be around someone else."

"Really?"

"Yes, I mentioned it to Gladys and she said she would be happy to do it. She's free all morning."

"Oh, wow. That's really nice of both of you."

"Oh not really, it's a little selfish actually. I just asked Gladys so we could spend some time together. I haven't had girl time in forever."

Paige felt certain that she had other friends she could spend this time with, but she didn't want to be rude and say no when they had already made all the arrangements. "Okay, I can do that. And I guess we could just wait and see if Lucy goes or stays home. Would that be alright?"

"Absolutely! I'll tell Gladys to be on standby, but either way, how about I pick you up about 9:15?"

"Sounds good."

"Great! I'll see you tomorrow then!"

"Alright, thanks." Paige hung up and felt overwhelmed at the thought of the next day. Instead of thinking about it any longer she finally got up and moved around the house to try to get some things done. She laughed when she turned from the chair and saw the pile of laundry in the floor that needed to be folded. *Maybe I should have let him come after all.*

. . .

Russell hung up from talking to Paige and sat in the quiet for a few minutes. He didn't know why, but he could tell from her voice that she was pushing him away again. He leaned back in his chair and closed his eyes, "Lord, why? Why does she keep doing this? Just when we start to get on the right track it's like she slams on the brakes...no like she throws the car in reverse. What am I supposed to do?"

Follow me.

"I do want to follow You, show me how. Show me what to do.

I've already shown you.

"You just want me to keep pursuing her?"

Don't give up, press on.

"Okay, Lord, I guess."

She needs to know that you're never going away.

Those words hit Russell hard. He realized that he didn't want to go away. Not now, and not at any time in the future. In following the call that God gave him and just trying to get to know Paige and help her, she had found her way into his heart. And he knew now that she would never leave. She needed to know that he wasn't going away because he never was.

Now he had to convince her of that. Already a plan was forming in his mind. He wanted to continue to pray about it, but he knew that the Lord was directing his every step.

Chapter 26

P aige opened the door Friday morning to find Gladys and Carrie had arrived together. "Good morning," she said.

"Good morning." Gladys hugged her as she came into the house. Carrie stepped in behind her and closed the door.

"Lucy is in the living room. I was surprised that she wanted to stay home, but when I told her you would come stay with her she lost interest in going to day camp."

"I'm so glad, we'll have some fun." Gladys went on through to see the little girl.

"Can I get you anything? Coffee or water? Have you eaten?" Paige asked Carrie.

"No thanks, and yes, I have. I'm all good to go if you are?"

"Sure. Let me just tell Lucy I'm going and I'll grab my purse." She walked into the living room and Lucy and Gladys were already chatting away. Gladys was saying something about a surprise in her bag. "Lu, I'm about to head out."

"Okay, see you later," Lucy called out.

"You mind Mrs. Pierce, alright?"

"I will."

"We'll be fine, Paige. Have a good time. Try to relax." She smiled.

Paige smiled back. She wanted to tell her that she would, but she wasn't quite sure. "Ready?" she asked Carrie.

"Yes! Let's go!" They walked down the sidewalk together and climbed into Carrie's car, a small SUV. "Excuse the mess, I mostly blame my kids."

"Oh it's nothing I'm not used to," Paige said.

"Oh yes, I'm sure you have your share of mess with that many. I don't know how you do it. I'm still figuring out how to handle two."

Paige gave a short laugh. "Most of the time you just do what you've gotta do."

"I guess that's true, well actually yeah, I know it is. Going from one to two was a challenge, but we just made it work. So I guess it's the same with more."

"Yeah."

"So let's talk about what we're going to do." Carrie couldn't hide the excitement in her voice.

"Okay, whatever you want to do is fine."

Carrie pulled into the parking lot of a shopping center and put the car in park before answering. She turned and faced Paige. "Okay, Paige, whatever I want to do? Really?"

Paige felt nervous all of the sudden. What could she possibly want to do? "Umm, yeah, I think so."

"Because I kind of have an idea, but I don't know if you're going to be up for it."

"Hmm, now you're scaring me."

"Oh it's nothing scary, it will be fun. But I just want you to know, we might just be running right past casual acquaintance and be becoming close friends in the next few hours."

Paige smiled. "Alright, what did you have in mind?"

"First I want to take you to the salon, I've called ahead and we can get our nails done, or...."

"Or....what?" Paige's eyes showed her concern.

"Or, if you're up for it, they have time for you to have a hair cut."

"A haircut?"

"Yes, and Paige, oh please hear me out. I think your hair is lovely, it's so long and pretty. But how long has it been since you've done something different with it? You know, just for fun."

"I don't know, I guess it has been a while. I haven't really made time for it, I guess."

"Then why not make time for it today? I mean really, if you don't want to, it's completely fine. I really do think your hair is so pretty, but if it would be nice for you to have it cut there's time for it today."

"Okay." Paige did think it would be nice, but she wasn't sure how much services at the spa would cost, so she wasn't sure if she should commit to it.

As if she could read her mind, Carrie spoke again, "And there's one more thing. I know you're going to say no, that you can't accept it and you're going to put up a fight, so go ahead and get that out of your system, but Gladys and Jim gave me money to spend today. It's for us to have a fun day, and they made me promise I wouldn't come home with a penny of it."

Paige shook her head. "Oh no, they didn't need to do that."

"I know they didn't, but that's the kind of people they are.

Paige, listen to me. You're a wonderful person. You're strong and independent and you work hard to take care of your family. But who takes care of you?"

Paige didn't have a response.

"Let me...Gladys and Jim, take care of you a little bit today. It will be so much fun for me, and it gives them so much joy to give you this gift. So just try to take it and accept it. Do you think you can do that?"

Paige gave a wry smile. "Do I have a choice?"

Carrie smiled. "Nope! Let's go!" She put the car back in gear and chatted away as they drove a few more minutes to the salon.

Paige sat quietly thinking about her hair and what she might be brave enough to do.

Forty-five minutes later Paige sat in the chair staring at herself in the mirror. After looking at some pictures with Carrie and talking it over with the stylist, they all agreed on the style she picked. Now she saw herself, her hair was cut just to her shoulders with soft layers framing her face in the front and enough shorter layers in the back to give her hair definition and movement. She ran her fingers through the locks and couldn't believe how much lighter it felt. "I love it." She smiled. "I feel like it's just been long and boring for so long, and now it's actually a cut with style. I really, really love it." She turned and saw Carrie watching her with a giant smile.

"I love it too." Carrie beamed. "You look amazing."

"Thanks. Thank you so much for talking me into this!"

"You're welcome, I'm so glad, it looks so great. But I think I know somebody who's going to like it even more than I do."

Paige blushed and rolled her eyes. "I can't imagine who

you're talking about."

"Oh come on, you know he's not going to be able to take his eyes off of you. You guys need to go on a date tonight just to show off the new look."

"Hmm, yeah, we'll see."

"Alright, come on, let's get out of here and off to our next adventure."

"What? I thought this was the adventure. What else do you have planned?"

Carrie's eyes twinkled. "I told you, Jim and Gladys made me promise not to come back with a penny, so we've got some shopping to do." She nearly dragged Paige out of the chair and out the door after paying for their salon trip. Paige felt like this day was a whirlwind that was only beginning.

At the mall Carrie was like a professional, moving them from store to store and searching out the best sales. Paige tried on jeans, dresses, tops, shoes, even a few pieces of jewelry, and Carrie even found time for her to sit at the makeup counter and try out new beauty products. She felt that the Pierces must have been overly generous when she looked at her shopping bags. Carrie had prodded and pushed along the way, reminding her about items of clothing she owned that were worn or that didn't fit properly. She left the mall with two pairs of jeans that fit better than any pants she had worn in years, a pair of shorts, one skirt, three new tops, two dresses, a pair of shoes and a few beauty products.

"This really is too much," she tried to argue with Carrie.

"Paige, when was the last time you shopped and bought new clothes for yourself?"

"I'm not really sure."

"This is stuff you really need."

"I know, but I could pay for some of it."

"Nope, today is a gift. You just have to accept it. Now, we still have time for a quick lunch before I need to get back to pick up the kids."

"Okay, but can I pay for my own lunch?"

"Nope." Carrie smiled.

"But surely we've spent all the money that they gave you by now." Paige was worried that Carrie would really be committed to spending the entire amount even if that meant they kept going.

"Oh, well, yes, we have, don't worry about that. Lunch is my treat." Carrie turned and walked quickly away from Paige before she could argue. "Come on, we'll put this stuff in the car and then we can go to this great little cafe close by."

Paige realized she had given up at this point so she followed after her and hurried to the car. In a short few minutes they had taken care of the bags of clothes and were seated at a booth in the nearby cafe. The waiter was bringing their sweet teas and left them alone to look over the menu. It was a lovely place and the options looked delicious for salads, sandwiches or soups.

"My favorite is the chicken salad," Carrie said as she pointed it out on the menu. "But their soups are really good too. In fact I think I'll have a half chicken salad and a half order of wild rice soup. You can split it so you get both."

"That sounds great," said Paige. "You talked me into it, I think I'll have the same thing."

Carrie got the waiter's attention and placed the order. Once he was gone she settled back into her seat, she seemed comfortable, but intent. "So Paige, I think we've talked about your family, and your work, and I've even asked you about your relationship with my favorite brother-in-law, so we've covered most of the basics. But the one thing I haven't asked you about is your relationship with Jesus. What's that like?"

Paige was surprised by this question, although she felt as if maybe she shouldn't be. She was fighting it, but she knew that God was working on her just the same. "That's a good question. Honestly, I don't know. I mean, I've been going to church my whole life, and at times I would say I had a good relationship with God, you know being the good girl. But ever since my parents died I guess it's just been distant. We still go to church, I want the kids to grow up there too, but it's just hard to trust Him anymore."

"I can understand that, and I appreciate that you can be honest about it. You've been through something really hard, something that changed your life forever, it's not easy to just keep going on as if life is perfect and there's no pain and sadness in the world. But a lot of people would just put up a front and say 'I know God's in control' and paste on a smile. I'm glad that you can say how you really feel."

"Yeah, I guess."

"Have you told him that?"

"Who?"

"God, have you told Him that it's hard for you to trust Him?"

"Umm, kind of. Not really straight out, I guess."

"You should tell him. Pray and tell Him that you find it hard to trust Him, and ask Him to give you the faith to believe in Him. And I promise you, if you really want it and ask Him, He will give you the strength to trust Him."

Paige thought about that as the waiter came back and delivered their food.

"Can we pray before we eat?" Carrie asked.

"Oh sure, go ahead."

"Lord Jesus, thank you for this food that you have provided. Thank you for the time we've had together today and bless our conversation here. And Lord, please help Paige to see You and believe in You, show her how to trust You. Amen."

They started eating and fell silent for a few moments.

"You know, Paige, I think sometimes it's hard to trust God because we only see this one little part of his plan. Our lives are a part of a much bigger story, from the beginning of time until the end of time, everything works together to fulfill his purpose. I know it's hard to see, but sometimes He just wants us to walk with Him and get through the tough parts so that He can show us the gifts that He has in store."

"Yeah. Russell said something like that, like I should think about what I have because my parents are gone."

"Exactly, he's right. And you know, so many people if they were in your situation wouldn't have handled it as well as you have. Think about what would have happened if you were younger, or if you had decided you couldn't take on the responsibility and your siblings got taken away and separated into foster homes?"

Paige shivered. "I don't even want to think about that."

"I know, it sounds so sad. But just think about that, yes it was horrible that they died, but what if the timing of it was the only thing that kept your younger siblings all together? You were old enough to be their guardian. You found the job at the club that allowed you to work and take care of them. Even those details worked out in his plan."

"I've never thought about that."

"I know, I don't want to make you think of the worst possibilities, but I just think that as sad as it was, it still worked out to the best it could have." Carrie paused and sipped her tea. "Paige, I can't sit here today and convince you to trust God, that's something that has to happen in your heart. But if you believe in Jesus, and believe that God sent his son to die on the cross for our sins so that we could be forgiven, that's pretty crazy to believe if you think about it right?"

"Yeah, I guess it is."

"Right, but if you do believe that then it's not that much of a stretch to believe that God has a plan and is in control of all the details, even when bad things happen. It was a terribly sad thing for His son to die, and He allowed that for our good. So maybe in the grand scheme of things, it's for good that you are where you are. Your parents were believers right?"

"Yes." Paige's eyes were tearing up.

"Then they are in a much better place than we are. We should be jealous that they already got to meet Jesus! They aren't hurting or toiling in life, they are in heaven, and you'll see them again one day."

"Yes, I know." Paige sniffled.

"I don't want to badger you, but will you think about what I've said?"

Paige nodded to assure Carrie that she would.

"Okay, there's one more thing I need to tell you. I know I told you that when I met Jack I wasn't looking for a relationship, and I fought it for a while, right?"

"Yes."

"Well, I don't want you to think I'm pressuring you into a relationship with Russell, but there's something I didn't tell you. I didn't lose my parents in the way you did, they're still living, but I lost them a long time ago. I wasn't brought up in a loving, Christian family like you were and like my husband.

My mom was a socialite who cared more about her appearance with people than she did her kids or our home, and my dad was both a workaholic and an alcoholic who would never admit it. My dad verbally abused my mom, me, and my sister constantly, and even though I can't say for sure, I think he physically abused my mother too. We were well off, so they planned and paid for my education, but once I was out of the house they didn't miss me, didn't call or worry about me. They were done. And since Jack and I were married we've had little contact. My parents are still legally married, to keep up appearances, but they're separated in every way that matters."

"I'm so sorry," Paige said.

"Thank you. It was difficult growing up, and for so long I wished they cared about me. And then I met the Pierce family, and at first I was so jealous. How come Jack had this wonderful, happy family that seemed perfect, and I had...well my family? It didn't seem fair. I had started going to church when I started college, it was something new for me, and I kept hearing how God was like a father. But I didn't want something to do with a God who was like a father, because my father was not good. And if God could give Jack this family and me that family, I didn't know if I wanted a God who would do that either. But the more I was around Jim and Gladys, the more I wanted a God who was a father like Jim was. He was loving and supportive, he spoke kindly to his wife and kids, and he provided for them. And I knew that's what God was like. And once Jack and I were together, I became part of their family too. They took me in without any questions, and they loved me like I was their own. Suddenly, I realized it. I had grown up in a family that I wasn't proud of, but God had always planned to give me a wonderful, loving family, and it was the Pierces."

Paige sniffled again. "That's so sweet."

"Today I've called them Jim and Gladys around you so that you knew who I was talking about, but to me one of the greatest gifts in the world is to actually call them Mom and Dad."

Paige swallowed hard to push back the tears. She knew that she would think about all that Carrie had said. She realized that she was often so preoccupied with her family and their struggles that she didn't take time to realize that other people had struggles of their own. She didn't want to be selfish.

"I know it's hard to trust God when it doesn't seem like He has given you the best," Carrie said. "But we just have to keep walking along with Him and letting Him show us his plan a little bit at a time. And most of the time we learn that the real best is yet to come."

Chapter 27

Paige managed to fill the weekend with activity and avoid for a little while thinking about all the things going on in her life. Saturday, she and Peyton spent the morning in the kitchen preparing the freezer meals that they had planned. Gladys had helped Peyton the week before by freezing a lot of the items ahead of time so they wouldn't spoil and writing instructions for modifying the recipes.

Russell had called a couple of times, but she didn't feel ready to talk to him. She felt like she needed to process everything that was happening.

On Sunday morning, she hurried the kids in at the last minute before the service started and took a seat in the back. She could see Russell down front with his parents, but he was facing the front and didn't see her. After the music started she could see him glance around as if he was looking for her.

The pastor approached the stage and asked everyone to open to 1st Thessalonians. "Today is our last Sunday in 1st Thessalonians," Owen said. "Please stand with me as we read chapter five, starting in verse 16." He paused while the congregation stood, then he began, "Rejoice always, pray without ceasing, give thanks in all circumstances; for this is the will of God in Christ Jesus for you. Do not quench the Spirit. Do not despise prophecies, but test everything; hold fast to what is good. Abstain from every form of evil. Now may the God of peace himself sanctify you completely, and may your whole spirit and soul and body be kept blameless at the coming of our Lord Jesus Christ. He who calls you is faithful; he will surely do it." He motioned for the congregation to be seated.

"Paul has just finished giving instructions to the Thessalonians and he is closing out his letter to them. Of course, Paul doesn't know whether he will ever see them again or even if he will write another letter to them - although we already know that he does, because we have Thessalonians part 2." The pastor smiled. "But as far as he knows, this may be the last thing he is able to say to them, so he is leaving them with a challenge and a bit of encouragement." Pastor Reed counted on his fingers as he spoke, "Rejoice always, pray without ceasing, give thanks in all circumstances. Why? Because this - this life that you're living, the circumstance that you're in, the things that you're going through - this is the will of God in Christ Jesus for you. Now it doesn't say that it's always sunshine and rainbows, and it doesn't say that everything in your life will make you happy. But it says we can rejoice because we are in the will of God. And we can rejoice because we have hope in Jesus. We can give thanks to Him in all circumstances because He is God and He loves us. And how do we really do this? Pray without ceasing. Talk to God. Tell Him how you feel, ask Him for His help. Ask Him what He wants you to do. This is His will for you, and when you pray without ceasing, you will walk with Him in a way that you can see that and give thanks in all circumstances."

Pastor Reed continued to speak, but Paige could barely hear. She brushed at her eyes before a tear had the chance to spill onto her cheek. *I'm not ready to rejoice* she thought to herself. *I don't like the way I feel and I don't want to give thanks in my circumstances.* Her heart stirred at the idea of talking to The Lord and telling Him how she felt, but she knew she couldn't do it here and now because the tears would come too easily. She heard the pastor as he was wrapping up the sermon, she had been so engrossed in her thoughts that she hadn't realized how the time had passed.

He invited everyone to join him as he closed with the prayer straight from the verses, "Now may the God of peace Himself sanctify you completely, and may your whole spirit and soul and body be kept blameless at the coming of our Lord Jesus Christ. He who calls you is faithful, He will surely do it."

After the final prayer, Paige saw Russell turn around and catch a glimpse of her. He waved, but she pretended not to see and begged the kids to hurry up and get to the car. They rushed out and she got them all loaded and in the car and was pulling out of the parking lot when she saw Russell emerge from the front door looking for her. She kept going and drove away.

Once they were home, Paige made sandwiches for everyone and the younger kids were begging to watch a movie, so she let them sit in front of the TV while they ate. Once they were settled she left them and went to her own room. Behind the closed door she immediately fell onto the bed and let the tears come. She let herself cry for a few minutes with no interruption.

Once she caught her breath she rolled over and stared at the ceiling. "Okay, Lord, I know You're working on me. I know you have something for me. You're using everyone and everything in my life to point me back to You. So here I am, ready to talk. But I'm scared. I'm scared that if I trust You, You will let me down. If I follow You, then I'm scared you'll take me somewhere that I don't want to go. Everybody keeps telling me that You have a plan, and You're in control, but I'm not sure I like it. But I can't get away from You, You're here, You're everywhere and I know You're real. I still believe in you, that you created everything and that you sent Jesus to die."

Then why can't you trust me with this?

Paige didn't have an answer. "I don't know." She buried her face. "I don't know. My whole life, everything was planned out, and my parents took care of us. I guess when I trusted You then there wasn't much to worry about. But now, everything depends on me, I have to take care of everyone."

But I will take care of you.

"Will You? How can I trust You?"

Ask and it shall be given to you.

"Lord, I think that I want to trust You, but I really don't know how. Will You give me the faith I need to believe?" She didn't hear an answer or feel like she was immediately better, but as she spoke those words she felt as if some of the walls around her heart began to crumble. For the first time in a long time she felt like she was beginning to open up to a life that had been locked away for so long.

Then she heard the kids arguing over the remote and she was reminded of the loss that would always be present. She wasn't always free to have a quiet afternoon in her room because of the people who were missing from her life. She tried to tell herself to take it in stride and keep walking towards the Lord. Even in the midst of this sister and mom role she was beginning to see that He was the one she needed to lean on.

Chapter 28

Russell stood just outside the restaurant door. It was Monday morning and breakfast was over and the staff had some time before preparing for lunch. He hadn't tried to call Paige on Sunday after he saw her leave church. He knew she had seen him, but he had stayed away. He wasn't sure what was going on. He had purposefully stayed out of the kitchen this morning, so he hadn't seen her yet. He had spent a lot of time over the weekend praying for her and thinking through what God had said to him. He knew what he wanted to do and he would follow God's leading. But he couldn't plan how she would react to him, and that's what worried him. He took a deep breath and opened the door.

He found Paige in the kitchen. When he walked in her back was to him and she was leaned over her desk writing on one of her clipboards. "Hey," he said.

She turned around. "Oh hey, hang on a sec." She finished making her note, then he could see her take a deep breath before turning around. "Hey, how are you?"

He took her in, her hair was down for only the second time that he had ever seen, plus he could tell that the clothes she wore were new. "Wow, you look nice, I like your hair."

"Thanks." She touched the end of her hair. "I'm still getting used to it."

"I like it, especially if it means you'll be wearing it down more often. You're so pretty with your hair down."

She blushed.

"So you're in between breakfast and lunch now, right?"

"Yeah, pretty much."

"Okay, good. Come take a walk with me?"

"A walk?"

"Yeah, outside, let's take a walk."

"Oh, I don't know, I might get in trouble with the boss." She smiled.

"That's alright, I checked with him and told him it was fine, he agreed with me."

"Oh alright, I guess I can spare a few minutes. You know I'm still catching up from last week."

"I know, come on." He ushered her out of the kitchen through the back door. They talked about work as they walked towards the wooded trail that wound around the golf course. "How was the breakfast crowd this morning?"

Paige beamed. "Great! It has been such a success so far! I walked around checking on tables and everyone was saying how good the food was and how they hope we keep doing breakfast like this."

"Sounds like it really will stick around 'by popular demand' after all."

"I hope so, we'll still have to see how it goes for a little while longer."

"Yeah, I'm just glad it's going well."

"Me too." They had reached the edge of the trail and the shade was a welcome relief from the hot June sun.

"I missed you last week. It was so strange to not see you every day." Russell fell in step beside her and casually reached for her hand as they walked. He was glad she didn't pull away as he wrapped his fingers around hers.

"Yes, it was strange. I guess I've gotten used to it."

"And you missed me too...?" he sounded hopeful.

She laughed. "Yes, I guess so."

"You guess so? I guess I'll take that." He let the silence hang before he spoke again. "Paige, I'm really very sorry for what happened to Lucy, although I know she's alright. I wouldn't have wished for it to happen, but I can't say I'm sorry that we got to spend the time together and that I was there with you."

Paige looked away. "I appreciate all your help, you know I hate to think about how it might have gone if you hadn't been there and suggested we go on to the hospital."

"I know, but everything is alright." He rubbed his thumb gently over hers. "It was all in the hands of God and He took care of her."

"Yes, He did."

"But I want you to know something." He stopped her and turned to face her. He took her other hand so they were standing face to face with her hands in his. "Paige, I want to be there for you. For all of those life experiences, for the fun times like at the Memorial Day party and at the park, and for the scary ones like Lucy's surgery, and everything in between. I want to be there and be a part of your life."

She shifted her feet and tried to look away, but he held her gaze.

"And I want to be there for your family too. For Lucy when she needs to be carried, because she's still a little girl but too big for you to carry, and for Joe to teach him to swing a baseball bat or a golf club. I want to help Peyton when she moves into her college dorm, and I want to be the one that Shep calls late at night because he locked his keys in his car."

Paige's eyes filled with tears, but she didn't wipe them away.

"Paige," Russell looked into her eyes and spoke directly to her heart, "It's not just about your family. You are the most beautiful woman I've ever met, inside and out. You care about people and you're kind to everyone you meet. I love to hear you laugh and I love the way your eyes light up when you're talking about something you are interested in. And I think it's cute when you bite your lip when you're not sure what to say next. I just get excited about the possibility of spending time with you or talking to you and I never want that to go away. I want you, Paige. I want to be with you, always."

She stared back into his eyes and felt the nearness of him. They were so close she felt like he could hear her heart pounding, she could feel the warmth of him.

He pulled her hand to his chest. "When I first met you I wanted to be your friend, to help you if I could, but now I care so much for you. You've made your place here in my heart. And I know that will never go away. I want to be there and take care of you always." His eyes never left hers. He only paused a moment to see that she had heard him before he slowly lowered his head until their lips met. He kissed her gently and briefly.

She barely moved, like she was afraid that the moment would burst if she flinched.

He pulled back and looked her full in the face, searching her eyes for her feelings. "Can you let me do that?"

For a full ten seconds it seemed like she wanted to say yes, to let him be in her life and not leave. But then she closed her eyes and when she opened them again she looked at him and said simply, "No."

"What?" The shock showed in his voice and on his face.

She realized he was still holding her hands. She dropped them and stepped backwards away from him. "No, I can't. I can't do this."

"Paige, what do you mean?"

"Stop, Russell. Just stop." She held up her hand to keep him back. "You can't talk like that, we can't talk like that. I'm sorry that I've let you go down this road, but there is no us. There is no future. There can't be."

Russell felt desperate. "Why not?"

"Because it won't work." She wiped her tears and turned to walk away.

He stepped in front of her. "Why not? Because of the kids? That's just an excuse. I love the kids. I love all of your family, I want to help you take care of them. Let me do that."

"But what happens when you're gone?" She started to cry harder.

"I'm not going anywhere. I'm not going away, this is what I'm trying to tell you. Paige, I want the future, I want forever with you. I won't leave you."

Her body shook with sobs and she took a gasping breath and it seemed to take everything in her as she nearly yelled, "But what if you die?"

The full weight of her sorrow hit Russell in the chest, he felt as if his heart stopped beating. He couldn't believe he had missed this, but she was actually pushing him away because she was afraid to lose him. He was too shocked to speak. Sadness filled him. He reached out and pulled her to himself, squeezing her tight as she cried. He wanted to promise her that that wouldn't happen, that she would never go through another loss like she experienced before, but he couldn't do that. He didn't know the future. He could do his best, but he couldn't make that promise.

She began to breathe more slowly and calm down. She pushed back and wiped her face. "I have to go," she said. "Please don't follow me."

She walked away leaving Russell standing on the trail alone and lost. He wanted to chase after her, but he let her go. He knew he couldn't convince her, and he didn't want to beg her. He knew she needed time, so he would give that to her. But he couldn't stop the hurt he felt. Hurt that she didn't immediately agree, and hurt that he had been so bold and she ran away. But more than anything, he was hurt that she had been through so much pain and sadness and he couldn't take it away.

He sank to his knees in the middle of the trail, and prayed out loud. "Lord, I know You have brought me here, You have led me to this moment for a reason. I see the hurt, I see her sadness, and I know that I can't take it away. But Lord, You can heal her. You alone can help her. You can give her joy that comes in the morning and new mercies everyday. Draw her to Yourself, let her see that You have a life for her. Teach her to walk in it and follow You. And Lord, if it's Your will, lead her back to me. I want to be with her forever. That's a desire you have placed in my heart. Please Lord, bring her back. Please."

Chapter 29

Russell sat at The Depot waiting for his dad. It was Thursday afternoon and he still hadn't spoken to Paige since their walk. All he had done was pray for her. He had wanted to give her some space and let her reach out to him when she was ready. But now he felt like the days were dragging on and he needed to do something. He wanted to get his dad's advice.

Jim walked in and spotted his son right away. Russell had already gotten coffee for the two of them and had it sitting at the table, he didn't want to waste time. "Hey, Dad."

"Hey Russ, how is everything?"

"Not very good actually."

"Paige?"

"Yes."

"I thought so, tell me what's going on."

Russell relayed the story. Of course, Jim already knew about their date and the emergency with Lucy, and about Paige's parents. He filled in all the other details ending with the walk on the trail and Paige running away.

"I haven't talked to her since then."

"Hmm." Jim leaned back in his seat as if he was contemplating what to say.

"Tell me what to do, Dad. I'm lost."

"It does seem like a very difficult situation. She obviously enjoys your friendship and she has let you in a little bit. But if she's so afraid that she'll lose you I can see why it would be hard to let you get close."

"I know. Do you think I should back off? Just try to go back and be her friend?"

"Wouldn't that just be like starting over?"

"Yeah, I guess so. But if she would let me be her friend, then maybe…" Russell trailed off.

"She's already let you be her friend, she seemed comfortable with that. So if you want to be her friend, then I say yes, go back and just be her friend. But if you want to be more then I think you did the right thing by being upfront about it."

"So now what?"

"You wait."

"Wait?"

"You believe the Lord told you to pursue her right?"

"Yes."

"And that He led you to tell her you want a future with her, right?"

"Yes."

"Then He will work it out."

"…Okay."

"But it might just be in His timing. He might be using this to do a work in her life, so you need to give Him time to do that. And allow Him to work on you in the meantime too."

"Hmm. Wait. Okay. Is that really the best advice you have?"

Jim laughed. "I'm afraid so. Listening to you I think you've done alright for yourself. I'm really proud of you, you know?"

"Really?"

"I am. When you came back here I saw you as this new independent person, you had become used to living on your own schedule and doing things your own way and for yourself. I could tell you didn't want to be considered the little brother anymore and were trying to make a name for yourself. But when God introduced you to Paige he changed you. You wanted to do something for someone else, you wanted to help her, and you saw the way she had sacrificed for her family. I think that had a real effect on you. You're not the same person who moved here even a couple of months ago. He has done something in you and I believe He's doing something in her too. And when you're both ready then you will be powerful together for His purpose."

"Thanks Dad. That really means the world to me."

"Just keep praying for her, and listening to His voice for what you should do next."

Russell took those words to heart, and agreed that he would keep praying. Something he hadn't stopped doing since he met her.

. . .

Paige sat in the comfortable chair in the empty bedroom upstairs. It had been her mother's chair where she had done her morning prayer time and where she could often be found writing "to do" lists or notes to her children. The empty room had been Zoey's, but she had moved into the room with Peyton when Paige moved to the master bedroom. One day Paige had cried over seeing the empty chair in the living room every day and so they moved it to the room upstairs. Now she had pulled it over next to the window and sat in the room with the door shut. The house was quiet since all the kids were at day camp or their own activities. It was Thursday and since she had worked extra hours the night before, she left work right after lunch. Russell hadn't been in for lunch all week and the days seemed longer somehow. There were things she could get done around the house, but instead of doing them she sat quietly in the chair. In the floor next to her was the Bible Russell had given her. Something about going to sit in her mother's prayer chair had made her bring it with her. So far she had just been thinking about everything that was going on. She hadn't seen Russell most of the week, but if she was honest with herself she had to admit she hadn't stopped thinking about him. She had tried to take some time to process things, but work had been busy and then the kids had been crazy at home, so she just kept putting it off. Now in the quiet it was all she could think about.

Did I mess up? she wondered. *Should I have never gone out with him?* An even quieter whisper in her heart wondered if she had actually messed up when she ran away from him.

She picked up the Bible from the floor and just like before she let it open to the Psalms. She wasn't sure what she was hoping to find, but she started reading the chapter that she came to, Psalm 9.

"The Lord is a stronghold for the oppressed, a stronghold in times of trouble. And those who know Your name put their trust in You, for You, O Lord, have not forsaken those who seek You."

Paige gave a long tired sigh. She knew it was time to make a decision. She felt tired and the weight of trying to be in control and keep everything perfect was weighing heavily on her. She was ready to give up that responsibility. "Lord Jesus," she spoke barely above a whisper, "I want to put my trust in You. I think I finally know that if I do that you won't forsake me. You're the only thing I can trust to stay forever. Will you always be with me?"

I will never leave you.

"Lord, I asked Jesus to forgive my sins when I was a little girl, but I don't think I knew what walking with You was really like. It's been a hard time, and I've tried to do everything by myself. But I'm tired, exhausted actually. I know that I can't do this on my own. Jesus, I give You my life. Will You be my Lord and Savior? I know Your word already says that You will. Thank You for forgiving me of my sins, help me to live and walk with You."

Open your heart.

"Open my heart?"

Russell.

It was as if his name had been shouted.

The tears came fresh. "Open my heart to Russell?" But what if something happens? What if he leaves or dies?"

Trust me.

A peace began to wash over her and for the first time since her parents' death she felt like she could breathe. It was then that Paige realized that trusting meant not worrying. If she really trusted God then she didn't have to worry. She didn't have to worry about the kids all the time, and she didn't have to worry that something would happen to Russell. She could trust that things would be alright. And even if something happened she had to trust that The Lord would take care of her anyway.

She sat quietly, but then a laugh started in her throat. It grew and grew until she laughed out loud. She laughed and laughed until her stomach hurt. She felt giddy with excitement and joy. Because if she could trust God with her life and her siblings, then she could trust God with Russell. And that would mean one very important thing.

She could finally admit to Russell how she felt about him without fear.

Chapter 30

I t was Friday night and Russell could hardly contain himself he was so excited. But at the same time he was more nervous than he had ever been in his life. Paige had called and said she wanted to see him, that she wanted to talk. She wouldn't say more on the phone, but said she wanted to talk in person. He told her he would be at her house and pick her up that night. He pulled in the driveway and looked at his watch. He was five minutes early. He thought about how much had happened in the two weeks since he had been there to pick her up for their date. He hoped this night would end differently than that one had. He decided he couldn't wait even five more minutes.

When he got to the door Paige answered before he even had a chance to knock. He stood there with his hand raised as she appeared. She laughed. "Sorry, I was kind of watching for you to get here."

"Oh good. Then I'm glad I didn't sit in my car waiting five minutes for it to be the right time."

"Me too." She smiled. "Everybody's already settled so we're good to go." She stepped out and pulled the door shut behind her.

Russell was surprised at her. She looked lovely as always, but she looked different somehow. She wore her hair down, and she had on a knee-length khaki colored skirt and a pink sleeveless top. She looked young and carefree. That was different. He hoped this was a good sign and not just something he was imagining because he wanted tonight to go well.

As they pulled away she asked where they were going. "Why don't we just see when we get there?"

"Sounds good, but I really want to talk."

"I know, we will."

"In fact, you know the talk we were having the other day? I would kind of just like to start over."

Russell's heart soared at those words. He was glad he had prayed about where they should go and that God had led him so perfectly. "That sounds good to me." He winked at her.

A few minutes later Russell pulled into the parking lot of the club.

Paige smiled when she saw where they were headed. Russell stepped out and walked around to her side. He opened her door and she stepped out too. He gave her a quick hug, then he took her hand and led her towards the trail.

It was dusk and not too dark yet, but there were fireflies in the trees along the path and it made the night seem to sparkle. When they approached the spot where they had been earlier in the week, Russell spoke. "Okay, so here we are. Now let's see, how did it go? Paige, I want you to know something, I want to be there for you, for everything. For forever."

She giggled as he tried to recreate the moment. "You don't have to actually say the exact same thing."

"I can try. Paige, I love your family. I want to help you, I want to be there for you and for your family. I care about you so much."

Paige was still giggling.

He stopped and turned a little more serious. "If I'm saying all this, is there a hope that your response is going to be different this time?"

"Yes, I think so. In fact, let me talk a little bit now."

"Alright." Russell gave her his full attention.

"I think by now you know me pretty well, which was something I was trying very hard to avoid. I didn't want to be friends with you or for you to work your way into my heart. But despite all my best efforts you have. You've made me care for you, and you've made me feel like the most special girl in the world that you care for me despite everything in my life. But I was afraid. I didn't want to let you get close if it meant that I might get hurt by losing you. I know it seems a little silly, but I've lost people close to me and I didn't think I could go through that again." She paused and let out a big breath before continuing. "But God has really been working on me. He's used you, and my sister, and your mom and your sister-in-law to show me that it's really time for me to open up my heart and trust Him. And I finally realized that if I want to live life I really do have to trust Him, and if I trust Him it means I have to stop worrying so much and be willing to risk something to gain something." She paused and then went on, "So I can finally admit it to myself and I can tell you that you've found a place in my heart too. You always take the time to listen to me and share with me, and I love watching you around the little kids. You are funny and smart and obviously you are very determined when you set your mind on something." She smiled. "But more than any of that You have made sure to point me to Jesus. You knew that I needed to trust Him when I didn't even know. I will always be grateful for that. And I know that you're not going anywhere." She took a deep breath. "Okay, so this is the part where you ask me again if I can let you be in my life."

Russell's smile lit up his face. "Okay." He cleared his throat. "I think that went something like this." He took her in his arms like before, then he leaned his head down and kissed her. Fuller and longer than before. Finally Russell leaned back and looked in her eyes. "Can you let me be a part of your life and take care of you?"

She beamed. "Yes, I can." He kissed her again, and this time he put his arms around her waist and lifted her into the air as he spun in a circle.

"I'm so glad to hear that." He set her back down on her feet and took both of her hands in his. "Paige Kelly, ever since I saw you in that church gym and asked if I could help you get Shep and you said 'No thanks, I can handle it', all I've wanted to do is take care of you."

"I can't believe you even remember that. Is that really what I said?" Paige took one hand away and covered her face.

He pulled her hand back. "Of course I remember it, you are unforgettable." She blushed. "Paige, I'm so thankful for you to trust God with your life and future, that is the most important thing in the world to me. And I'm grateful for the way it changed our relationship. I want you to know this. I love you, Paige."

Tears filled her eyes. "I love you too, Russell."

She gasped as he knelt down on one knee. "I can't promise that everything will be perfect, and I can't promise that nothing will happen to me. But I can promise you that every day that I'm alive, I will love you, provide for you and take care of you. If you'll just let me." He reached into his pocket and pulled out a small box. When he opened it she saw a beautiful solitaire diamond ring. "Will you marry me?"

This was more than Paige could bear. She covered her face with her hands as the tears rolled down her cheeks. She took a deep breath and shouted, "Yes! Yes of course I will!"

He stood and hugged her tightly. He took her hand and placed the ring on her finger, then he took her face in his hands and kissed her.

When they finally pulled away she was breathless. "Oh my goodness!" Paige said. "Is this really happening? Are we crazy?"

"Yes, and maybe yes," he said. "But I don't care. I have prayed so much for you and about this and I have absolutely no doubt in my mind that you're supposed to be my wife."

"I can't believe this is happening to me. This is about the last thing I would have thought would be my life right now. I can honestly say that I know that God is so good."

"Yes, He is. He has been good to us, and we can trust that He has great things for us in the future."

She kissed him again. "Yes, I'm just glad that you will be by my side."

"Yep, you're never getting rid of me now. And you know what else?"

"What?"

"You just gained a whole new family too."

She laughed. "Well I hate to tell you, but I think they have already taken me in. They didn't want to wait to see what would happen with you and me."

"That's alright. I already knew this would happen, and I think they did too. We were all just waiting for you to figure it out."

"Well, I'm glad I did."

He kissed her once more, then took her hand and they walked on down the trail. It was the first steps of their new journey together. And together was the way they both wanted it.

About the Author

Hannah Jo Abbott is a wife, a mom of four, and a homeschool teacher. She loves writing stories about life, love, and the grace of God. And she finds inspiration and encouragement from reading the stories others share. Hannah lives with her husband and children in Sweet Home Alabama.

For updates on new releases and free books join the newsletter!

You can connect with me on:
- http://www.hannahjoabbott.com
- http://www.facebook.com/hjabooks

Subscribe to my newsletter:

✉ http://www.hannahjoabbott.com/mailinglist.html

Also by Hannah Jo Abbott

Dream with Me
Want more stories from The Kelly family?
Read Peyton's story now!

She's following her dreams.
He's following his heart.
But does God have a plan for them
together?

FREE NOVELLA - Just Maybe
Don't Miss Carrie and Jack's story!
   Get it for free when you sign up for
newsletter updates: www.hannahjoab-
bott.com/mailinglist.html

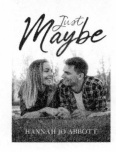